Harini Chakrapani is an Ooty born, Chennai bred, Dubai and New York-based writer who also likes to call herself a nomad. Her love for words began when she heard her English teacher use the word 'perilous' and went on to write her first story titled 'A Perilous Vacation'. Since then, she prefers to spend hours reading sci-fi, fantasy, gothic fiction, writing and browsing *www.dictionary.com*.

Her résumé includes a degree in Tourism Management from Ethiraj College, Chennai, and a stint in journalism with celebrity and lifestyle magazines, *Masala!* and *Pose Dubai*. Currently, she's a student at the City University of New York's Graduate School of Journalism.

The Secret of the Mantle is her first book.

The Secret of the Mantle

Harini Chakrapani

Om Books International

First published in 2015 by

Om Books International

Corporate & Editorial Office
A-12, Sector 64, Noida 201 301
Uttar Pradesh, India
Phone: +91 120 477 4100
Email: editorial@ombooks.com
Website: www.ombooksinternational.com

Sales Office
107, Ansari Road, Darya Ganj,
New Delhi 110 002, India
Phone: +91 11 2326 3363, 2326 5303, 4000 9000
Fax: +91 11 2327 8091
Email: sales@ombooks.com
Website: www.ombooks.com

ISBN: 978-93-85609-38-1

Printed in India

10 9 8 7 6 5 4 3 2 1

To

Mumsy, Appa, Archie, and Migy, for loving me, and
Shreya, for telling me that mermaids can also fly!

Eram quod es, eris quod sum
—Horace
(And Death says to the living, 'I was what you are, you will be what I am.'
—Horace)

Contents

Part I

Dr Chary

1

A Dark Secret

The palatial house that stood on top of a hill, with a view of vast ice-capped mountains and a charming blue lake, still remained a prison for its owner. Tall, thin, and reclusive, 65-year-old Dr Chary had spent nearly three-fifths of his life in Chenpalle, a small town in Himachal Pradesh, and a fifth of his life in sheer loneliness at this particular house.

He stayed inside most of the time. There was no need to go out even for groceries. A maid had been hired to take care of that. She also paid the bills and drew money from the bank whenever Dr Chary fell short of it. The rare occasions on which he left the house were marked by a visit to the museum, where he could absorb the rich colours of Galan Gregorovic's palette-knife paintings all day long and the bookstore that lay downhill in the Bazaar Street. Nothing gave Dr Chary greater joy than reading.

Dr Chary had no friends; no one came to visit him or talk to him. His closest neighbours were 10 kilometres away. Indeed, all his life he had been a loner, but his transformation into a recluse began when he lost his wife 14 years ago. Though he would never admit it, her death had made him very depressed. There were days when he wouldn't do anything, but just stare at the walls and cry.

Still, the old man hadn't entirely given up on life. He loved to write and continued to do so even after his wife left him. Writing was what brought him great fame and fortune. He was after all the Dr Seuss of India, with 36 books to his name. The most successful of these were *Nine Too Many, Kapil's Freckles, Found And Lost Again, The Magical Den, The Water Hole, Pensive Pensie, The Poor Little Prince, The Turtle And The Serpent, The Eye In The Sky, The Seven Seers* and *A Dwarphant's Long Tale* that had recently been made into a film.

At the moment, he was writing novel number 37, titled *The Mouse Witch Witchen*. He had been stuck on the story for four years; no new ideas came to him. There were days when the book seemed ridiculous. After all, who wanted to read about an insignificant thing like a mouse, especially one that was blind and wanted to travel around the world in a magical mousetrap? There were days when Dr Chary just couldn't write. There were days when one could say he had lost his marbles, because he was yelling at the walls or talking to himself.

It was a very stressful time and Chenpalle's picture-postcard setting couldn't do anything to soothe the writer's nerves. The only one who could help the old man was his grandson Naveen, with whom he shared his birthday—Naveen was born on September 23, 2000. He hadn't met his grandson yet, but had only seen pictures of him—the photographs of the little bundle of joy, with his pink toes and dark, sparkling eyes, much like the mouse Witchen, instantly brought a smile to Dr Chary's face.

Yes, he wasn't all alone as he often thought. He did have a family—a son named Akshay, daughter-in-law Meera, and his grandson Naveen, whom he loved very much. But he kept away from them because he didn't like being with people or talking to them all the time. He wanted to see his family, only for, let's say, an hour a day, and then wanted them to disappear altogether. But strangely of late, he just couldn't be by himself. He wanted to see Naveen desperately but couldn't tell his son that.

Dr Chary was sitting on a chair with his head resting on the table over some scraps of paper, in which he had written about the mouse Witchen's pink toes turning pale when she gets caught in a mousetrap.

The sun had just risen. Its rays beamed into the house through the open window. Dr Chary could feel the warmth on the table. He looked up and saw the golden orb shining gloriously above Chenpalle's ice-capped mountains. The whole sky was blushing a deep orange. Still, the sight didn't make him smile. After all, it was another morning, another day, and that made him realise how time had passed and he was still stuck with the book. The air smelled foul. But why? He realised it was because of him. After all, he hadn't bathed in days. His head hurt. He hadn't eaten, brushed or shaved. Those things were distracting and could keep him from writing, so he couldn't think of wasting his time on them. Indeed, Dr Chary was a mess and so was the house around him. The maid had apparently not done her job. After all, hadn't he specifically asked her not to come to his house until he called for her? But why had he done that?

'The experiment,' Dr Chary said under his breath. The whole thing was just so *odd*. He didn't want anybody to know about it. Once it was over, it always messed with his mind, leaving him with violent fits of temper and full blown panic attacks for days. And he didn't want his maid to put up with that, for she was a kind lady. At his age, he wasn't sure if he could handle it.

Dr Chary took off his clothes and walked into the bathroom. The last time I went underwater, did I remain submerged for 33 or 35 minutes, he asked himself. He thought hard but couldn't answer the question. The answer was important to him, so he went back to his study to pick up a thick diary from the table. Once he returned to the bathroom he turned on the tap to fill the bathtub. Hot water gushed out with a fury, spreading out on the white porcelain floor, making bubbles near the drain. After plugging the drain, the writer shifted his attention to his diary. Now he flipped through its pages. He didn't know where exactly he would find the answer to his question because he had a habit of making notes wherever there was an empty space. And so he ended up reading bits of his past entries, from here and there:

MARCH 18

I don't like being dropped off at school. I am 14-years-old. Why can't Amma get that? Arjun suddenly talks funny. He blows air into your face when he has to say any word that begins with an 's'. Apparently, he has a lisp. His best friends, Girish and Pankaj, picked on him today.

My timing today was 12 minutes and 23 seconds. Throat burned a little. I could have stayed longer. But, Ramesh Sir, our new swimming teacher, blew the whistle. I will try to sneak into the pool after school on Thursday.

APRIL 9

Why didn't the river drag me inside? Why did it get Appa? Did I do something wrong? Amma's still crying. It's been over 10 years. Why can't she forget Appa and move on?

I took 14 minutes and 53 seconds. I am getting better... Amma's yelling at me. She wants me to do my homework. But I can't. I really can't concentrate. There are a million thoughts in my head.

MARCH 19

Arjun Nolachit called me a white freak today. I was inside the pool for 23 minutes and four seconds. He was there the whole time watching me. I don't know how I didn't see him when I got in. Anyway, when I came up for air because my chest had begun to hurt, Arjun Nolachit called me a white freak because my face had turned completely white. He probably watches me every now and then. Should I be worried?

Dr Chary flipped through a number of pages in between. He didn't have the patience to read each and every entry.

MARCH 2

I don't have any friends. Well, everyone's afraid of me. They think that if they talk to me or touch me they'll get white patches on their skin like me. The doctor says it's just a skin condition that sets in when the cells responsible for colouring our skin suddenly stop functioning. But it's certainly not a disease that's contagious. I tried explaining that to everyone but they wouldn't listen. Girish and Pankaj taunt me all the time by calling me a panda, or a chessboard, because my skin has two colours; black and white. Honestly, they have been doing this for years now and it doesn't hurt me anymore. I am happy being on my own; reading and writing. Still, there are these two boys who joined school last month who want to be friends with me regardless of what I look like. But I can't hang-out with Shyam and

> Balaji. They're just stupid—talking about girls, picking their noses, pulling pranks on everyone... My best time today was 18 minutes and 13 seconds. It's definitely abnormal. Why am I feeling so restless now; can't stay in one place without thinking this is not where I should be or this is not what I should be doing.

Next he read something scrawled in a corner of the page:

> Amma is getting real sick. I don't like going to the hospital; the noise, the long wait for the doctors, and the smell of sickness. Today, I stayed underwater for 27 minutes and 28 seconds. (I don't care what day it is; Amma is dying anyway.)

Dr Chary took a pause and sighed heavily. Four decades had passed since his mother's death, yet the memories were still raw. But he didn't want to dwell on them—that was not why he had sought this diary. He then turned over the pages in haste looking for the entry about the longest time he had held his breath underwater.

His hands however stopped at a page. There were clippings glued to it from newspapers, books and magazines. Here was all the research he had done as a teenager, related to his abnormality.

- Two or three minutes, at best, is the average time a human can hold his breath underwater. Beyond this time, it has been observed that because of the lack of oxygen and the build-up of carbon dioxide, the mind blacks out, the heart stops beating, brain cells get damaged, and the body shuts down permanently. It's called carbon dioxide poisoning.

- 1959. Robert Foster. Canadian. Survived for 13 minutes and 42 seconds underwater, on a single breath, inside a pool. Record unbeaten. Reports say that he had filled himself with pure oxygen with the help of a machine, for 30 minutes before the stunt.
- Pearl divers in Japan were known to last upto five minutes underwater without any air supply.
- A fisherman in Tuvalu, the little-known island nation in the Pacific Ocean, attempted to stay for nine minutes and 52 seconds in a tank. No reports to suggest whether he had filled himself with oxygen before this attempt.
- In 1945, South African swimmer Lesedi Mehrtens held his breath for 10 minutes and 31 seconds.

The next entry read:

> AUGUST 17
>
> I don't want to be different. When people look at me I know they can see it. I am scared. I don't want to change. What if they find out what's going on inside me? Will they lock me up in a zoo for visitors to come and stare at my oddity? Amma's dead… I never told her. But I think she knew. She knew I was different from the beginning. Why did she hide it? But why am I different? Not knowing the truth makes me so anxious. I can't get any sleep. I wish Amma was still here to hold me, be with me, calm me down, make me sleep. I feel I am all alone.

The memories were painful. They made Dr Chary's heart ache. Tears streamed from his eyes and blotted the numbers below the August 17 entry. Oh no! He was sure that was the last record of the longest time for which he could remain submerged in water, without having to come up for a single draught of oxygen.

As Dr Chary was trying to decipher the numbers, he was reminded of his last feat that had been achieved years ago. The night after the feat, he had had the most restless sleep; full of panic. He woke up with a start, sweaty, cold and nauseous with his heart pounding wildly. A voice within kept telling him that he had frittered away all his time in doing things that were inconsequential when all he had to do was find out why he was different. Then his legs had stiffened, his chest tightened, his throat and nostrils closed up and he couldn't breathe. Panic had gripped him for a whole month post that event. It only petered out when he found a pen and paper and began to scribble away all his thoughts. Once they were out of his mind, he felt considerably lighter. Writing became his salve; it gave him peace. And to preserve the peace, he did two things. He made writing his profession. Secondly, he kept away from swimming pools, so he wouldn't be tempted to try the experiment again.

But all that had changed a week ago, when he came across a painting of a fish inside a glass jar. The fish looked so serene, so relaxed; in its element. Dr Chary knew that's how he felt when he was submerged in water and thus felt a fierce urge to revisit his past and try the experiment again, even though it was a double-edged sword.

The bathtub gurgled and water was now overflowing from it. The tap had been running for a long time. Dr Chary ran to turn it off. He then cleaned a dust-laden tiny clock that he had kept in a remote corner of the room (within the frame of the exhaust fan) where his eyes would never look for it, for he hated keeping track of time. But that wasn't true always. When it came to his abnormality, knowing the measure of time gave him immense happiness. He had once thought about it for a very long time, about why time had mattered. The answer was simple. Nothing brought him as much peace as staying breathless underwater. Still, he was terribly afraid of its aftermath when anger, panic and restlessness roused within him. He was afraid even more so, of what those emotions would transform him into when they completely possessed him. That was the reason why he suppressed his abnormality. But there were times when he could silence his fears too, especially once he got into the water. When he stayed breathless for some time, it meant that he hadn't let fear deny him his real nature for those few minutes. That realisation made him feel liberated and that was the significance the numbers bore for him. Thus, time was necessary now, to revisit his abnormality.

After turning on the stopwatch, the writer slipped into the steaming tub and held his breath. It was so good to be afloat again, he thought. As the warm water caressed his skin, he felt his worries slipping away. He felt weightless. For several minutes, he lay at perfect ease; his lungs content with the store of oxygen. There was no struggle, no need to come up for more air.

At length, however, his peaceful sleep was being disturbed. The bathroom door was open; a shrill sound from the drawing room came unobstructed. It persisted! It was relentless! Why wouldn't it stop?

Dr Chary rose above the water. He was now staring at the clock. Had an hour passed since he had been in the tub? This was scary! The shrill sound came again and he realised it was the phone. Could he have stayed submerged indefinitely had the phone not disturbed him, he asked himself? What was going on with his body? Did he not need oxygen at all? The phone continued to ring continuously, making a shrill noise in the stillness. He had to answer it so the noise would stop. He got out of the tub, put on a bathrobe and hurried to the drawing room.

'Hello, Dr Chary's residence,' he said with annoyance, after picking up the phone.

A long silence followed. His sharp ears could pick up muffled snivelling in the background. He used the time to suppress his own excitement about his outrageous feat.

'Dad! It's so great to hear your voice... I have missed you.' It was his son, Akshay.

Dr Chary was quiet for some time; he was so happy to hear his son's voice. But Dr Chary couldn't tell him that, because he was never the sort to express his feelings openly. Also, he wanted to tell Akshay that he missed him too, his wife and Akshay's mother, Aarthi. Memories of his wife came back. Why had Aarthi left him? Why had she been so weak? Why had she embraced death? Why hadn't she fought back? Ever since she had gone, his loneliness had been so overwhelming.

There were so many thoughts in his head, but Dr Chary couldn't let them out. He didn't want Akshay to think his father was weak and needed his son's help to get his life in order. Added to that, he believed if Akshay came to stay with him, their familiarity would breed contempt. Thus, the writer swallowed his emotions.

'How is Murjan? Is it a clean town like they say? Wait, you're not calling me from there. The calling code reads different. Where are you?' He could hear echoes of his own voice. Clearly, he had been put on a speaker phone.

'Dad… I called to tell you just that. I have good news… we have moved to Darmas. We're going to be here for a long time. I know how upset you're that you haven't seen your grandson yet because of my hectic travel schedule. Anyway, Meera is fed up shifting houses. She keeps a record, you know, the number of times we have changed apartments. I am bad at remembering these things. We've practically lived in over 53 apartments in every state in the country. Anyway, she put her foot down last month and went to… umm…meet her uncle…Uncle Romas. He offered me a job in his firm in Darmas. It's a desk job. I couldn't say no. There's absolutely no travel involved, unlike my previous job. Isn't this great news, Dad? I like the job very much. Meera likes it here, being close to her uncle and teaching at one of the schools owned by him. She set up our house in less than a week. I don't know what I could do without her. We have a maid too for Naveen. Aren't you happy, Dad? This is what I wanted all my life.'

Dr Chary's eyes lit up as he smiled.

'So Darmas is where you are going to stay. I am happy that you like it there. But I've heard that summers are brutal and that the pollution is so thick that you can't see the sky. That's not good for my Naveen… How is *my* little grandson? I'd love to see him,' Dr Chary added in a very feeble voice.

He hoped that Akshay had both heard him and hadn't. He was embarrassed after expressing what he thought were soppy emotions. Why had he given free rein to his emotions for his grandson?

Akshay was surprised. Although his father's voice had been faint, he could discern the force of his father's emotions from the long embarrassed silence. But his father was always so stolid. Had time changed him? Now, Akshay wanted to open up too, let his father know why his wife had put her foot down in November against this constant shifting of houses. She also wanted Dr Chary to stay with them.

> 'Don't you think it's your duty to look after your father?' Meera had asked him in a scathing tone one day, and then, after bouts of hysterical crying, added, 'I can't live this life of a nomad. You hear me. I want Naveen to grow up with his grandfather around him. That's all I want.'
>
> 'Father won't listen. He loves being by himself. Don't you understand that?' Akshay had retorted, but Meera had walked out of the room by then.

Akshay was guarded about what he expressed now, 'Meera and I would love it if you came here…stayed with us, that is. It is a big house. We have five bedrooms and a big library. She's filled it up with her great grandmother's collection. She remembers how much you loved it when you saw it first.'

He knew dwelling over emotions would repel his father.

Dr Chary shook his head. His mind was ready to reject the offer. He didn't need this distraction. He had a book to write.

'I'm really happy for the three of you. But you know Akshay, there is so much to be done here. I have just finished my draft. The publishers aren't happy with it. They want certain parts to be rewritten. So, I am constantly meeting with people, researching, to get the right sound of things. You have a routine going on there and I wouldn't want to disturb you,' he lied, before adding, 'besides, the heat and the pollution there wouldn't suit me.'

A long pause followed again.

'Dr Chary...please...we *insist*. We really want you here.' It was Meera this time, 'It's a lot cleaner where we live. Trust me. The house feels so empty without you. Especially the library! I have these dreams of you reading out to Naveen... I know it's too early for him to understand all that but I can't imagine anyone but you being the best influence on him... As for book research, Uncle Romas would easily be able to connect you with a mixed bag of people in Darmas. I don't know if you still remember Uncle Romas's daughter, Nitya. You helped her write her very first book three years ago. She talks about you all the time; about how you encouraged her. She's in Graam right now working on something new. She called me up last night and told me if you came down to Darmas, she'd leave all her work to come see you. She'd be thrilled; she practically idolises you. For our sake, please do consider a short visit; at least, if you can't stay for a long time. We all miss you so much.'

Dr Chary heard intermittent whimpers of his grandson. He was stirred. He listened. His son was on the line now.

'Dad, there's something else. I couldn't say it earlier. Umm... Everytime I visit you, I get so scared... You look different...*older*. It is true that none of us is getting younger... It pains me nonetheless to admit that I have missed many years of your life...that I couldn't care for you when you needed me, that I so selfishly left you all alone in that cold damp place because I was on the road all the time. But I had no choice back then. Things are different now. I don't have to travel anymore for work. I have a house of my own and you can stay with me for as long as you like. Please do consider how I feel. Give me a chance... If you don't like Darmas, then I can quit my job and be with you. I am sure I can live *without* care, off your money.'

Akshay's voice lost its trembling quality. He laughed after the quip. He wanted to make the moment light for his father.

'Akshay, there are a *few*...' began Dr Chary and then stopped. He felt a heavy pain in his head, as though it had taken a hard blow. The cordless phone fell from his hand and he grabbed his head. Tears fogged up his vision. Minutes later, the pain subsided. Dr Chary sat on the chair, bewildered. He thought he had heard a voice. It was so faint. The phone rang again. He didn't answer it. He didn't want to speak to his son. He knew Akshay would badger him with questions about why he had hung up on him so abruptly. His son was too sentimental. If he knew his father's head was hurting, he would travel all the way to be with him. Then he would beg his father to move to Darmas. Dr Chary was a tired man. He couldn't argue with his son, but at least he could be aloof like he had been for so many years.

The phone kept ringing. Dr Chary was annoyed. It seemed that Akshay's will to get his attention was as tenacious as his was to ignore. He gave up and decided he'd speak to his son and let him know what was really in his mind.

He began, 'I really can't come, Akshay. You should stop bothering yourself with the whys and why nots! There are reasons I'd like to keep to myself unless you want everything to turn unpleasant between us. Tell your wife I may be old but not useless to spare all my time to babysit her son.' There was an angry inflection in his voice that he now found shocking! It was as if someone else had spoken those bitter words. He waited for his son to say something, but Akshay seemed to have just gone quiet. 'Akshay. Akshay, are you there?' He asked weakly.

Then he checked the calling code. It wasn't Akshay. It was someone else calling him from Chenpalle. Now he could hear sounds; quick and rough, very much like the nib of a pen scritch-scratching paper.

'Dr Raman Chary? Good morning. I hope you're very well,' a lady greeted.

'Yes… Who's this?'

'Good morning. I'm Anita Shah, calling from director Jerome Ray's office. Would this be a good time to talk?'

'Uhh…what? Jerome who?'

'Umm...Mr Ray… Well…umm,' the words sounded as though they had been uttered through clenched teeth. The woman on the other side was getting annoyed.

'He directed the film adaptation of your book, *A Dwarphant's Long Tale*. Since *A Dwarphant's Long Tale* is going to hit the theatres this coming Friday, Mr Ray thought it would help the promotional campaign immensely, if you could do a book-reading session on Sunday.'

Dr Chary scratched his head and tried to grasp all the details. Anita repeated her request, with undisguised impatience.

'Well… Anita… I'm afraid I don't have the time for such an undertaking… There are certain travel plans in the pipeline. I guess the film will do just fine without my interference,' replied the writer.

The truth was he didn't like public appearances. There was a certain image he was expected to project at these events and that made him terribly nervous. Plus, now that he had done the experiment, he knew that he was definitely going to be more peevish and jumpy than ever before. Hadn't he already had an outburst?

'If you could send us a copy of your schedule I am sure we could accommodate a one-hour session before the coming Friday,' said the secretary in a very composed, professional manner.

Dr Chary was annoyed. He felt as though he was being forced to cooperate.

'What…what is this? Why don't you understand? I said there are plans in the pipeline. I'm occupied with other things. Isn't that clear enough?' His nostrils flared in anger.

'Uhh… Dr Chary, you signed a contract earlier, which was forwarded to us by your agent. It states clearly that you'd provide us your complete assistance for the screenplay which you have so amply given and for the promotion once the film is complete, for a fee of course. Your agent has already collected the cheque for the book reading event. However, if you are still unwilling, I can have Mr Ray speak to you; to make things *clear* enough.'

'Oh! Vimal Verma,' Dr Chary muttered. That was his book agent; the man who oversaw all the contracts concerning his books and the films based on his books. Clearly, Vimal had signed this contract for *A Dwarphant's Long Tale* too.

Dr Chary had in fact given him the permission to forge his signature because he didn't like to waste his time reading legal documents and signing them. Clearly, it was wrong to trust Vimal so implicitly, he now thought. After all, he was a greedy man and whenever there was an opportunity to make money, he couldn't pass it up.

His head began to throb again; this time with more severity. He couldn't argue any further. Besides, the breach of contract could land him in the thick of a courtroom drama and the old man was too tired for all that.

'All right… I'll be there. When and where am I expected?' he asked gruffly.

For few minutes there was silence at the other end; the secretary seemed shocked. She hadn't expected the writer to give into her demand so quickly. So she thanked her lucky stars and gave him all the details before he could hang up on her.

After ending the call, the writer went into the bedroom and slept for the rest of the day, groaning in pain and distraught with fear.

When he woke up, he could distinctly remember hearing a woman's voice. Her words seemed absurd for she called him the White Death's Equal… Whatever that meant!

2

Meeting with Vimal Verma

Dr Chary checked his phone first thing in the morning. He hadn't slept well at all because of a splitting headache, the voice of the mysterious woman and the constant ringing of the phone.

There were 32 missed calls on his phone; mostly from Akshay. He had no intention to talk to his son and rehash the drama of the previous night. He wasn't going to Darmas. Chenpalle was his home and grave. The rest of the calls were from his book agent and director Jerome Ray's office.

'Vimal,' Dr Chary said to himself. His face hardened with rage at the thought of his greedy agent. He knew he was going to fire him once he was done with the book-reading business. Shortly, he picked up the phone and punched in director Jerome Ray's number. There was something he had forgotten to ask.

'Director Jerome Ray's office. How may I help you?' asked the secretary with a robotic lilt in her voice. It was this annoying, calm, indifferent tone that office-goers in general maintained whether they were angry, excited, bored or in pain.

'Anita. Hello. Raman Chary here. I just noticed I had several calls from your office yesterday.'

'Of course, Dr Chary. Good morning. I'm so terribly sorry about yesterday. I apologise for inconveniencing you. We are working under tremendous pressure. Mr Ray wants everything to go in perfect accordance with his plans. How are you Dr Chary? I hope you had a good day...yesterday.'

Dr Chary kept quiet. He liked people to express their motives directly. There was no need for cordiality. It was just so insincere, so contrived!

The secretary feared this silence. She had heard about the writer's mood swings. The book agent, Vimal, had warned her that even if the old man agreed to the reading event, he could very well cancel at the last minute. She had nearly hyperventilated on hearing this. Mr Ray had given her a huge responsibility—to make sure the event was sensational in every which way possible—and she could not let him down.

'Is everything all right, Sir?' she asked in as gentle a tone as she could manage, thereby masking her impatience.

'I had a bad headache. But now I feel okay. Other than that, everything is where it should be.'

'I hope you got the address right. I'll repeat it just in case. Hotel Neemowalia, Thiabar Street, opposite Picot Mall. You're expected in the conference room on level 2C at 12.30 p.m. From there you'll be escorted to the auditorium where you'll read the first chapter to the audience.'

'I wanted to ask you about who I can expect at the event.'

'We will send a car with a chauffeur to your residence at 11.45 a.m. on Sunday. Mr Ray insists that you shouldn't have to strain yourself unnecessarily to get here.'

'There won't be any need for that. Tell him I can take care of myself. Now would you tell me about the crowd?' His irritation was palpable.

'Oh, but he doesn't want you to drive. You haven't been keeping well. And the forecast says it could rain on Sunday. The roads get so terribly flooded. The driver can take care...'

'Bah! No one takes care of me,' Dr Chary interrupted angrily. 'Now stop wasting my time and give me the details about who I can expect.'

The secretary had never heard Dr Chary's voice shoot up with such fury before. More menacing, it seemed to her, was his heavy breathing between words. Her lips curled into a smile. She remembered what her boss had said. The old man was always volatile and that was why the event was going to be sensational.

'I'm sorry. I don't have all the details now. Let me give you a call as soon as I get the information from the organisers. In the meanwhile, I think Mr Vimal Verma will join you at home to briefly discuss the presentation.'

'What in the blue blazes! I did not invite anyone home. Call him back. Tell him he's not welcome here. I can do the reading myself.'

The secretary wasn't surprised. The writer was, after all, a recluse. The book agent, who had kept tabs on the old man through the maid, had learnt that he hadn't stepped out of the house in two years. This was further substantiated when the writer repeatedly declined the director's pleas to visit the movie set, approve the filming, interact with the crew and even attend the special, star-studded screening of the film where Mr Amitabh Bachchan himself was present. Now, who could say no to meeting the legend!

'He's on his way, Dr Chary. We didn't think it was appropriate for you to waste your time so we prepared the material for the presentation ourselves.'

'All right. I'll see to that. And I'll expect your call shortly. Let me make it clear, I don't want a big crowd. Kids are fine. I don't want too many people from the media. I don't like the things they write,' said the writer gruffly.

'Whatever, you crazy old recluse! If you're so afraid of people, why don't you stay home. Oh wait, you can't do that because you want money,' said the secretary under her breath, pulling the phone away from her mouth.

But, Dr Chary had heard every single word. After a pause, he retorted, 'I don't do anything for money. It means nothing to me. I can write it all away to you. I am doing this for myself. I just feel I need a break, that is all.'

The secretary turned red with embarrassment. Her voice ran with apologies but the writer ended the call abruptly. However, he thought about the phone call. The secretary was right. He had become crazy, irritable and a recluse. It was all because of his wife passing away and also his writing.

With this came the realisation that he did need a break; he did need to calm down. And no one could help him but his grandson Naveen. He would leave for Darmas after getting over with this book-reading event.

Just then, the doorbell rang. It was Vimal Verma, the agent. Dr Chary greeted the man at the door.

The writer's appearance was a shock to the agent; he took a while to recover. Only two years had passed since their last meeting, yet it seemed that the writer had added 20 more years to his age. Dr Chary had shrunk to a skeletal frame. And his face? It could give anyone the chills. Pale as a ghost and marked with blue-green veins, wrinkles and dark circles under the eyes, a medium-length grey beard and a moustache. The head was so delicate that it seemed it could crack open with a mere nod. The old man looked very much like he was on the verge of dying, only if it weren't for the warm lustre in his coal black eyes and the smile on his face. But what was the reason behind it? Was Dr Chary thinking about his grandson? The maid had told the agent that whenever the old man talked of his grandson he seemed happy.

Vimal noticed the house. Had the maid been slacking? Apart from the weather, it had endured the apathy and fits of outrage of its owner. And, there was a heavy musty odour. The paint had peeled off from the walls, the curtains looked torn, the carpets were stained and the furniture was piled with dust. Vermin could be seen crawling about.

For a long time, Vimal waited at the shoe rack in the veranda, peering into the house, wondering if he needed to remove his shoes. Dr Chary understood the agent's discomfort.

'Keep your shoes on. Who knows you could help squash the bugs around here,' said the writer as he inspected the house with equal surprise and disgust as Vimal.

The agent wasn't amused.

'Apparently, my maid has been slacking behind my back, and if it weren't for you, I wouldn't have noticed the state of the house so closely,' said the writer. 'It's good to see you, Vimal. Make yourself at home,' Dr Chary added.

The agent stepped inside, laid down his briefcase and numerous files in the drawing room. After a short while, the writer joined him on a heavily soiled silk canapé. For minutes, there was silence. Many thoughts popped up in Vimal's mind. He was here on a mission; to find the sensational stuff Anita, the secretary, and the director Jerome Ray were looking for. The old man was a lunatic; he looked like one and his house certainly seemed like a place where a sick man lived. But why wasn't he being nasty, vicious, fitful or withdrawn? Why was he happy and kind? The film would do very well if it got publicity. The writer's zany side had to be unravelled to the public. What had Mr Ray said to him in private during one of the team meetings? Ah yes, it was, 'I think he's given up on writing. But we don't care about that, do we? What we really care about is to get back all the money we've put into this "dwarphant" film and then some more. You're going to help me in this endeavour, Vimal. Want to know how? All that the film needs is good publicity and I can't think of anything better than an exposé on the country's greatest writer, the warped genius Dr Chary. I am telling you, the old man is bonkers. You're going to pay him a visit, talk to him, try his patience, and let him show you his zany side and how he explodes with anger. So you can take pictures of the very moment.'

Then, Jerome Ray had slipped his hand inside Vimal's pocket and the book agent smelled a wad of newly printed notes.

'It's been a long time since we last met. How have you been?' asked Dr Chary at length. The concern was so forced, so pretentious.

'Yes...erm...I am all right. I did try to contact you a couple of times,' Vimal admitted with hesitation. In truth, a 'couple' meant over thousands of calls in the last two years. Vimal knew the writer's phone number so well that he could even say it backwards.

'I see you have brought the material with you,' Dr Chary said, eyeing the papers that Vimal had brought with him.

'Ahem...yes,' said Vimal, somewhat absentmindedly.

He was thinking of the future, of how Dr Chary would react when the newspapers published stories about his zany side.

'I'd like to brief you about the session on Sunday,' Vimal said finally. 'It will be an hour-long affair. There will be kids in the audience, as you already know. So we thought you could talk to them about your personal experience as a writer and inspire them to write. I have the speech ready here. The speech will be followed by a question-and-answer session in which you'll field questions from budding writers. Anyway, that is the plan for the first half of the session that should be wrapped up in 22 minutes to be precise. In the second half, we'll have the book-reading. If we skip the preface, then the first chapter can be read in 28 minutes. That'll leave us with 10 minutes for the film's cast and Mr Ray to make a surprise appearance. It'll all be grand,' finished Vimal.

'You seem to have struck a *thick* friendship with the director and his secretary,' remarked Dr Chary dryly whilst thinking of the contracts Vimal had signed on his behalf.

Money indeed is the strongest foundation for friendship, Vimal thought to himself, but said, instead, 'I only represent your interests, Dr Chary.'

'You do a fine job young man. But you don't do me justice. I can't omit the preface even if it means Mr Ray cannot make his *surprise* appearance on the stage. If it weren't for my work then he wouldn't even be up there in the first place.'

Vimal's smile froze. The old man's pride was sharp as a thorn.

'Oh! Pardon me. I have been very impolite. Would you care for some tea or coffee? I'm afraid that's all I can offer at the moment. I should head down to the supermarket today,' said the writer before sauntering into the kitchen.

'I'd like tea please,' yelled Vimal, with some reluctance. He couldn't bear the thought of drinking tea in this squalid place. But he couldn't leave. Dr Chary had given him time to snoop around.

With some nervous hesitation he fished out a camera from his briefcase. Click! Click! Click! He soon had all the pictures he needed. Only a sick man could live in a house like this. It was time to note down all that he had seen. He fished a scratch pad from his bag and scribbled away. Mr Ray would be so thrilled and happy with his effort, he told himself. Vimal's eyes scanned the room again. At a distance, he saw crumpled balls of paper strewn on the floor and ink spilling from a jar onto the mess. Was Dr Chary working on something? Click! He took another picture. Just then he heard the writer's footsteps and ended his spy work.

As he sipped on the horridly bitter tea, he asked curiously, 'Are you writing another novel, Dr Chary? The reports are false, right? I never believed you had retired.'

Dr Chary shook his head. He didn't want to discuss his next book. He was so drained. The agent kept quiet. He suspected the writer was absorbed in his thoughts. So he let him be.

The silence unnerved Dr Chary for it let his thoughts flow uninterrupted. They weren't all happy; some of them were quite disturbing. Maybe it was a side effect of the experiment or maybe it was because of his latest novel, *The Mouse Witch Witchen.* Writing it had been so horrifying! After all, it wasn't an innocent tale of adventure as it appeared to be on the surface. There was such an appallingly macabre element in it—of mice eating mice, that intrigued Dr Chary. The writer was well aware of the ghastly changes that had come upon him during the writing process. He even took fright sometimes when he looked at his reflection in the mirror.

'I had a few ideas. I couldn't work on them. Anyway, I am so sick of the whole thing. I guess the reporters got it right. Maybe it's time to quit.'

Dr Chary looked as though he had surprised himself with the admission. And now when he had said it, he felt calm and happy.

Vimal panicked! If Dr Chary gave up writing, where would he go? He wouldn't have a job. No, the writer had to change his mind.

'You had experienced all this before too with *A Dwarphant's Long Tale*. It's just a phase. Don't give up. Your gift of storytelling is something you need to share with the world.'

'I don't want to be enslaved. I fear that there's no escape from this house or...my mind. These thoughts won't stop. My head throbs in pain. I...I'm losing it... I need to put an end to this. I have to leave. I can't do this anymore.'

Was the writer having a meltdown? Vimal had witnessed it several times before. Indeed it was torturous to be Dr Chary. Suddenly, the book agent pitied the old man.

'Why can't you be with Akshay? Where does he live now?'

Dr Chary pursed his lips and closed his eyes. Memories of his son, Akshay, flooded his mind. He missed him terribly. At length he spoke, 'As a matter of fact, I'm going to do just that. He is in Darmas now and maybe I'll go and stay with him there.'

The writer opened his eyes. There was that lustre again.

The agent was pleased to learn about Dr Chary's plans. Visiting his son would thoroughly refresh the old man and maybe help him write his next book. With that hopeful thought in his mind, Vimal handed the writer his copy of *A Dwarphant's Long Tale*, which had proved itself to be one of the bestselling books of all time.

'I have a paperback. It folds very easily. I thought you'd like to read from it at the event,' said Vimal in good spirit.

Dr Chary took the book from him with a smile on his face. The book agent left soon after that.

3

A Dwarphant's Long Tale

The book-reading event at Hotel Neemowalia didn't kick off as planned. Dr Chary was expected to be present at the venue at 12.30 p.m. but there was no sign of him, and it was already quarter past one. The organisers were in a tizzy trying to contact the chauffeur, who was meant to bring Dr Chary to the venue.

'What's going on? Where is Dr Chary?' asked director Jerome Ray, trying to keep a tight rein on his anger.

'I am sorry Mr Ray. All we know is that he got into the car. That was the last message relayed to us by the chauffeur. We have been trying to reach him ever since, but the chauffeur hasn't been answering our calls,' replied Anita, heavily distraught.

'Shut up… Shut up… Don't waste my time with these excuses. If Dr Chary doesn't show up in the next 15 minutes you can say goodbye to your job.'

It was quite a frantic scene at the hotel—just as Dr Chary had wanted it to be.

'Don't answer that,' ordered the writer as he saw the chauffeur—a young, oily-haired man—reaching out for his ringing cell phone, on the dashboard of the limo that he was in.

'But Sir, the organisers are calling. They want to know where we are. Why are we still circling Bazaar Street, Sir? We are already very late,' remarked the chauffeur as he stared nervously at the writer's reflection in the rear-view mirror.

'The show doesn't start until 2.00 p.m. We have a lot of time to spare. Let's go get some tea.'

'But Sir, I'll lose my job.'

'Bah… Didn't I promise you that I'll pay you 100 times the salary you make in a year. Guess you don't believe me. Well, let me see what I can find,' said the writer as he dug into his wallet.

He flashed a wad of 1000-rupee notes and then generously donated his wallet to the chauffeur, who was stunned.

'Now would you kindly take me to Mana Manaji's café?'

The chauffeur's face broke into a euphoric smile. Mana Manaji's café served the finest tea in all of India. The tea leaves used packed in a potent flavour. It was believed that even a whiff could knock out the blues and give the drinker a burst of energy enough to keep one awake for two days in a row! That's why even a tiny cup of tea was insanely expensive. But it seemed to the chauffeur that the old man could easily afford to buy, not just a cup, but the whole shop.

Dr Chary wasn't much of a tea drinker. He was just hoping to draw all his energy from observing nature during the scenic uphill drive from the Bazaar Street to the tea shop.

And he was right.

Everything around seemed so crisp and new—the whooshing song of winds, rolling dances of fallen leaves, bobbing heads of flowers, curving folds in the mountains, soaring flight of birds, and the very invigorating scent of the air that he breathed in. At the end of the detour, both Dr Chary and the driver felt blissful.

However, their bliss didn't rub off on the organisers. They glared at the duo as soon as they arrived at the hotel. A plump, curly-haired woman in charge of the event barked into her walkie-talkie and informed the rest of her crew that the writer had arrived. Dr Chary took note of the disgruntled woman. The device in her hand crackled again.

'Smile. Smile. We're good. We still have 12 minutes before the show starts, so don't annoy him. He's a moody man and could walk back home right now if you rubbed him the wrong way,' warned a voice on the other end of the walkie-talkie.

The woman, immediately realising her folly, flashed her best smile as the writer appeared right in front of her.

'Welcome, welcome Dr Chary. Was the drive comfortable? I hope everything was pleasant. You look so bright. No signs of rain today. I love that colour on you,' cooed the lady.

The writer did look dapper in a red turtleneck sweater, a black mackintosh coat and fitting trousers, with his grey hair combed back neatly.

'We're getting late,' reminded the writer. He wanted the woman to flare up at the irony. That was the whole point of this act of rebellion, wasn't it? He wanted to send a message to Jerome Ray that just because a stupid contract had been signed, it didn't mean that he could be controlled.

'Not very...now let me take you inside,' said the woman as she kept her temper in check.

Dr Chary found himself at the threshold of a heavily-crowded conference room.

Apparently, the who's who of the country was present here; that's what the curly-haired woman had whispered in his ears. Dr Chary hated these people; they all seemed phoney to him, with their fake foreign accents and superficial knowledge about art and culture acquired over a summer trip to Europe.

The writer looked at each one of them condescendingly.

'Forget reading the book, I bet not one of them knows the name of my book,' muttered the writer to himself. Just then, a familiar face materialised before him. It was his conniving agent, Vimal Verma.

'Dr Chary, welcome, welcome, welcome,' said Vimal.

At once silence fell into the room. The crowd eyed Dr Chary as he was escorted inside. The writer stood before a smug-faced man with a buzz cut and a bespectacled woman scribbling in her scratch pad.

'Jerome Ray,' said the man and stretched his hand forward.

Dr Chary didn't shake his hand. Instead, he pressed his palms together, in a *namaste* and greeted Jerome.

Jerome Ray felt slighted but he didn't show it.

'We were expecting you here an hour earlier. Is everything all right?' the woman next to him asked. Her voice was familiar. She was Jerome's secretary, no doubt.

'That's none of your concern. Now I am here to read, not chit-chat. Clearly I am in the wrong place because the people here don't look like they read,' said the writer, surprising everybody, including himself, with his scathing and insolent tone.

The papers were right; Dr Chary was a cranky old man.

Jerome Ray just smiled. It was good to see the old man so ruffled. After all, that was what he wanted. The secretary's pen moved across the scratch pad with a fury noting down Dr Chary's acerbic remarks that she could share with the press.

'Dr Chary, hope you had something to eat along the way,' said Vimal out of concern.

'As a matter of fact I did not.'

'We can get you a sandwi...' began Vimal.

Then, director Jerome Ray chimed in. 'Show starts in three minutes,' before adding, 'I hope Vimal briefed you about the time slots.'

Before the writer could answer, the curly-haired woman behind him, who was in charge of the event, cleared her throat to say, 'Are you ready to step onto the stage?'

'Yes,' said the writer.

'There's a clock on the wall. Just in case you have to watch the time,' she suggested.

'I'll let it watch me,' replied the writer as he glared at the director.

Jerome Ray balled his fists while the secretary cursed the writer in her mind because he had had the final word.

A smug smile appeared on Dr Chary's face now as he was led down a hallway by the woman. Midway, however, his smile changed into a grimace because he felt his chest shudder and ache. When he rubbed it, the book he was carrying, slipped from his hand.

'Are you all right, Dr Chary?' asked the curly-haired woman as she picked up the book.

'Yes, let's go.' The writer shook his head to clear away all the negative thoughts. There was no need to worry. It was just a spasm. He had felt it before when he was stressed about his book.

They entered a sprawling ballroom. It was done up in a way to evoke the very setting of *A Dwarphant's Long Tale*. There were hills, trees, vines coiled around pillars and stairs leading up to a temple; all made of cardboard. The audience sat atop rocks and not chairs. Candles alone lit up the scene. It was all very dramatic. Dr Chary walked towards a lectern fixed right in the middle of the stage.

The wooden boards creaked with every step. The writer seemed unsettled. There were a lot of people in the room and he realised he had to speak to them. As he reached the lectern, the audience united in welcoming him with a thunderous applause. Cameras flashed. He caught a twinkle of awe and joy in a child's eye, who was seated right in front, and his confidence returned. He imagined his grandson sitting in the audience and the thought made him happy.

Dr Chary surprised his audience; his speech was clear, funny and witty. The book agent and the secretary were stumped. Even the speech wasn't the one they had written. It had been completely changed by Dr Chary at the last minute.

'I didn't expect him to be so proper and composed. When he got in first, I thought, I saw a flash of lunacy in his eyes. And he did lose his temper, didn't he? Don't tell me tonight won't be sensational,' remarked the director with heavy disappointment.

Vimal Verma didn't know what to say.

Dr Chary opened the book *A Dwarphant's Long Tale* after the question-and-answer session. His eyes brimmed with tears. Memories of how he had written one of his best novels ever flooded his mind. He began:

> '*Once upon a time, when a day lasted as long as a month, and a month stretched on for a year and a year seemed as long as a decade, there lived a young dwarphant named Kanlin. If you don't know what a dwarphant is, then allow me to explain.*
>
> '*A dwarphant is an animal that looks exactly like an elephant. Perhaps, you could call it a long-lost cousin of the elephants. "Why are they long-lost?" you would ask. I would say simply because we don't see them around*

anymore. So they probably got lost somewhere in time. Next, you would ask, "If they looked like elephants why don't you call them that?" I would answer just because a dwarphant looks like an elephant, you can't call it one. A dwarphant and an elephant are different, in three ways.

'A dwarphant is very short, like a dwarf; that's why it was called a dwarphant. Now, what do you get when you combine the words, dwarf and elephant? A dwarphant, right? A full-grown dwarphant adult could only reach up to four feet in height or less, although it is said that there was a dwarphant called Rudat who surpassed that limit when he grew to a height of four feet and ¼ inches.

'Now, have you ever seen such a short elephant before? Not a baby elephant, I am talking about a full-grown adult elephant. Now hold on for the next important difference. A dwarphant is impossibly black, including its eyes and tusks, as if it were clothed by the night sky. And the third reason why dwarphants can't be called elephants is because they don't have tails.

'Now, let's get back to our story. Young Kanlin was a dreamer who lived for 1587 years; the longest by far for any dwarphant and envied by all for it was a glorious life replete with adventures, thrills, treasures, food and tales—tales that were remembered by his children, grandchildren, great-grandchildren, great-great-grandchildren, until they were eventually passed on to me, even though I am not a dwarphant.

'I was told that Kanlin's tale must be read on a Sunday because no matter how fast or slow you read you will end up finishing the book on a Sunday. And thus for me, the magic of Kanlin lived on forever.'

'Why did he read the preface? I thought I told you to tell him to exclude it. We're losing time, Vimal,' the secretary lashed out at the book agent.

'I did. He wouldn't listen,' Vimal replied defensively.

'He never does,' the director added with displeasure.

'And dear audience, isn't it a strange coincidence that I read to you on a Sunday, just as the tale is supposed to be read,' said the writer.

The crowd egged him on. After years of isolation, this sudden meeting with people overwhelmed the writer. His heart beat with a violent force. Soon, his enthusiasm gave way to fatigue. Despite the chill in the hall, because of the air conditioners, he began to sweat. And despite his discomfort, he continued to read. As he turned the pages of the book, his arms hurt. Every page seemed to weigh as heavy as a rock. Sweat dripped from his forehead and he pulled out a handkerchief to wipe himself.

'Check the air conditioning,' someone yelled from backstage.

'*Chapter One: The Worst Birthday Ever*,' Dr Chary read. There was a change in his voice. It seemed devoid of any emotion. The people who were observing him intently, thought it rather odd. Dr Chary continued:

> *'Kanlin slept very well every day as though no day was bad and no worry worth losing his sleep over. As soon as he closed his eyes he saw happy, cheerful dreams and instantly fell asleep. That's why he couldn't understand why his parents or his brother complained of bad sleep. Kanlin was always the earliest to go to bed and the last one to wake up. All dwarphants had varied durations of sleep, but unlike their cousins, the elephants,*

(who according to the dwarphants slept rather poorly and worried too much) they slept a minimum of 12 hours, which in our time could well mean for 15 days.'

Dr Chary's stomach rumbled. He hadn't eaten since morning. He should have had that sandwich Vimal was about to offer him. Perhaps, then he wouldn't feel as sick as he did now.

'But Kanlin was different. He outdid everyone by sleeping a minimum of 20 hours or more. Sleeping was the only way dwarphants could recharge their magical powers. So, the dwarphants slept a great deal, and so did Kanlin, with the hope that when he got up he would feel a great magical power surging within him.'

Dr Chary lowered the microphone, rubbed his stiff neck, and then continued to read.

'Other dwarphants envied him. They assumed Kanlin had a simple, easy, carefree life and that's why he could sleep for long. But they were wrong. Without a doubt Kanlin slept the longest, but what they did not know was that he was a very, very unhappy dwarphant.

'Sleeping was the only way by which he could forget his unhappiness. When he was asleep, he saw dreams in which he was everything he wasn't in real life—a valiant dwarcerer (a dwarphant sorcerer) who could conjure powerful magic; loved and respected by everyone in the forest, including his brother. You see, the reason Kanlin was unhappy was because he was a weakling, a coward in real life, fiercely hated by his brother.

'On a particular Sunday morning, our hero, the dwarphant Kanlin, woke up with a start.

'"Happy Lefaphant," his mother greeted, as his father circled around him and trumpeted jubilantly.

'"Stop it…stop it. I was trying to get some sleep. What's wrong with you all?" yelled the dwarphant lying a feet away from Kanlin on a lush green field.

'"Ranag, it's your brother Kanlin's Lefaphant. He's 11-years-old today. It seems your memory is as poor as the elephants. Now will you stop being so touchy. Get up and wish your brother," admonished Kanlin's father.

'Ranag picked some stones and hurled them at his parents with his trunk.

'"He's not my brother. My brother Kanlin is dead. This dwarphant you're cosseting now is a piece of filth you found in the swamps, brought home and wanted me to call Kanlin. Well, he's not Kanlin. He is just a piece of filth and that's all I'll ever call him."

'Kanlin, who had heard every single word of his brother's hurtful rant, broke into tears.'

Dr Chary suddenly became conscious of the people staring at him. He realised that he was drenched in sweat. His voice had shot an octave and his heart was raging. Every throb felt like a bullet slamming into his ribcage.

Children, seated in the front, moved uncomfortably in their places. It was obvious that they were scared. Their parents threw each other questioning glances. What was wrong with the writer?

Dr Chary's excitement grew. It seemed as though he had no control over his body. His hands flipped a number of pages in between before he continued with his narration.

'Ranag kicked his brother Kanlin's leg from behind. Kanlin let out a cry of pain before falling to

the ground. His shin hurt terribly and his eyes were wet with tears.

'"*Daydreaming about Carsani, were you?" taunted Ranag, as his posse chortled.*'

'What's he doing? He's skipped chapter one and is reading chapter two now. There's something wrong. I should go check on him,' said Vimal, worried, and watched the writer from his seat near the stage.

'Well, you're not doing anything, Vimal. Stay put. Did you hear his voice? He sounds like a mad man. This is the sensational stuff I had been hoping for... We're going to be rich,' sang Jerome Ray, as the writer's voice blared through the speakers fixed to the walls.

'"*Who's Carsani?" asked Ranag's friend; a dwarphant with round ears.*

'"*You numbskull...he was one of the greatest dwarcerer of all time," remarked another dwarphant in the group.*

'"*Shut up... You're all numbskulls, but you know who's the biggest numbskull? It's this piece of filth grovelling on the ground. Want to know why? He thinks if he dreams about Carsani he'll become as powerful as him. Well, I am here to burst his bubble," said Ranag, as he repeatedly kicked Kanlin's behind.*

'"*You scum... Stand up on your legs right now," demanded Ranag.*

'*Although he was in a lot of pain, Kanlin managed to get up. He knew if he didn't listen to Ranag he'd only hurt him more.*

'"*So you think you're Carsani, huh? Let's see if you can defend yourself against me," said Ranag, as he looked at Kanlin's trembling, bumbling self and laughed derisively.*'

Dr Chary heard a ringing noise in his ears. It was feeble but it pricked him like needles. Then a voice said, 'Where are you? Can you hear me? Answer me.'

The voice was the one he had heard the previous night.

Dr Chary was puzzled. It seemed the voice came from somewhere near—almost as if the woman who had been talking to him since the previous night was standing next to him and whispering these words in his ears. But the truth was that there was no one around. The writer thought he had imagined it all and continued to read in his high-pitched voice:

> '*Ranag walked back a few metres, away from Kanlin.*
>
> '"Apsaryati," *he yelled and launched himself into a run.*
>
> '*Before Kanlin could blink, a body had slammed hard into him, throwing...*'

Dr Chary stopped abruptly.

'Serf, heed my order,' yelled the woman angrily. Then the ringing noise echoed. It seemed to tear through his skull.

'Stop it,' he screamed. His whole body convulsed. Suddenly he saw a burning flash of light in front of his eyes that faded away to reveal his wife holding her throat, gasping for breath until her life was gone. His own breathing grew laboured. A sharp pain jolted his chest and he fell on the floor to the sounds of cameras clicking, lingering gasps and screams.

4

Teeth in the Closet

Dr Chary knew he was alive. His ears were at work; picking up sounds—his heart beating, a steady beep of some machine, a fluctuating bulb, the buzzing of the air conditioner, a wobbly chair perhaps? His nose hadn't taken rest either. It was busy picking up the smells—blood, chlorine and a slew of chemicals. Was he in a hospital? The realisation brought to his mind the image of his wife lying on a hospital bed, wan from sickness, and with her spirit to live, broken.

'Aarthi, wake up… Aarthi,' he yelled as he got up with a start. He found monitors, tubes poking the veins in his hands, IV bags and green curtains all around him.

A woman in a white uniform rushed into the room. There was a syringe in her hand. She smelled just like his wife—full of chemicals.

'Aarthi, Aarthi,' he yelled without a pause.

'Dr Chary, calm down… Everything's all right,' she said, as she gave him an injection and patted his forehead. The writer felt his muscles relaxing and slowly sleep overcame him.

The next time he regained consciousness, he heard voices; very feeble that seemed to come from afar. Still, because of his sharp hearing, he could pick up every spoken word.

'Don't get him too excited. His health could be at risk again,' said a woman.

'Yes definitely, thank you,' said a man.

Something creaked. It was definitely the sound of the door opening. Now he heard footsteps. Then, cold, trembling fingers pressed against his forehead and a heavy, musky odour hit his nose. It was such a familiar scent. Dr Chary opened his eyes.

For a whole minute, Akshay didn't say anything at all. He looked at Dr Chary. He was happy indeed. But there was a perplexed expression on his face—while his lips parted widely in a toothy smile, his eyes were startled. He barely recognised his father. This weak, balding, emaciated man lying on the bed didn't look anything like his father. His father was a man who had a head full of shiny black hair. His father was a man who had such strong arms that he nearly crushed Akshay whenever he asked him for a hug; a man who was so broad-chested that it was difficult to find a shirt that could fit him. How Akshay envied his father while growing up because he always looked so dull and stunted in front of him. But now it had all changed.

Eventually, Akshay learnt how to suppress his shock for his father's sake. The nurse had warned him that Dr Chary could have another heart attack if he got too excited.

'Just keep calm. He's alive. That's all that matters,' Akshay muttered to himself.

'Akshay,' Dr Chary called, as the corners of his lips lifted up into a smile.

'How are you feeling, Dad?' asked his son, a tall, well-built man, dark and debonair, with a collared shirt, square glasses and a goatee.

Dr Chary looked around him and realised that he was in a hospital.

'If it weren't for the pictures you sent me and your favourite cologne that you're wearing, I wouldn't have recognised you.'

His voice was low and feeble and Akshay had to lean towards his father in order to hear him.

'Yes, of course…I hadn't realised that. I have changed, haven't I? How do you feel?'

'Uhh…a bit weak.'

'That's why I am here—to feed you and help you get strong. Remember the arm wrestling matches we had when I was in school and how I beat you all the time. Well, we are going to have a match pretty soon. If you want to beat me, you'll have to start eating everything I feed you,' Akshay lied of course. He knew his father intentionally let him win every single match, just to make him happy.

Dr Chary smiled again and asked, 'How did I get here?'

Akshay remembered what the nurse had told him. He had to be sensible about how he responded.

'You have been under the weather,' Akshay lied again.

Just then a rap was heard on the door. The nurse walked in with a tray of food and medicines.

'Can I take care of that?' asked Akshay.

'Yes, certainly,' replied the nurse and she laid the tray on a table and left.

Akshay picked a steaming bowl of oatmeal from the tray, put some sugar in it and gave it a stir. With just a few spoonfuls of the creamy nutty meal, Dr Chary's voice gained strength. Even his eyes seemed livelier.

'How is my grandson?' he asked.

'He sleeps all the time. I wish I had that luxury. I wish I could go back in time.'

'Don't we all wish that.'

'Meera wanted to come see you but Naveen had to be given his monthly shots. Her uncle, Romas, is in Cyprus on business. We couldn't find anybody else to take care of Naveen.'

It was time to give his father medicines; he had to come to terms with the reality that his father had had a heart attack that had nearly killed him.

And it wasn't just Akshay. Dr Chary too realised what had actually happened to him when he read the names of the medicines; they were the same ones the doctors had given his wife when she had had a heart attack.

'I want to take you to Darmas with me,' Akshay expressed his desire.

'Of course! Finally you know what you should be doing,' said Dr Chary with a smile, while remembering his meltdown at the book-reading event and wishing Akshay had come to him earlier before it had happened.

Dr Chary was discharged from the hospital the next week. However, he couldn't fly to Darmas immediately. The doctor had advised him complete rest for a few more weeks. Akshay took the instructions to heart and made sure his father never left his bed, except for going to the washroom. Dr Chary didn't see the daylight for many days. When the sun was up there, it marked the start of a new day. One had to deal with the hustle and bustle of life; the milkman, newspaper boy, vegetable vendors ringing the door bell, the sound of traffic.

But more importantly, realising that it was a new day made Dr Chary restless somehow. He would come to Akshay and tell him, 'It is Friday already, I heard the spinach vendor outside the door. She only comes on a Friday. I haven't written in a while. I am wasting my time. Everything's such a big waste.'

Akshay didn't want his father to be anxious. So he fed him well, even gave the old man pills to make him sleep and miss the sun. Wasn't that what the doctor had asked him to do? All that thinking had taken a toll on Dr Chary. The doctors said the writer had tired himself out.

Night or day, Akshay did not get a wink of sleep. Even his father's sleeping pills didn't help. There were so many things to deal with…

The newspaper reports about his father's mental health; they were brutal. They said the writer had had a breakdown and was in urgent need of psychiatric help. They backed up their allegations with evidence—before and after pictures of the writer alongside pictures of the *mad man's house*. The first time Akshay read them he had been terribly hurt. In order to prevent his father from finding out what was being said about him, Akshay had cancelled the newspaper subscription and cable connection and asked his wife to do the same in Darmas.

His father's restlessness had to be contained; Akshay had to distract him by taking him out for walks, talking about Naveen, cooking or cleaning the house with him, and cracking jokes. The latter was tough as Dr Chary rarely laughed; it seemed the funny bone was missing in him.

The big question, of whether or not his father should continue to stay in the Chenpalle house after his recovery, plagued Akshay. The house could be worth a fortune, however, Akshay was ready to abandon his childhood home for free. After all, there were so many painful memories here of his mother's long battle with cancer. Perhaps, that was why his father had fallen sick. Staying in this house also made Akshay sick with sadness; thinking of his mother's illness, how his father had rushed her to hospitals when her condition deteriorated, how his father remained hopeful even when the doctors gave up hope and how relentlessly he cared for his ailing wife, often foregoing sleep and food just to make sure she was all right.

Although he'd never express it in words, Dr Chary loved his wife dearly. He was devoted to her in a way Akshay could never be. His was not a typically happy marriage; he was not in love with his wife Meera. But he didn't want his father to learn about that and become upset.

One day, while he busied himself with cleaning the house as Dr Chary was asleep, he entered the room his father usually kept locked. Akshay was able to open it with a bunch of keys he had found in a flower pot just outside the room. His father had a habit of hiding keys in pots and he was well aware of it.

Akshay stood pleasantly shocked as he looked around the room. Situated in a nook of the palatial house, this room was a testament to just how much the old man missed his wife. He had carefully preserved all of his wife's things—hair clips, shoes, perfumes, nail polishes, her favourite cassettes, books, paintings, and even the jewellery she wore. Akshay felt his throat constricting with emotion, for every object evoked a different memory of his mother. When he opened the closet behind his mother's bed, he got another shock. Stored alongside his mother's clothes was an object whose presence was nauseatingly disturbing. It was a necklace—not made of precious stones, but human teeth—yellow, decaying, malodorous human teeth.

When he overcame his shock, he was reminded of what his father had once told him, 'Son, do you really want to know why I married your mother? Well, it may sound weird, but I was really attracted to her because of her beautiful pearl-white teeth.'

5

A New Beginning

Dr Chary's first step into Darmas was memorable, but not in a pleasant way. As soon as the exits of the plane were opened, his nose was assailed by a strong stench from the dirty airport surroundings. The drive from the airport to Akshay's house was smelly too. After all, Darmas, located in south-west Tamil Nadu, was known as the city of factories that belched an effusive mass of gases and dust into the air day or night. In fact, things were so bad that it wasn't unusual to be swathed in dust if one took a walk in Darmas.

Everything about Darmas was so overpowering. One could go deaf listening to the clamour of the traffic and the multitude of people swarming the streets. As for the sights, one could find a man eating, next to someone who was just about to throw up. But these things didn't seem to bother the writer too much. He was just excited about meeting his grandson.

Akshay pretended to be happy and cheerful for his father's sake. In truth, he was very disturbed. Had his father really gone bonkers? His father had loved his mother dearly, no doubt, but the fact that he had actually preserved her teeth to remember her was just bizarre. And how did his father get his hands on his mother's teeth? Had he somehow managed to steal them from the dentist when he wasn't looking? Akshay remembered those long and painful visits to the dentist when his mother's decayed and chipped teeth had to be removed. His mother once used to have the most beautiful set of teeth. But the radiation therapy for her cancer treatment had ruined everything about her, the least of which was her beautiful smile.

Presently, the taxi pulled over at a bower ensconced in the long shadows of mango and coconut trees. This was Akshay's house; an oasis of calm amidst the ruckus of Darmas. The environment definitely had a soothing effect on Akshay. For some time his worries didn't niggle him as much.

'I never thought I'd ever set foot in the city of factories or the *city of filth* as I call it. Yet, here I am and it doesn't look that bad. It's a new beginning. Now let's see my grandson,' expressed Dr Chary with a beaming smile.

Akshay had never seen his father so happy in the past weeks that he had spent with him in Chenpalle. After paying the fare, he stepped out of the car with Dr Chary's luggage in his hands and a broad smile to match that of his father's.

Dr Chary was ravenously hungry. Standing before Akshay's house, he could smell the oily puris, and the spicy, tangy curry to go with them. The aromas had come wafting from the neighbour's house, which was a stately villa, just like Akshay's. There were some fine houses in the vicinity, the writer observed.

'You have made good money son,' Dr Chary remarked.

'I haven't…it was Uncle Romas's gift to Meera,' said Akshay with disdain. Although he didn't want his father to know the truth, the words just spilled out of his mouth.

Dr Chary's face registered surprise, then disappointment. 'But... Akshay...' he began with some hesitation, and ended with, 'you could have asked me son... I would have definitely helped.'

'Dad... I don't want to talk about it... It's a new beginning...time to forget the past... You said that...so let's just stick to that,' said Akshay gruffly, surprising his father yet again.

Despite his words, Akshay thought about the past; how Meera had orchestrated getting the house for herself even though she knew Akshay couldn't afford it. She had fallen in love with the house when she had first laid her eyes on it.

> She had come to Akshay and said, 'Let's get it.'
>
> 'No, we can't. It's in the most posh neighbourhood of Darmas... We don't have that kind of money,' he had replied.
>
> 'We can borrow from your father and pay him back in instalments...'
>
> 'Enough! I am not going to ask him for any money. He's done more than enough for me...spending on my education, buying me every single thing I could dream of as a child.'
>
> 'Isn't that the kind of childhood you want for Naveen too? Besides, if your father has done so much for you, don't you think it's time to thank him in some way. If we had our own house in Darmas, Dr Chary could come and stay with us. You have neglected him, Akshay, and that's not right.'
>
> Akshay didn't know what to say. He felt really guilty.
>
> Then a week later, she had admitted to him, quite awkwardly, 'Umm... Uncle Romas... Well... I told him I liked the house...and umm...how ideal it was for Naveen to grow up in that house. So he bought it for us.'

Akshay had been horrified but Meera had argued that they would now have a permanent place to stay. They had bickered over this for months. But Meera had been stubborn about holding onto the house, making Akshay go through several more guilt trips about not looking after his father. In the end, he had no choice but to tell Meera's uncle that they would move into the house only if he was allowed to pay back the money in installments.

And it wasn't just this one episode; Akshay and Meera had had several fights because she came from a rich family and always wanted more of everything. Akshay tried to provide as much as he could but Meera was never content. Although he had a rich father himself, Akshay refused to ask for help.

A very pretty, petite woman, with light brown hair and eyes, dressed in a flowing white embroidered sari, emerged from the house. She opened the gate and broke the awkward silence between the father and son with the words, 'Dr Chary, finally! It's so good to see you.'

'Meera, it's good to see you too,' said the writer, before hugging his daughter-in-law.

Meera loved the writer. She had read his books as a child and idolised him. Even after marrying Akshay, she couldn't call him anything else but Dr Chary, the name by which he was famous among his readers. Her father-in-law too didn't object to it.

Dr Chary noticed two sedans parked in the garage adjoining the house. He wondered if Romas had helped Akshay buy the cars too. But he decided to push away his resentment; after all, it was time for a new beginning.

'Don't you get started on how thin I have become. I have heard enough of that already. Now where is my grandson?' he asked Meera.

Although Meera was shocked because her father-in-law wasn't just thin, but a bag of bones, she didn't express it as per Akshay's prior instruction.

'You're only here to see him, aren't you? He's upstairs, sleeping. It's the first room on the left. It's amazing how he looks so much like you when you were a baby. Akshay showed me your pictures, Dr Chary.'

'Akshay never misses an opportunity to embarrass me, does he?' remarked the writer. Then his eyes fell on his pale hands and the odd, scattered, black spots on them. At once he was reminded of his skin condition. What did Meera mean when she said Naveen resembled him? Did he have his condition too? Dr Chary didn't want his grandson to be called a panda or a chessboard by his classmates and suffer discrimination like he did. He walked into the house and climbed up the stairs in a hurry. A slight pain began in his chest because he was anxious.

If he has it, it's okay. With time the white patches will grow larger, the skin colour will even out like it did for me. It will get better, said Dr Chary to calm himself down. The pain in his chest disappeared.

He now stood inside a cool, dark, curtained room. His grandson was lying in a wooden cradle near the window. There was a soothing piece of music playing. He caught glimpses of Naveen—his satiny black hair, round mouse-like ears, a sharp nose and pink puckered lips—whenever the curtains fluttered due to the breeze and let in feeble shafts of sunlight. Meera was right. Naveen did resemble him. But what about the colour of his skin? There seemed to be no white patches on his face. But what about the rest of his body that was hidden by his clothes...

Dr Chary parted the curtains to allow more light in the room. He had to make sure his grandson wasn't abnormal. So he rolled up Naveen's sleeves and his pants. Much to his relief, his grandson's skin was flawless—dark brown, like chocolate, no spots whatsoever. Standing there, while looking over Naveen and holding his soft, tiny baby fingers, all his worries seemed to disappear. He felt so light, as if he was riding a wave of happiness. He wanted to stay right there and be caught in this moment for eternity.

6

Marita

Two weeks passed by in Darmas. The writer wasn't sure if he had recovered entirely. He did feel immensely happy being around his grandson but there were those nights of unspeakable horror. He dreamt of graveyards filled with piles of rotting corpses and a white cloaked figure; a menacing white phantom standing atop them all. He was swinging a long sharp weapon and slashing the bodies of people Dr Chary knew—his wife Aarthi, son Akshay, daughter-in-law Meera, and the apple of his eye, Naveen—as they came flying past him. Dr Chary couldn't get a wink of sleep after that.

Either he saw those terrible nightmares in which his loved ones were slaughtered or the flash of a white light that didn't seem to disappear even if his eyes were open.

In the morning, the morbid thoughts lingered on. That made him sick. He felt nauseous, restless, and his body was in pain. Sensing that this ordeal was because of the underwater experiment—for it always played with his mind—Dr Chary got back to writing. But unlike before, it didn't help him calm down.

Then one day, when Meera appeared in his room with Naveen and his eyes fell upon his grandson, something extraordinary happened. The white light, that he often saw, disappeared, and he calmed down instantly. After the incident, Dr Chary thought of his grandson as a healer.

So, whenever the nightmares came, the writer would drag himself out of bed and tiptoe to Naveen's room. He would open the door carefully so as not to disturb Meera who slept beside her son. Then he would flash a feeble torchlight upon Naveen until he would find the calm amidst the storm of his restless thoughts.

But one particular night, Dr Chary realised he couldn't keep running to his grandson's room whenever he had nightmares. What if Meera saw him staring at her son with a torch? What would she think? Would she call him a freak like the papers did? Dr Chary had read the news on the plane when Akshay was in the washroom and known that his son had tried to hide it from him all along.

'I want to be with him. That's the only reason why I'm here,' Dr Chary said, one day when he requested that Naveen be shifted to his room.

'So much affection for him and so little for your own son, Dad? I'm jealous.'

'I'm selfish, Akshay,' his father had said in jest, smiling. 'I just feel better when I'm near him. When you are my age, perhaps you'll understand. Watching the young beside you gives you a strange feeling of comfort, that even when you are gone, you would have passed on a bit of your wisdom, your unfulfilled wishes, a bit of yourself to them...that you'd still remain.'

Akshay's eyes were moist when he heard his father, for those were the very words his mother had said to him when he was young. Now his mother was gone. He couldn't bear losing his father too. He had to keep him happy and healthy in Darmas. That was his duty. The next day, Naveen was moved into Dr Chary's room. At the end of another week, Dr Chary emerged a happier and calmer man.

On a particular Friday afternoon, the writer woke up from his nap quite suddenly. The sun was blazing down upon him; the windows had been opened, the curtains parted. Dr Chary looked for Naveen, as he did every time he woke up, but his grandson was nowhere to be seen. His cradle was empty. The old man sat up in a daze. Seconds later a voice boomed into the room. It was Meera.

'Oh! You're awake. I'm sorry. Did the maid disturb you? I had asked her to bring Naveen downstairs. Oh wait.' Her eyes scanned the room.

'And she's cleaned it too. I had specifically asked her not to do that. I'm so sorry. Let me close the window.'

'It's all right. I am quite awake. Don't intend to sleep all day long.'

'Well, in that case, let us get ready for a grand feast. Akshay wanted to announce it but he just got a phone call from work. So I came up instead to check on you.' Meera looked at Dr Chary expectantly. After all, it was her birthday—she had mentioned it to him the previous night—and hoped he would wish her now.

'I'll be there,' Dr Chary replied gruffly.

Meera was surprised. Why was Dr Chary angry? Was it because the maid had woken him up?

'I apologise for the maid disturbing you,' she said with embarrassment before leaving the writer to himself.

Meanwhile, Dr Chary was equally surprised, wondering why his voice was laced with such anger.

He went downstairs and entered the dining room. It was exactly the sort of place he didn't want to be in; there was a big crowd of people. They all looked so phoney—laughing and chatting about inane things and pretending to show concern. Dr Chary recognised some of the faces. They riled him, especially that uncle of Meera's, Romas Kinkar.

He was a big sweaty man with a bald pate and a squashed nose that snorted air like a pig and sharp eyes that spotted everything, even ants.

Even though he was annoyed, Dr Chary couldn't think of going back to his room for a scrumptious feast was laid out on the dining table; golden roasted potatoes, long grained rice that was steaming hot, tangy sambhar, wholesome avial, fried appalams, dosas that glistened with ghee, at least a dozen chutneys, sweet and creamy payasam, and Dr Chary's favourite treat, rasgullas dipped in a pulpy mango syrup.

The people gathered there greeted Dr Chary. He exchanged pleasantries in the same falsely cheerful voice. Then he took his seat by the table next to Akshay.

'It's Meera's birthday. I couldn't help it. This party came up quite suddenly. She seemed to miss her family,' Akshay whispered into his father's ears. He knew he had upset his father with this social gathering.

'Well, of course it's her birthday. And you can't expect everyone to be a recluse like me, can you son? Birthdays ought to be celebrated and you can't do that without people.' He spoke evenly, his voice neither conveyed surprise nor happiness on learning about Meera's birthday.

Dr Chary talked very little to those near him. There were the neighbours, Mr and Mrs Lachenpas, next to Akshay. On his left sat the birthday girl, Meera, and her uncle. Dr Chary exchanged some words with Meera out of courtesy. He wanted to avoid Romas Kinkar altogether.

He hated the man with a vengeance. There was no one as phoney, uncouth and vicious as him. He swore like a sailor, perspired like a pig, and spat like a snake about to take down its victim. However, Romas was persistent in trying to get Dr Chary's attention. He succeeded when he asked Meera to swap places with him. Dr Chary's discomfort grew.

'Your film is doing really well, Chary. It's impressive; 15 crores in two weeks! What a fortune! Of course, I haven't had the time to get that information. I have been so busy with my overseas trips. I heard it this morning from the caddie. Apparently, everyone's been struck with the dwarphant delirium. Congratulations.'

Akshay glared at Romas and then at Meera. He had warned his wife that no reference was to be made about his father's work, especially the film. The makers had said so many nasty things about Dr Chary. But wait, was the remark expressed genuinely, Akshay wondered. The film had done well. Perhaps Romas had just heard about the success and was thrilled to express himself. The man was so busy all the time. His crazy schedule saw him travel across seven continents, seven times in seven weeks. He had especially taken out time to make it for Meera's birthday. He loved her dearly.

'I suppose it is. Thank you for bringing me the news. You know it's been a while...' Dr Chary began, only to be interrupted by Romas.

'Yes, Chary. You have seized the moment as they say. Tell me how did you do it? You must coach Nitya, my daughter. She's lost her mind writing poetry and stories about tribal land disputes. Who wants to read that kind of crap? There's no money in it, you know that. I told her, follow Chary. He's made it big because he writes for kids. You know what she tells me, "I listen to my heart, Daddy." Bull crap. She doesn't have a college degree. She's wasted five whole years of her life to write about tribal land disputes. Imagine that. Teach her the tricks, Chary. Knock some sense into her.'

Dr Chary was about to lose his temper. His face had been bathed in Romas's spit. He clenched his fist, but realised that he had to be decorous for Meera's family and friends were here.

'There are no tricks. You only write about what you're interested in. My advice to her would be to continue to do what she believes in. I have read what she's written in the past, but I'd like to see her latest work. Could you send it to me?' he asked with genuine interest this time.

Romas ignored Dr Chary and turned to chat with a freckled woman in the room. He obviously thought the writer's advice was absolute crap.

Dr Chary felt slighted. This was the indifference that had staggered all his efforts to socialise with people.

'You sent her to Graam?' The freckled woman asked.

'Oh I did not. Does she ever listen to me? I warned her it was a dangerous affair dealing with those tribesmen in Graam. They haven't evolved; still animals that can attack you. She just nodded. You know how little she really speaks and she still calls herself a writer.'

He laughed as though it was a very funny joke, and then continued, 'Anyway, I was sure she wouldn't go. But the next day, while I was about to take off to Lisbon on a charter plane, her mother called me up to say, "Nitya is in Graam. She left last night."'

Dr Chary wished he could plug his ears with cotton. He didn't want to listen to any of this chatter. He turned to find his son trying to sit down. Apparently, he had gone into the kitchen. Next he found Akshay mouthing a message to Meera. He kept doing it over and over again. Didn't Meera get it? Was she dumb? Or did she choose to ignore Akshay because he had more work for her, the writer wondered? After all, she had so many things on her plate—taking care of Naveen who had been crying without a pause, serving food, clearing the dirty dishes from the table, and calming down the other boisterous children in the room.

By then, the noise in the room had reached a crescendo. People were talking aloud and gesticulating like they were deaf. This whole room was a circus.

'What is it Akshay?' Dr Chary burst out.

There was pin-drop silence now. All the faces turned towards the old man in shock. Dr Chary felt uneasy. Within a few seconds Naveen resumed his cries.

'Please excuse me,' Dr Chary said feebly. He pushed his chair back and stood up. Akshay did not look at anyone except his father. His eyes were full of concern. He followed the old man into the kitchen.

Within minutes, the chatter in the dining hall resumed. Dr Chary could hear echoes of it in the kitchen. The room was a circus no doubt. He leaned against the wall and closed his eyes. He wanted to forget what had happened. Akshay waited for his father to gather himself, and then said, 'I'm sorry, Dad. I shouldn't have let Meera go ahead with this. I'm really sorry. I messed it up, didn't I? And you have only just arrived. It was selfish and thoughtless of me to force you into coming here. I should have just quit my job and stayed with you in Chenpalle, away from all this. You were much better there.'

'No, I wasn't. I was much worse. Don't lie to me. And you didn't force me. No one forced me. I came here on my own because I was afraid...of myself...of the loneliness I had caged myself in...I know all about it, Akshay. The breakdown at the book event, the horror-stricken faces of children. Then, there was the stroke. In a way, I'm glad I had it. It brought an end to my madness. I dread to think what else could have happened if my heart hadn't stopped that day.'

'You are not mad, Dad. Stop saying that. It hurts me so much to hear you mention anything about that day. I thought I had lost you... The doctors spared no hope. It was a nightmare. Please don't ever bring this up. What happened now at the table was just stress. You are, and have been, gravely stressed for some time. The reporters don't understand all this. We have been through so much.' Akshay swallowed a lump in his throat. He thought about his dead mother and the closet in which Dr Chary had stowed her decayed teeth.

Then he continued, 'So if you don't like someone, or something, you just need to tell me, all right. You don't have to put up with anything. I don't care two hoots for those people sitting there or what they think about you or us.'

With that, Akshay hugged his father. Dr Chary held onto him tighter. Tears fell from his eyes. 'I'm not losing myself, am I, Akshay?' The many thoughts that he had padlocked within were now agitated. They wanted to break free.

'No, you are perfectly well. Again, no compromises, you don't like it here then tell me. We'll leave. I'm here for you always. You're not alone.'

Meera was standing at the threshold, listening.

'I can kick these people out…especially Uncle Romas… I know you don't like him.'

'It's not like that Akshay… Anyway, so what were you trying to tell Meera at lunch?'

'I wanted her help in the kitchen. The maid sprained her ankle and took off. The raita's undone, the yoghurt is set, the veggies are in the fridge, they need to be chopped.'

'Oh. Come on. Your mother and I perhaps pampered you too much. And now, Meera has to suffer. The poor child! It isn't fair. You need to share responsibilities like your mother and I did. That's how things should be. Hand me the cutting board and the veggies.'

'Absolutely not, Dr Chary! The guests are all waiting for you. Please join them, that is, if it is okay with you,' interjected Meera as she walked into the kitchen, while picking up the cutting board and the bowl of veggies.

Dr Chary whisked them away from her and said, 'No, no, child. You give them company. As for me, no one needs an old crab in the room.'

'Dr Chary please.'

The writer wasn't ready to give up. Akshay kept quiet. He was happy he didn't have to do the chore.

'Please come and sit with us. You shouldn't have to be alone in the kitchen. Besides, it's really hot in here,' Meera pleaded.

Dr Chary agreed. Akshay followed him back to the dining room.

At first, Dr Chary was a bit embarrassed thinking of how he had lost his temper. But he noticed that the convivial atmosphere still lingered in the room. The crowd had possibly forgotten about his outburst.

Romas was still sitting in the chair next to his. Akshay asked him if he wanted to swap places, but Dr Chary said he was perfectly comfortable. He didn't want to make a scene yet again.

The writer, however, was irked listening to Romas's brags. Didn't Romas ever get tired of talking? Why did everyone like him anyway? And that included his son. Why hadn't his son come to him and asked him for help to buy the house? Had he felt closer to Romas?

Before his anger could surge, he tried to distract himself with the raita preparation. He picked the carrots first from the large bowl of vegetables. As he peeled them, a smile came upon his face. Slowly, the smile turned into a chuckle; the carrots—pale, swollen and hairy—reminded him of Romas's fingers. He wondered how it would feel to peel the skin off of Romas's fingers instead of the carrots and shook with mad delight.

Now, he picked the knife and chopped a carrot—that he imagined to be Romas's finger—in half. He imagined the blood oozing out of the severed finger and hearing Romas's agonising cries as the knife's blade reached his bone and abraded it. He laughed dementedly, but his laugh was drowned by the ruckus raised by the children playing in the room. No one noticed him for they seemed to be engrossed in inane gossip.

Dr Chary himself seemed to be oblivious of the crowd around him. It was as if he had completely disconnected himself from the environment and was purely absorbed in his own madness. He began to chop the carrots feverishly. His skin prickled with goosebumps and a shiver passed through his body.

Then something strange happened; a white dot popped up in his line of vision. Soon, it multiplied itself into hundreds, thousands, millions, billions, trillions, gazillions, until all he could see were luminous flashes of light framing his vision in a circle-like corona. A venomous voice within him boomed, 'Marita.' Upon hearing it, Dr Chary's hand tightened around the knife and moved away from the cutting board. The corona disappeared. Dr Chary—who seemed to be in a hypnotic trance now—stared at Romas's chest. The voice told him to stab his heart, where life was contained, and uproot it. Somehow, Dr Chary felt compelled to listen to it.

Just then, the wall clock tolled. Its loud chimes shook the writer out of his trance. The knife fell from his hand. He now stared at the faces of the people around him. They were absolutely clueless about the revolting thoughts that had crossed his mind seconds ago. His chest tightened in shock. Minutes later, he quietly slipped out of the scene to his room upstairs.

Dr Chary was in the bathroom now. There was an unrelenting turmoil in his head. Questions that needed immediate answers—why had he run away from the people downstairs? Why did he have such appalling thoughts all his life?

He plugged the drain of the washbasin before filling it up with water and ducking his head inside. The water relieved the pressure in his head but not for very long. For soon, he heard the mysterious woman again, this time telling him, 'Leave Darmas and come to me…for you are the White Death's Equal.'

Dr Chary pulled his head out of the basin. He looked around the room but couldn't find the source of the voice.

Where was she? Why was he still imagining her? Now, the ringing noise echoed in his ears.

'Life is a curse; full of pain and suffering,' said a voice.

It was different. It didn't belong to the woman. But it was also familiar.

'Marita,' spoke the voice and Dr Chary instantly recalled hearing the same venomous voice that had urged him to stab Romas Kinkar earlier.

Shortly, loud raps came from the door, but Dr Chary hadn't heard them. His hands closed around his throat for the oxygen that he inhaled stung like poison now.

When Akshay found Dr Chary, he didn't expect to relive his worst nightmare. His father was coughing, gasping for breath, turning blue just like his mother did 14 years ago. Akshay's mind urged him to help his father, but his body refused to obey. It remained neither still nor in motion—a flaccid, throbbing mass, stricken with panic. Just like the day his mother had choked on her cancer medicines and died right in front of him. That day, his father had been out shopping and when he returned, he discovered that his son had passively watched his mother suffer and die without doing anything to help her.

Meera was the one who responded to the emergency now. She used her hands and words to calm Dr Chary's nerves. Within minutes, the old man's breathing returned to normal and he lay down on the bed with Meera's help.

'What happened?' asked Romas who had just come upstairs after noticing that both Akshay and Meera were missing from the dining table.

'Nothing really... Dr Chary is just a bit stressed. He needs to rest. Akshay, will you please go downstairs and ask everyone to leave? Tell them I fell all of a sudden and hurt my back. We don't want any noise around so Dr Chary can have a good sleep. He will be all right when he wakes up,' said Meera with confidence. Her calm manner seemed to have a positive effect on her husband. For as soon as she had spoken, Akshay snapped out of his stupor and did as he was told.

The crowd took a while to disperse; those who were still pecking at their plates found it extremely rude and those who were genuinely worried for Meera, were alarmed. Like Mrs Lachenpas, the neighbour, who insisted on staying back to help. She apparently knew some massage techniques to relieve back pains. Akshay thanked her and told her that Meera just needed to be alone for a while.

When his eyes, by chance, fell upon Naveen who was asleep in his stroller, Akshay realised he had forgotten all about his son and that he was still getting used to fatherhood.

'I know you're hiding something,' said Romas, noting the deep distress in Meera's eyes.

'He tried to take his life,' admitted Meera weakly as though she was still in disbelief about what had happened.

'Really?' asked Romas. Oddly, there was a hint of excitement in his voice. Even his eyes lit up suddenly. Meera wondered for a brief moment if her Uncle Romas did take delight in Dr Chary's misfortune sometimes, just as Akshay had told her. But she brushed aside this thought once the worry returned on her uncle's face.

'His hands were wrapped around his neck. He was choking himself,' said Meera.

'And his skin's wan…his skin's wan…' mumbled Romas to himself, before adding, 'this is disturbing. First, the book-reading event and now this! He should be taken to a doctor…a good one, mind you. Let me call Dr Chandrika

Chetak. It's very difficult to get an appointment with her. But I may be able to pull a few strings. Should I do it?' asked Romas as he flashed his fancy brick-sized cell phone.

'Yes absolutely...she's the best one in the country and that's the right way to go about this. He needs to see a doctor. There is something afflicting him and he is perhaps afraid to discuss it with us. A doctor should be able to help. Except I don't know how I can talk to Akshay about this.'

'Well, your husband just has to come to terms with it. He is an adult. It's time he acted like one. I'll let you handle him, Meera,' said Romas before leaving the room.

Akshay and Romas crossed paths at the stairway, with the latter on the phone.

'Hello, is it psychiatrist Dr Chandrika Chetak's clinic? Yes...yes...yes... The patient's name is Dr Raman Chary... Yes... I can give you my phone number but I'd like to talk to the doctor first. Can you tell her Romas Kinkar is on the line,' spoke Romas on the phone in an intentionally loud voice as if he wanted everyone to hear him. Some of his spittle landed on Akshay's face and some on Naveen whom Akshay was carrying in his arms.

'Uncle,' said Akshay and shot him a questioning glance. But Romas seemed to have not seen or heard him at all. He was now pacing about the empty drawing room downstairs with his face stuck to the cell phone.

'Meera, what's going on? Why is Uncle Romas talking to a psychiatrist?' asked Akshay.

Meera bit her lip. She didn't think she would have to confront Akshay so soon. 'Dr Chary has been unwell. You saw what happened today.'

'What happened today, Meera? I'd like to hear it.'

'Oh! But you saw it, Akshay. He wasn't okay. He tried to...' Meera swallowed the rest of the words. She knew Akshay didn't want to hear the truth because it was just unthinkable.

'Tried to what?'

'Kill himself. You saw it, Akshay. He was choking himself. If I hadn't stopped him he could have...'

'Stop it... So you and your wiseacre uncle concluded that my Dad's gone bonkers and needs psychiatric intervention?'

'That's not what I meant.'

'So what did you mean?' asked Akshay angrily. His voice shot an octave.

At once, Meera closed the door and the windows. She didn't want the noise to reach the neighbours.

'You always raise your voice at me, Akshay. I have told you a million times I don't like it, yet you continue to do so. It's humiliating. But I am not going to bring up the past now. Your father's not been well and you know it too. Just the other day, he went about searching the whole house to find out where a certain ringing noise was coming from. None of us heard anything but he kept insisting that the noise was there and was driving him insane. Are you telling me there's nothing wrong with your father?'

'You know it Meera. He's just stressed with the book and everything. There's been so much going on. He'll be okay if he gets enough rest.'

'No...that won't solve it. What happened today was shocking! Dr Chary is a threat to his own life. You have to come to terms with it. Clearly, your mother's death has taken a toll on his physical and mental health. And the only way he can get better is through psychiatric counselling.'

'Clearly, Uncle Romas has put that thought in your head. It is his plan and you are in on it. He's never liked

Dad and is jealous of the wealth he's made on his own through pure talent and not chicanery like him. And now he wants my Dad to see a shrink, so that word gets out that he's loony and the whole world makes fun of him. Well, I'll tell you what I want. I want that bald, scheming, venal vermin to get out of the house right now.'

'Firstly, Uncle Romas would never do that. He respects your father. Why else would he ask him to mentor his daughter Nitya? Besides, your father's mental illness has already been made public without my uncle's so-called scheming, as you call it. And secondly, why should my uncle get out of the house when the house belongs to him?'

'Thanks for reminding me, Meera. I'll show myself out right away.'

Akshay angrily stomped across the room to leave Naveen in the cradle. His hand was upon the doorknob now, twisting it furiously and kicking it as though it was Romas's bald head.

Meera knew Akshay meant what he said, that he was ready to abandon the house, his family. After all, this wasn't the first time she had witnessed his tantrum. But she couldn't let her husband walk away from her like he had in the past. They had a baby now.

'Akshay... No... Please listen. How can you leave your son? I shouldn't have said it. I know it hurts, but think logically. I only want to help your father. A doctor could help...'

'No... I can take care of my father. Believe me when I say that.'

'I do.'

'Then, can you please ask your Uncle Romas to...'

'I will talk to him right away,' said Meera and left.

7

Memory is Misery

Things went out of control sooner than Akshay had anticipated; in fact, it happened 10 days later, on a Monday.

Akshay was in the office that day; having taken a week off earlier to look after his father and lift his spirits. He had requested Meera to call in sick for a day and spend time with his father because he had an urgent meeting to attend. Meera agreed. That Monday morning, the maid walked into the kitchen. Her brows were furrowed in worry.

'Madam, there's something I want to tell you,' she said.

'Yes, go on,' urged Meera.

'I found blood in Dr Chary's room.'

Meera skittered up the stairs panting and panicking. But soon she tripped, and ended up twisting her ankle. As she hobbled into the bedroom to find Naveen blissfully asleep in the cradle with an adorable smile on his face, she wondered if she had overreacted. But just about then, her eyes caught sight of bright incarnadine stains on Dr Chary's bedsheet and her panic returned.

The flushing of the toilet was heard.

'Good morning, Meera,' said Dr Chary with surprise after coming out from the bathroom.

Meera did not greet him back. The writer followed her gaze to the bloodstained bed and then to her baby. Dr Chary could understand that an alarming fear had possessed her. How could he make her understand that he had been crippled by the same emotion too? Should he tell her the truth about how he had suffered while bleeding from his ears? Would she believe him at all or distance herself even more from him?

'Oh! My shaving cut's made a mess. We need to change the sheets now, don't we?' stated Dr Chary, matter-of-factly. His voice did not betray his fear. It would do neither of them any good to dwell on fear.

Meera's eyes moved to the writer. His beard and moustache seemed to be intact. She couldn't see a cut anywhere on his face. Obviously, he was lying to her. What was he trying to hide? Had he attempted to take his life once again, by cutting himself?

'Do you hear it?' asked Dr Chary worriedly; his emotions returning, as his eyes searched the room for the source of the noise he could hear.

Meera looked vaguely at the writer.

'The ringing noise...every time I hear it, my ears start bleeding,' confessed the writer, fearfully. The ringing grew sharper. Dr Chary waited for his ears to bleed so that Meera would believe him, but nothing happened.

'Please tell me you can hear it,' he said and looked at his daughter-in-law with beseeching eyes.

'I can't Dr Chary. There's no noise here.'

Dr Chary was now stunned too. It seemed that he had been imagining the whole thing. Was he indeed losing his mind? The thought was so unsettling.

'Dr Chary, I know your wife is no more. But you still love her and miss her. You have been lonely and that is a bad state to be in. It makes you sad and terribly restless, with a million odd questions running in your head about the meaning of life, your very existence. And when you don't get the answers to those questions you end up hurting yourself. But why would you want to put yourself through such pain, punish yourself when a doctor can easily answer your questions and ease your worries. Let me take you to the doctor. I promise you, at the end of the visit you'll feel calmer. And I know it may seem scary to admit that you need the help of a psychiatrist, but we all have our problems. I have been seeing one for years now. Trust me, the doctor can help you calm your nerves with medicines.'

Dr Chary felt instantly comforted. Meera had been so prescient. It seemed as if she had read every thought in his mind. Right now, all he wanted was to get back to being calm. Clearly, writing hadn't helped him as it did in the past. But Meera had assured medication could cure him. She was confident about it. Maybe, he ought to try it. Plus, Meera had confessed to consulting a psychiatrist too.

'Thank you Meera for understanding,' he said.

Meera waited awhile. She expected Dr Chary to ask her why she was seeing a psychiatrist, but he didn't.

Sometime later, the writer and his daughter-in-law found themselves in a new place; a building made entirely of glass. This was Dr Chandrika Chetak's clinic, located in the boondocks, surrounded by lush greenery.

'Good afternoon, Mrs Meera Chary. How are you? I didn't know you were Mr Romas Kinkar's niece. He is one of the most notable patrons of the Chandrika Chetak Foundation. Would you like some tea or coffee before you see the doctor?' asked the receptionist aloud toadying to Meera from her oval glass desk.

'I am not the patient. It's Dr Raman Chary,' said Meera, and remembered how the receptionist had refused to give an appointment at such short notice till she had brought up her uncle, Romas Kinkar's name.

'Oh yes, madam,' replied the receptionist having caught a glimpse of the old man who was sitting along with a slew of patients in rows of chairs.

'There's a form that we require the patient to fill and sign. The doctor will see him as soon as that's done,' informed the receptionist, before escorting the duo to an adjacent room. Meera whisked the form away from the receptionist and began to scrawl the details as Dr Chary's weight and blood pressure were checked by a pudgy, pimple-faced nurse whose chin was oddly marked with hair. Here and there scabs could be seen interspersed between flesh coloured bumps. Meera cringed, watching the sore patches of skin, before turning her attention back to the form. There were about 10 dozen questions in the 10-page form. Meera answered each one of them. She wasn't perturbed by the time-consuming exercise. In fact, she was glad that they would finally have all the answers for Dr Chary's erratic behaviour.

In the meanwhile, Dr Chary's face was worn with worry. He wondered what the psychiatrist would find out about him, whether she would conclude he was abnormal as he thought himself to be since his childhood.

'You'll be okay, Dr Chary. Feel free to tell the doctor everything. It'll help you immensely. Trust me, you won't be judged,' reassured Meera.

Dr Chary looked at Meera with pleading eyes. He wanted to tell her what he couldn't and refused to utter what he should have. Wouldn't he end up in the psychiatric ward if he revealed hearing the ringing noise, the strange voices urging him to kill himself and those around him? After a heavy pause, he asked, 'Will she have medicines to calm me down?'

'Yes, she will.'

That's all Dr Chary wanted to know. He couldn't tell the doctor the whole truth but he could admit a part of it to get the medicines.

Just then, the pudgy nurse returned to the room. 'Dr Chary,' she called.

The writer looked up with a start. Meera handed her the form.

'The doctor would like to see you,' she said politely and added—'Mrs Meera Chary, could you kindly wait for the patient in the next room? The server will bring you refreshments in a bit. I am so sorry but visitors aren't allowed inside, so that the patient and the doctor can have a frank and healthy discussion.'

'Of course,' Meera replied before stepping out.

The writer now followed the nurse to Dr Chandrika Chetak's room, which was located at the end of a long hallway behind the reception. It was bright inside, with the sunlight streaming in through the glass walls and ceiling.

For minutes, Dr Chary waited at the threshold along with the nurse and stared at a solemn figure seated by an oak desk, reading something with profound interest with her head leaning. Evidently, the nurse was trying to let their presence be known by knocking on the door, clearing her throat, tapping her shoes on the floor, but never once daring to speak.

'Is there a problem?' asked Dr Chary, losing his patience. At once the nurse gasped and thwacked her head as though he had done something terribly wrong.

'Who sent him here?' asked the solemn figure with her eyes still fixed on the many files laid out on the desk. The voice was bold and full of authority.

'Rrrr...Romas Kkk...Kinkar, Dr Chetak,' the nurse answered timorously.

'Ah...yes...I remember now... Is this really important?'

'Mr Kinkar...ttt...thinks so.'

'Remind me why.'

'The patient is suicidal.'

'They're all suicidal. Tell me something new.'

'It's his skin...'

'What about his skin?'

'It's depigmented.'

'So?'

The nurse asked Dr Chary to wait, while she mustered up courage to cross the threshold and come closer to the desk where her boss was. 'Finally, I think we can now solve the mystery of the White Death,' the nurse said.

Upon hearing the name, Chandrika Chetak let out a throaty sound before pounding her fists on the desk. It was an outlet for all the anger, annoyance, and exhaustion that she felt on hearing about the White Death. But it didn't relieve her, for she began to exhale heavily, bearing the pain of her emotions. The nurse came forward to tend to her boss and blocked Dr Chary's view of the psychiatrist.

The pace of Chandrika's breathing slowed down. But the sound that was heard next was just as fierce as before. 'Why must I keep doing this, day in and day out, trying to find the White Death?'

The nurse stepped back. The only way to placate her boss was through words. Now that she had been given an opportunity to speak, she needed to be careful with her choice of words; choose only those that her boss wanted to hear. Experience had taught her that empathy was what an angry person needed the most.

'I know you are angry because you have been doing this tirelessly for so many years without getting any reward. It all seems so futile…it drains your energy. It isn't easy at all.'

'Tell me who the White Death is? Give me a reason why I must continue to find him, even after all these years.' Chandrika's voice had lost its fierceness, it was now a soft cry; a desperate plea for reassurance. Chandrika knew who the White Death was. She perhaps needed to hear from someone else why her life's mission was worth living for.

'The White Death is the dispenser of death. He is the twin brother of Life. He is…the reason whatever…is born must die.'

Again the desk was pounded upon, Chandrika's violent temper had returned, sending files of papers crashing down upon the floor. 'You know I can't stand this cultural babble. Just cut to the point.'

The shaken up nurse replied carefully, weighing the merit of every word uttered, 'He has the power to kill; to snatch life from the living, breath from the breathing. You want to study the many mysteries of this power because knowledge is all that you seek.'

Chandrika chuckled to herself softly while a wisp of a smile animated the nurse's face. Finally, it seemed she had said the right words to diffuse Chandrika's temper. She knew Chandrika valued nothing more than the pursuit of knowledge. Reiterating it had drawn her attention away from anger to what was more important to her.

'Bring him in,' ordered Chandrika.

Dr Chary seemed more confused, astonished and worried than ever before. He had heard the name of the White Death. The bodiless voice that spoke to him had uttered that name every now and then. Still, he didn't know what to make of the conversation that had just transpired. Had he imagined things that didn't exist like the white flashes? Was his mind playing tricks on him, making him see the unreal like a madman? But what if he had heard right? What if there were strange things going on in the world too and not just in his mind? Was this the connection he was waiting for? Just as he considered this possibility, Meera's face came to torment him. The way she had looked at him when she discovered the bloodstained bed and heard about the ringing in his ears, with terror-stricken eyes as though he was a deranged monster on the loose who would harm her baby… as though her baby meant nothing to him but fresh meat. Would merely talking about his abnormality make him that monster feared and reviled by all, removed from society, caged and separated from the ones he loved the most; Akshay and Naveen? He couldn't bear the possibility anymore. His only resort was to suppress his thoughts just as he had done all these years.

'Take a seat,' said Dr Chandrika brusquely, pointing to a comfortable leather recliner, once Dr Chary was brought inside by the nurse.

Dr Chandrika Chetak was a short, muscular woman in her late thirties with something very crude, wild and compelling about her. She had an untamed, frizzy mane, a unibrow, the faint trace of a moustache and a beard.

Her face was narrow and stretched like a horse, swarthy but marked with blisters and white patches just like Dr Chary's had been years ago. As for her eyes, they were sharp, tawny orbs like an owl's.

Despite his reservations, the writer settled in quite easily. The recliner, the fur mat underneath it, and the shelves of books around reminded him of his favourite bookstore in Chenpalle, transporting him back to a time when everything was well and normal, bringing him a moment of peace.

Just then, an electronic melody was heard, disturbing the writer's peace and drawing him to the present.

'It's Kinkar calling me…he's desperate for Dr Chary to be examined…and I hate that I have to listen to him… Get the sun out of here,' ordered Chandrika after throwing away a bulky, chiming device at the nurse, who missed getting hit by the skin of her teeth.

'Yes doctor,' said the nurse; her calm voice belying the irritation she felt. She then pressed buttons on a remote that activated the wall fans and screens across the transparent walls and the ceiling of the uniquely designed glass room.

'You can leave us now,' said Chandrika to the nurse. The nurse handed over the patient file and then closed the door behind her.

'Are you a widower, Dr Chary?' asked the doctor matter-of-factly reading from the patient file.

The writer was grossly offended. But he didn't know how to let his feelings be known.

'Yes, I am.'

'When did your wife die?'

'Uh!…1986.'

'1986…1986…all right,' said Chandrika Chetak and then fished out her glasses from the drawer. They seemed like an ordinary pair until she tapped on the round lenses and they magically began to glow white.

'Relax Dr Chary... Relax... Just lean back on the chair and relax,' instructed the doctor in soothing whispers.

Dr Chary was drawn to her voice, drawn to her glasses. He listened to the doctor and once he did what he was told, he felt very calm, very peaceful.

'How did your wife die, Dr Chary?'

'Cancer.'

'Do you still love her?'

'I...my life feels like a complete waste...without her.'

'Did you try to kill yourself because you miss her?'

'I... I...love her... I am,' began Dr Chary.

'Go on... Did you really want to die because of her? I think you know... Tell me the truth.'

'I...sometimes...for as long as I can remember, I have felt that my life is a complete waste... That there's no purpose... I wanted to kill myself because I was fed up with life. I wanted an...'

'You don't say... Well...well,' Chandrika's voice quivered with excitement as did the rest of her. Just then a bell rang and the pudgy nurse stepped inside the room.

'Do it now. I don't have all day,' said Chandrika Chetak, and immediately, the nurse poked the buttons on the remote. The air began to smell foul now, redolent of mouldy fruits, faeces and rotting meat. The nurse fought her urge to vomit and soon fixed a gas mask on her face. The doctor however was unperturbed. Even the writer didn't react, perhaps because his mind was too relaxed.

Shortly, something even more strange happened. Images flashed on the doctor's glasses of an ancient chamber with pillars, stairwells, statues, ornate doors, a vaulted roof, and dead bodies strewn all around in various stages of decomposition. These images lasted for a minute after which the light went out from the glasses. When they glowed again, words echoed from the glasses.

'The blood is getting warmer.'

'Life grows within him.'

'Fools tarry not. Kill your Master, bring death to the White Death before the Prana grows too strong.'

The light disappeared again and when it reappeared, Dr Chary saw images of seven robed giants encircled around a platform on which a body lay covered with a white sheet. Strange voices were heard. The light faded away. Just as soon as it returned, it presented another image of a giant pulling a sword from its scabbard fixed to his waist. When the sword was nearly out, his hood fell back slightly revealing a face mask and two milky orbs from the centres of which white light shone. And then, the scene dissolved away and what lingered on was the image of the supine body covered with the white sheet. The sheet-wrapped body reminded Dr Chary of his wife. And instantly, a past memory triggered; every moment of which was inexplicably beamed onto Dr Chandrika Chetak's glasses.

Dr Chary saw his younger self in his own house in Chenpalle, lugging shopping bags and standing before a partly open door. He was peering into his wife's bedroom now where she was coughing, gasping for breath, squeezing her throat. No doubt, she had choked on her own medicines. It had happened before. Dr Chary had helped his wife back then. But now, he wasn't alarmed; he had no intention to save her. Hadn't she punished herself enough with all those chemo sessions, surgeries, medicines and their side effects? It was time to stop living like this. Embrace death. Death was serene, blissful.

Dr Chary clasped the door knob. His fist tightened. He whispered his wife's name, 'Aarthi,' and at once, saw her fall on her back. Then a moment of serene silence and stillness followed only to be broken by a cry. The writer flung the door open. He found his son Akshay squalling uncontrollably. After all, the poor child had watched his mother collapse in front of him. Dr Chary called his wife's name again, pressed his ear against her chest. But there was not a sound; her heart had stopped beating and her body was still, she was dead. Then, he pulled a sheet from the bed, covered her body and whisked his son away from the scene of death.

'I cou...couldn't do anything, Dad. My legs just wou...wou...wouldn't move,' Akshay stammered through his cries.

'It's okay, Akshay. Your mother is in a better place now.'

'I let her die. I killed her. Didn't I? I killed her.'

'No Akshay, it wasn't just you,' he said, as he tried to console his son.

I watched her die too because I wanted her suffering to end, Dr Chary whispered to himself.

Dr Chary got up from the recliner with a start. He had snapped out of his entranced state because of guilt. Slowly, the remorse gave rise to waves of shock and sadness that passed through his body, jolting him just as it had 14 years ago. His head fell into his palms and he cried and called his wife's name lugubriously. The nurse rubbed his shoulders to comfort him. The doctor on the other hand didn't seem to care for her patient as was her duty and the nurse could easily sense that. Chandrika was caught up in her own personal agony; berating herself and banging her hands on the desk and finally picking up her cell phone, answering a call and throwing it back again.

'Doctor...I understand the patient didn't connect with the memories you shared with him but you...do have to calm down,' advised the nurse after pulling out her gas mask. The sickening odour had disappeared as soon as she pressed another button on her fancy remote.

'I can't...that pigheaded Kinkar wants me to see another suicidal patient ASAP... Who does he think he is, wasting my precious time. I want to tear the skin of his bones... Throw this obnoxious wailing school girl out of the room... The White Death...doesn't exist... You hear me. The White Death is dead.'

'Doctor, please calm down... Please, it isn't good,' begged the nurse, as she noticed her boss suddenly looking hairier than before, on the verge of transforming into something wild and fierce.

'Get him out of here now,' yelled Chandrika.

'But doctor, what about erasing the patient's memory of what he saw?'

'I can't deal with that right now. Just leave me,' ordered Chandrika.

The nurse dragged Dr Chary to the next room. Once she gave him a shot, the writer calmed down and stopped repeating his wife's name.

'Your wife's death has taken a toll on you. You suffer from stress, depression and hallucinations. The doctor would like to see you, day after tomorrow, to continue to treat you, especially for the very disturbing hallucinations you had during today's session. I will fix an appointment for you right away.'

Dr Chary nodded. Just then, his daughter-in-law Meera walked inside and the nurse briefed her about the situation.

Why isn't she telling Meera about the strange things that happened in the room, Dr Chary wondered. He wasn't sure if they were indeed real or he had imagined them just as the nurse had told him. But he couldn't ponder too long for the injection the nurse had given him made him feel very drowsy.

The drive back home passed like a blur for Dr Chary (all he could remember was Meera begging him not to tell Akshay about this visit to the doctor). But it wasn't so for Meera. She was tense, aware of every single minute and thought in her mind. After all, she wanted to reach home quickly so Akshay wouldn't find what she had been up to.

They were back home after a long time. Meera parked the car in the garage. Akshay wasn't home yet. Meera was relieved and helped Dr Chary out of the car. But, just when she stepped on the porch, to her horror, the door opened revealing Akshay.

'Oh... Hi,' said Meera.

Akshay didn't greet her back. His eyes were scrutinising the bag in Meera's hand; the name and address of Dr Chandrika Chetak's clinic was printed on it.

'Are you all right, Dad?' asked Akshay worriedly, stepping forward and wrapping an arm around his father's back.

'Just...very sleepy,' Dr Chary replied. His eyes were barely open and his voice a feeble whisper.

'Let's go upstairs,' said Akshay and escorted his father to his room.

As soon as Dr Chary was inside, sleep overcame him and he passed out on the floor. Akshay had to lug him to the bed.

'Meera,' said Akshay indignantly as his wife walked into the room. There was a tic in his cheeks.

'You're raising your voice again... Naveen is sleeping,' said Meera while turning her attention to her child lying in the cradle.

'Bet you didn't expect to see me. But my car broke down and I had to take the taxi to get some important files from home. Now the reason I took this long to ask you what you have been doing is because I wanted to give you enough time to think of a good lie to explain what's going on with my father.'

Meera knew that she would have to tell him everything now, 'I am not going to lie to you Akshay, because you already saw the medicine bag from Dr Chandrika Chetak's clinic. Yes, I took him there and whilst he was talking to the doctor about the past, he had a breakdown. So they had to give him a shot to calm him.'

'I told you not to take him to a psychiatrist. But you didn't listen to me. You went behind my back just like you did when you begged your uncle to buy this house for us.'

'I am sorry, Akshay. But you are bringing up two different issues. Right now your father needs therapy. He is very disturbed. He hallucinates.'

'Shut up! I told you it was that scumbag Romas's plan and you went ahead with it by completely disregarding what I had told you.'

'And I told you why your argument made no sense at all. I can't believe you are bad-mouthing my uncle despite all that he has done for us. Oh wait a minute! I know what this is about. You don't want to accept the truth that your father could be depressed. Maybe because you know that leaving him all alone in Chenpalle after your mother was gone could have led to this. But if you are going to wallow in your guilt and not do anything practical, you could lose your Dad just as you lost your Mom.'

'Enough. Just shut up. Shut up. Shut up,' yelled Akshay and slapped Meera hard on the face. Meera was stunned. She couldn't believe what had just happened.

'I have put up with everything—you humiliating my family and me having to live like a peasant. But this... this is the last straw, Akshay.' She then grabbed Naveen and stomped out angrily.

When Dr Chary awoke the next day the house was empty—Naveen, Meera, Akshay were all gone. The only real signs that revealed they had once been with him in this house were Naveen's feeding bottle, Meera's wedding ring and a note from Akshay which read:

> Dad, sorry to leave you. Work's come up. I should be back by lunch.

Dr Chary waited for his son. The hours passed by. But Akshay didn't return. Even the maid didn't show up. The house was unusually empty and quiet. But what was even more unusual was the fact that Meera's wedding ring was lying on the floor, as though it had been discarded. He tried to remember the previous night—his secret visit to the doctor with Meera, Akshay steering him upstairs. Had Akshay found out that Meera had taken him to the doctor against his wishes? Had he then fought with Meera over it? Oh no! It was his fault. He couldn't stay here anymore. It wasn't right. He had made a mess of things. His son shouldn't have to suffer. Suddenly, the mysterious ringing noise blared into his ears and when it stopped, he heard the woman's voice again. The voice said, 'Come to me, Dr Chary. You are the White Death's Equal.'

Part II

Ricchay Gupta

1

The Hunt for Dr Chary

There was a slight nip in the air. Still, the man driving the luxury sedan, with its windows rolled down, was drenched in sweat. It was unusual for the night temperature to drop so low in Darmas. Did the man in the car not feel cold? Of course, he did. His hands and feet were trembling.

In the next couple of hours he had to kidnap his victim at gunpoint. The thought of putting a gun to someone's head was making him terribly nervous. However, this wasn't his first time. He had abducted 30 people in the past. He remembered each of his victims—their names, how they talked, behaved, smelled. These memories of his victims haunted him, hurt his mind and body like he was stricken with a disease. They couldn't be forgotten so easily. The thoughts remained as if to punish him for the sins he had committed.

His victims had all been killed. Not solely by his doing. Ruchira bore culpability too. She was his friend, his partner in crime, who lived near the Arabian Sea.

All the 30 people were dead because they were not special. When the first three died in quick succession, Ricchay had gone into deep shock. He hadn't been able to talk, eat or even find a minute of calm. His conscience constantly pricked him like a thorn in his chest. But with time, things had got easier and the thorn fell out.

Ruchira had explained to him, 'Ricchay, we're doing this for the greater good. This is the only way we can find the one who can challenge the White Death. He is coming for us all; we need a saviour urgently.'

Ruchira's words had made it easier to get on with life, or so he thought, until he had to come to terms with accepting the death of his last victim, a seven-year-old girl called Padma.

> 'I really thought Padma was special,' he had said to Ruchira.
>
> She shook her head, her eyes were red. 'I thought so too. She stayed underwater for a long time until dusk… for 15 whole minutes…and then suddenly it was all over. She had drowned.'
>
> Ricchay wasn't listening. He had blacked out, as though a speeding train had slammed into him. The shock had been as severe. When he woke up, he imagined the little girl, Padma, smiling adorably at him. She smiled all the time, even when he had kidnapped her. That day, he had told her that he was going to take her to the beach for a swim and she had believed him. She had been so happy and excited. She had expressed how she loved nothing more than the water. Thinking of the past had brought painful questions to his mind. Hadn't Padma been in the water, in the bosom of the Arabian Sea, when she died? Was there a smile on her face then? Of course there was. But how long did that smile last before she began to choke? How much did it hurt when the sea—something that the little girl loved so dearly—flooded violently into her young body, crushing her delicate lungs.

No doubt, Ruchira had watched all this happen as a passive bystander. She couldn't have helped the poor child because she needed to know if Padma was indeed special, that her survival instinct would kick in at the very last minute and save her from drowning to death in the Arabian Sea. That was the reason Ruchira hadn't saved her or any of the other victims who were thought to be special.

Still, the child's death was devastating. More so because Ricchay had become a father of a two-month old baby girl called Ajari. Every time he looked at Ajari, he wondered how he'd feel if she was snatched away from him, thrown into the dark cold water of the Arabian Sea and put to test by Ruchira to see if she could hold her breath underwater. If Ajari failed—that is if her body couldn't adapt to the water; learn how to breathe in it—and she died, then Ruchira would simply tell him with tearful eyes how she was positively sure Ajari was special.

Ricchay Gupta stopped the car. His hands couldn't hold onto the steering wheel. His fear engulfed him. He had felt this way not only because he was on a mission to kidnap victim number 31, but also because he had realised this could very well be his last mission. It was dangerous and the chances of his survival seemed rather slim. Still, he was willing to take the risk because both Ruchira and he believed that Dr Chary was special. He was destined for greatness. Even if he didn't know it now, he was going to stop every mortal man from dying of disease, murder, war and accident. Yes, he would be the healer and have the power to cure every fatal disease or injury. Not just that, he would protect the earth and every living, breathing creation from any grievous harm. He would do so by duelling with and vanquishing the embodiment of death, destruction and decay: the White Death. The White Death was real, existed from the time life was first created on this planet. Even though one couldn't see the White Death in this time and age, one could feel the presence of the White Death's evil power tempt one into confusion, greed, indolence, pride, fear, anger and hate. Religious texts around the world had different names for the White Death: Life Slayer, the Lord of Death, the Devil. The White Death's purpose had been to augment the evil in men, to overpower the good, surge forth and destroy creation.

Indeed, this mission was both alike and different from the ones before. In his mind, Ricchay went over the notes he had made. Dr Chary was believed to be special just like the 30 others before him. But this belief wasn't just based on the fact that he fulfilled every term of an ancient prophecy about the planet's saviour, one of which was his ability to stay underwater indefinitely. There was something else to prove that Dr Chary was special—a book written by him about a time and place in which the White Death had existed. That's what Ruchira had told him and he had to take her word for it for she herself belonged to a different era and showed him things from the ancient past, talked to him in such veritable detail about the genesis of life, its many mysteries and descent into chaos and degeneration that no amount of imagination could ever conjure. As a sworn protector of life, Ricchay was prepared to deliver Dr Chary to his fellow protector Ruchira but what he wasn't prepared for was the life-threatening obstacle along the way that gravely distressed him.

But how could Ricchay overcome it? Death was certain, no doubt, at the hands of the hostile army—the deranged worshippers of the White Death—that stood between him and Ruchira. Especially because he was ill-armed with just a pistol and a stone in his pocket when he knew the army would hurl grenades at him and maul him with its brute strength. Still, there didn't seem to be any other way out because Ruchira didn't trust anybody but him.

Indeed, Ricchay Gupta felt powerless. Strangely, this feeling had sunk in long before his mission to abduct Dr Chary. All his life he had been weak and vulnerable. He didn't like himself and neither did his parents like him. While growing up, he was aware of how his parents neglected him even if he cried for attention. He was not the best in studies and he was bullied by kids for being dull, fat, ugly and was always confused. Even as an adult, life wasn't pleasant. He hated his job but was forced to do it. His career was built on lies.

Ricchay now yanked his wallet from his pocket to look at a picture of his wife holding their baby daughter. Why had Kadambari married him? What did she see in him? She was the most beautiful and talented woman he had ever met. He was the ugliest, weakest person he had ever known, yet Kadambari had fallen head over heels in love with him. It was just preposterous. She deserved someone better; definitely not him. He was a liar, a wimp, even a murderer. Ricchay shook at the realisation and wondered how Kadambari would react when she discovered that he had been responsible for the death of 30 innocent civilians.

Ricchay dropped his wallet and yanked a shiny semi-automatic pistol—with the silencer attached—from his pocket. He pressed its long barrel against his chest now.

The safety latch was set off. His heartbeat raced. It was time to punish himself. He closed his eyes and pulled the trigger without thought. Click!

'Tut...tut... How selfish are you! You don't look like you care about anything else in this world but yourself. But do spare a thought for people dying of starvation,' said a voice full of censure.

Ricchay looked up. A thin, bald, lightly freckled man in woollens peered into his car. His gibbous eyes were rimmed with dark patches of skin as though he hadn't slept in a while.

'Who...are you? What do you want?' asked Ricchay, stunned. There was a numb spot on his leg where a ball of ice had been resting. From within its misty walls an object gleamed; it was the very bullet that had shot out of the pistol to kill him. But its movement had been hindered because of the ice ball that the bald man had placed mysteriously between the bullet and Ricchay.

'You are selfish, aren't you? Never paid attention to a word I said. My abettor is starving and you'll make a perfect meal.' The man smiled at Ricchay revealing a set of unnaturally white teeth.

He now pointed his hand at Ricchay and whispered a magical chant, '*Unhissa*.'

Ricchay let out a yawn, dropping his gun. He felt so terribly tired and drugged with sleep. His eyes could not focus. 'Follow me,' said the bald man. He held Ricchay's hand and led him inside a van parked behind Ricchay's sedan. The air in the van was nearly frigid. Ricchay sat next to the bald man just behind the driver. The long seat opposite him was occupied by a strange, trembling figure lying underneath a pile of woollen blankets.

'Drive, drive,' the bald man yelled and the driver stepped on the accelerator at once.

'Are we still checking on that ringing noise?' asked the driver.

'No, we can't risk it. We don't want Chandrika Chetak's minions back on our trail,' answered the bald man.

'Maun, can you please spray some perfume?' The bald man requested the driver.

At once, the driver pressed a button. Puffs of mist floated around. The car smelled floral now.

The bald man reached into a duffel bag lying on the floor and fished out a box of syringes. He picked one from the set and examined it.

'We can't risk it. We can't have this man bleeding in the car. The smell of blood will alert them. They'll find us,' he said to himself.

The driver seemed to have heard the bald man. 'How do you know it was Chandrika Chetak's lackeys who gave us a chase?' he asked.

'It's simple, Maun. Chandrika Chetak is the only one who is trained in the magic of intrusion. She can get inside your head, examine your memories, remove them and put new ones in. It's a special ability. She's a big doctor here in Darmas. That's how she treats her patients. Apparently, she's taught her minions too. Did you see their faces? They were all wearing those circular glasses to get inside my head. Luckily, I distracted them. If they had seen Labya they would have found out about the ringing noise and the Corestone because she's been thinking about it often.'

The bald man now shook as if out of fear. He then fastened a pressure band around Ricchay's arm, felt his vein and pierced it with the needle, meticulously, like a nurse.

The syringe filled up with Ricchay's blood and although he could see the bald man draining the blood from his body, he couldn't object to it. He was just so very tired.

The bald man took a long, hard whiff of Ricchay's blood and his pale eyes gleamed with excitement.

'Why is everyone looking for the Corestone? I don't know anything about it because no one tells me,' said the driver.

'I'll tell you later, Maun. Please drive us to the Darmas cemetery first. Chandrika's lackeys could give us a chase again. If we head to the cemetery we can be sure they won't bother us. Lots of rotting bodies there; the hounds won't be able to bear the stench.'

Now, he fed the syringe into the shivering body wrapped in the blankets and said, 'There there, Labya. There's been too much drama in a day. Now take all the nourishment you need.' After that, he pushed back the sleeve of his sweater to reveal a jewel on his wrist. Ricchay's eyes lit up as he recognised the jewel. After all, he had the same one in his pocket. It was called a braceband—a solid band of metal with a white stone fixed in its centre. The stone glowed fiercely on the bald man's wrist and he smiled at it.

'Even if they find us, we are prepared to fight. Now, Maun, you were asking me about the Corestone, right?'

'Yes, Master Besar.'

'Tut…tut…Maun, I am not your Master. I am not worthy of that respect. Our only Master is the all powerful, the eviscerator of life, the death-giver, the White Death, and it is the White Death who will free us from the shackles of life…until death,' said Besar, and pushed his index and middle fingers into his neck.

'Until death,' repeated Maun. 'As I was saying, the Corestone is an object designed by our Master, the White

Death himself. Its powers are inconceivable. They say, once Master had forged it in the White Age several thousands of years ago, Master was able to not just rule the world, but also massacre millions of innocent lives in a matter of seconds. That is why it is imperative that we find it and fulfil our Master's purpose—the destruction of life on earth.'

'But how do we know it exists when we don't even know about our Master's existence,' said Maun, before asking to be forgiven for his insolent remark.

'No, no, no, no…never ask for forgiveness. And never believe completely. Disparage and doubt always. Only then will the evil within you grow. You're right, we don't know where our Master is but we do think the weapon could be around because of the ringing noise.'

Just then, loud moans were heard. The chill within the van diminished and the figure wrapped in blankets awoke with a start. She opened her mouth with a vicious growl and retractable fangs tore through her gums. She was ready to pounce on Ricchay and nourish herself with more blood, but she was stopped by Besar with a solid jab to her face. Hurt, she growled louder than before, and flashed her fangs at Besar.

Ricchay shook with horror as he realised he was in a car full of bloodsucking vampires. They were the worshippers or followers of the White Death. But why were they here in Darmas? He had to call for help, he had to alert the Council—the special police unit capable of duelling with vampires and suppressing them—by making contrails in the sky with the braceband. If only he didn't feel so tired, he could slip his hand inside his pocket and get the braceband out.

Of course, that was what his instinct told him because it was evident that he was in danger. But the truth was, Ricchay didn't know how to use the braceband; sometimes it worked, sometimes it didn't. And when it did, he had no control over it and disaster struck.

'Labya, calm down, will you? We have had too much drama,' said Besar to the female vampire who had short, wavy, perfectly coiffured hair framed around a pale, thin, heavily-powdered face.

Labya was still in a rage. So, Besar pricked Ricchay's hand, drew out more blood and fed the syringe into Labya. Within seconds, her breathing eased.

'You know you're very crude and messy with this whole sinking-your-fangs-into-flesh business. You have always been that way. I can't let you make large, gaping holes in this man's arm and watch the car being soaked with blood. The stench will definitely alert the werewolves—Chandrika Chetak's lackeys. They'll instantly know where we are. Do you hear me?'

'Don't you dare raise your voice. And don't you dare forget who you were before I elevated you—a werewolf grovelling in filth, begging to be transformed to a vampire. I was the only one who paid you any attention, listened to you, helped you, elevated you. If it weren't for me you and this driver would be licking the feet of every vampire,' said Labya.

'That was 50 years ago. Am I still to prove my worth as a vampire?' asked Besar, clearly irked.

'No matter how hard you try you'll always be a werewolf in my eyes,' replied Labya.

'Well, if I was still one, I wouldn't have disembowelled that werewolf today.'

Labya laughed derisively. Now creases were visible on her perfectly smooth skin. 'How very vain of you! It wasn't a werewolf. It was a rabbit hopping about in the sanctuary,' said Labya, while aligning the pearl pendant of her chain with the tapered neckline of her tailored dress.

'He wasn't a rabbit. You saw him. When I killed him, he changed into his original self—a werewolf. Just to remind you Labya, that rabbit was a morphone, or in other words, a werewolf who can transform himself into other animals.'

'Oh yeah! You were one too, weren't you? A little frog picking flies with its sticky tongue. I am sure we are going to need rabbits, frogs and ants in this mission to end the world.' Labya laughed out aloud and added, 'If you hadn't been so daring we wouldn't have landed in trouble. I can't believe we are running scared from the very werewolves we conquered and crushed eons ago.'

'They're Chandrika Chetak's lackeys—the morphone I killed and two other werewolves. They're dangerous, Labya. They know how to get inside your head with magical glasses. Before they kill us to avenge the morphone's death, they'll want to extract our memories. We can't let them find out about the Corestone. And just to make things clear, we landed in trouble because of you. Because *you* think the Corestone is here in Darmas. We covered almost every inch of the city, even the underground sewers, looking for the relic. We even deprived ourselves of blood for nourishment because you didn't want us to waste time on feeding. And look what came of it. You couldn't hold up, went into severe hypothermia and altered the weather. Darmas is possibly one of the hottest cities in the country. And it was almost freezing outside. If the Council got wind of it they'd be on our trail too along with the werewolves. I was the one who brought you this human meal. His blood gave you the warmth you needed to keep you from dying. I was the one who saved you, so cut me some slack.'

'The Corestone is definitely here. The werewolves have got it wrong. They're in the wrong place wasting their time. I can hear it. It rings when it is being used. And someone is using it.'

Then she slid open the window, peered outside and asked, 'Where are we going, driver?'

And then, just as suddenly, she yelled, 'Stop the car. Stop the car. Let me concentrate.'

'You're doing it again. If we stop the car we'll be in trouble again,' warned Besar.

'I won't say it again. Finding the Corestone is vital. With it we can be powerful again, destroy the werewolves, the Council, this planet and carry out our Master, the eviscerator's mission.'

'Until death,' repeated the three vampires in unison by pressing their fingers into their necks.

Ricchay Gupta suddenly seemed more alert; like he had overcome his body's weakness; hearing the name of the White Death had made him feel fear and hate. Every fibre of his being now was excited. The White Death was evil and so were the minions who served him. He had to stop them all. He was a life protector. Wasn't that why he had been on this mission?

'Drive us back. All the way back. The ringing sound is coming from somewhere behind us,' yelled Labya at the driver, Maun. The latter hoped Besar would protest, but he remained quiet. Was he afraid of Labya? Perhaps so, especially after she had reminded him of his servile beginnings.

The car now got back on the same path it had left behind.

'Faster,' urged Labya and smiled as the driver stepped on the accelerator. She was happy to be in charge of her coven once again.

'What if they follow us again?' asked Besar.

'Their noses are hypersensitive, remember. The city is way too polluted for their own good.'

'But what if they…'

'Finding the Corestone is of utmost importance. If the werewolves find the Corestone before us they can unlock its power and use it to crush us. We can't risk that.'

'Driver, take a right turn now and get into this lane. The noise is coming from here. Yes…yes. It's growing louder,' yelled Labya and stuck her hand out of the window pointing at a house as the car came to a screeching halt.

'I'll be back. Watch over the human. He's our meal,' she reminded.

'But Labya, don't you want me to come with you?'

'No,' said Labya harshly. She didn't want Besar to accompany her as she wanted to be the first one to lay her hands on the Corestone.

Time passed. The riders in the car got restless. Maun and Besar were afraid the werewolves would find them. Also, as they were vampires, they had hypersensitive hearing. They could pick up Labya's excited voice and movements inside the house. They too wanted to be with her and see the Corestone.

As for Ricchay, checking the time on the clock did not help; the numbers were changing so quickly. With every minute gone, he realised he was getting closer to being sucked bloodless by the vampires. But how could he save himself? He felt unarmed even with a weapon, almost as if the braceband inside his pocket were a bauble. But it was wrong to call it so. It was a powerful, magical device that could spout fire and burn these vampires to ashes. But he didn't know how to use that magic. Ricchay wondered if he should take out the bauble and let the vampires know he belonged to the Council, so they would be scared of him. No, that was risky business! Because if they found out the truth, they would kill him instantly. After all, by serving the Council, he was their adversary. Ricchay waited quietly.

Another 10 minutes passed by. The riders were at the edge of their seats now in anticipation. Ricchay's eyes lit up. He had thought of a plan to save himself and he acted upon it at once.

Stealthily, he grabbed the syringe lying on the floor of the vehicle and nicked his arm with it. He then stuck his arm out of the window. Red gleaming drops of blood now spilled onto the ground. And just as he had anticipated, the quick, heavy sound of the blood plopping onto the road drove the vampires wild.

He saw them lunging at each other and sparring to get the first taste of his blood. Besar overpowered Maun by shoving him back to his seat and turned towards Ricchay. But Maun recovered quickly.

Ricchay's heart pounded. He squeezed his wound to enable a steady flow of blood. If the vampires were wildly excited before, now they were frenetic; scratching each other bloody with their claws that emerged out of their hands. Then they exchanged a series of blows before knocking each other out cold.

Now Ricchay drew his hand inside and smiled despite the pain. The first part of his plan had worked. It was now time for part two—dumping the bodies of the vampires and driving away to Dr Chary's house. But just as he was about to get a hold of Besar's body, Dr Chary came to him.

Ricchay was stumped.

The writer was thrust into the car by Labya. For a moment, Labya sat still and analysed all that she had sensed was happening in the car while she was away—the noise of her abettors quarrelling with each other, the syringe in Ricchay's hand, the bleeding wound in his arm, the blood of the vampires on the car seat and the lump in Ricchay's pocket… Labya thought to herself if that lump could be a braceband?

'You are from the Council, aren't you?' she asked aloud, sensing that her abettors had been tricked into fighting each other over Ricchay's blood that she no longer felt the thirst for since she had already fed on it. Her face turned pale with horror.

She looked out of the window. Her eyes moved skyward.

'Oh no!' she exclaimed, imagining she had seen contrails in the sky.

'*Rasavi*,' she shouted a chant and Ricchay found his hands bound hard by clay. Labya did it to ensure he could no longer use his braceband. Just then she realised a car was charging towards them. It was easily five kilometres away but still she could hear it—a werewolf's tail scratching the seat of the car, the key being slammed into the ignition and turned clockwise, a foot crushing the brake, the air being sucked into the engine; mixing with the fuel with a loud gurgling, the furious bobbing of the pistons, a series of explosions and the engine roaring to life. Yes, she could hear the faintest of sounds. After all, she was a vampire and the breed was gifted with hypersensitive hearing.

'Impossible! The werewolves are here. But how could they bear the pollution in the city? They must have smelled Besar and Maun's blood. Well, there's no time to waste now. I need to get to the cemetery,' said Labya as she quickly closed the windows, jumped into the front seat and stepped on the accelerator. The car whizzed out of the lane.

If they catch up and attack me, I'll use the Council scum as a shield to protect myself, she muttered to herself.

After a pause, she asked aloud, 'Where is the Corestone?'

'I... Uh... I really don't know what you are talking about,' replied the writer, gulping in fear. He was shaken up for Labya had been asking him the same question repeatedly in the house with increasing menace.

Ricchay stared at the scraggly bearded man with high cheekbones sitting opposite him. He had no doubt that the man was Dr Chary for he had seen enough pictures of the old man before starting out on his mission.

Although a part of him was happy and relieved to find Dr Chary—for that was the most vital aspect of his mission—but the other part worried about why the writer was in the car. Why was the vampire interested in the old man? Did she know about Dr Chary being special; that he could be the only challenger to the White Death? But that seemed impossible. Almost no one knew about Dr Chary's ability or his possible role in bringing order to the chaos in the world and letting all living beings circumvent death, except for his friend Ruchira and him. No, it wasn't that. It had to be something else. Ricchay had heard the vampires talk about the Corestone but had not a clue about what it was.

Just then the car screeched, swerved and trundled into a new track.

'Bah... Stop telling me the same thing over and over again. Who are you? Where have you hidden the Corestone? It's certainly not in your house. Who are you?' asked Labya, as she checked the rear-view mirror for her pursuers.

Dr Chary stole glances at the bodies of Besar and Maun slumped against the seat next to him and at Ricchay. He was horrified imagining Ricchay flashing pairs of fangs at him just like the woman who was now driving the car.

'Be quiet... Shhh!' Ricchay mouthed and turned behind to find a car following them.

'No...no way,' yelled Labya from the front.

Suddenly, the car that was behind gained more speed and drew closer. Labya panicked and turned the steering quite sharply. The tyres squealed agonisingly and the sudden turn nearly threw Ricchay off his seat.

Bang!

The car hit something hard, perhaps a rock, and came to a screeching halt. Ricchay's head hit the seat and he slumped. Besar and Dr Chary slammed hard into Ricchay, and everyone was knocked unconscious.

Moments later, regaining her consciousness, Labya felt her forehead. There was a long wet line of blood running from her hairline to her eyebrow. Apparently, her head had slammed against the steering wheel. The gash stung and hurt deeply. But there wasn't a thing she could do about it. The werewolves were around; she needed to think of a way to defend herself. Instantly, a plan came to her mind.

She now opened the car door, yanked all the inert bodies and threw them on the moonlit ground of the Darmas cemetery. It was close to midnight and the crickets were abuzz. Their chirping seemed to cut through her head and reverberate through every bone and tissue. It was frightening.

Could the force of the echoes shatter her from within? No, it wasn't right to give in to the paranoia. There was a task at hand. So, with a finger pressed against her ear she began to sniff the ground like a dog. A minute later, she clenched and unclenched her free hand. Soon, menacing white claws grew out from her fingertips, beneath her perfectly manicured finger nails.

Much to her distaste she now found herself digging a particular spot on the ground and her nails filling up with dirt. The sight made her cringe in the same way as the sewers or the dumpyards in the city; sites she had been to in the past week whilst searching for the Corestone. She shook her head, unwilling to accept that she had engaged in this dirty, uncivilised activity that was characteristic of the werewolves.

A corpse that was buried in the pit, unearthed after Labya finished digging up. It was dark, well-decomposed, infested with flies and maggots and gave off a powerful stench—both sweet and pungent—that Labya knew was enough to make the werewolves die of nausea.

The sharp foul odour brought the fallen to their senses—Ricchay Gupta, Dr Chary, Besar and Maun.

Dr Chary began to panic almost instantly and was ready to run. Labya could sense his fear through the sounds: beads of sweat popping on his forehead, the heart hammering deafeningly loud, his toes crunching the grass underneath, the vein throbbing in his neck, his breathing turning rapid and shallow and his eyelashes fluttering wildly. The sounds were too many and they roused Labya. Her excitement was so high and manic that she feared it could kill her. She was convulsing now and knew she had to snap out of it. So, she kicked Dr Chary hard in the gut and the writer fell on the ground.

Labya calmed down instantly. Now, only two distinct sounds echoed in her ears—that of the writer writhing in pain and the crickets chirping.

Besar by now had gauged the situation, 'Labya, I can hear them. The hounds...they're coming for us. I can hear them. They're confident their gas masks would block the foul smell of the cemetery.'

'I know...that's why I have been thinking of a plan of action,' said Labya, whilst eyeing the rotting corpse, and added, 'Maun, you'll focus on ripping their gas masks. Besar, you'll build me an igloo.' Both Maun and Besar agreed.

'Who's the human; the old man there?' asked Besar, pointing at Dr Chary.

'A thief...a dirty little thief.'

'What did he steal?'

'The Corestone. Master's Corestone.'

'How do you know?'

As Besar asked the question, the air felt hot and heavy. Silence set in. It was dull, dead; the crickets couldn't be heard anymore. It was like the calm before the storm.

2

A Grave Battle

A cloud of fire burned brightly in the sky.

'*Agnivasati*,' chanted two werewolves in unison as they emerged from the thicket surrounding the cemetery. Mottled fur covered their large, beefy bodies and rubber gas masks concealed their faces. The cloud that was directly above the vampires churned, ready to spew a rain of fire.

'Besar, what are you doing? The fire will pour down upon us any minute now,' yelled Labya as she found him staring at the driver who had moved away from them to tackle the werewolves.

Besar was worried about Maun's life. After all, Besar was also a werewolf once; just like him.

'I can't leave Maun. He's my own; my brother.'

Labya spat on him as if she had heard the foulest thing ever.

'Don't you dare forget our Master's teachings. Love weakens you. Feel hate. Sever all the ties. Let the White Energy flow out through your fingertips.'

A loud rumble and boom echoed. Both Labya and Besar looked skyward to notice the first streak of fire hurtling towards them from the cloud above.

'*Stalikrati*,' chanted Besar, pointing at the braceband on his wrist. Soon, walls of ice grew out of the ground and sealed Besar, Labya, Dr Chary and Ricchay within an igloo.

Both Labya and Besar looked up, watching the liquid fire raining upon them, and listening to the menacingly loud hisses of the shower trying to burn their ice shield. Although Besar was nervous—unsure of how long he could hold up against the torrential downpour—Labya seemed to be calm, perhaps because she had already chalked out a plan to thwart the werewolves and was positively sure it would work.

There was a smirk on Labya's face. She wanted to demonstrate her power over Besar. After all, she was born a vampire and not bitten into one like Besar. She now held her braceband close to her lips and began to whisper a series of chants. Besar was curious about what tricks Labya might have up her sleeve. Still, he didn't let himself get too distracted and focused all his attention on keeping the ice house sturdy from the onslaught of the fiery rain.

'*Vatahata*,' chanted Maun, who was outside the igloo and directly in the line of fire.

A powerful gust of wind shot from his braceband and pushed away the fire towards the trees surrounding the cemetery. Leaves and barks burst into flames and a thick smoke arose.

The werewolves sneered; the counter attack was the weakest they had ever seen.

'*Agnivapan*,' chanted the werewolf with a dull grey coat of fur and eyes that matched his skin, while his partner, with wheatish-brown fur, focused his attention on melting the igloo with his rain of fire.

The air began to heat up. Maun broke into beads of sweat and then he saw it; another cloud of fire in the sky. But this one was different. It began spinning like a vortex, ready to swallow him inside its fiery belly.

'*Vatahata*,' yelled Maun once again. But this time, much to Maun's horror, the wind fanned the flames.

The vortex now descended upon him. He ran to get away from it but it followed and lifted him up with its force. He was a hair's breadth away from being sucked inside the column of fire. However, that provided hardly any relief, for the heat emanating from the vortex was enough to burn his scalp. Maun cried. The vortex pulled again. He could now see licks of flame dancing around him, searing the skin on his face, neck, and shoulders. His cries turned into agonising screams. One more tug and he was sure to be sucked into the belly of fire. No, he decided that instant, he couldn't accept this fate.

'*Himcaun*,' screamed Maun as he ducked from the flames and pointed at his attacker, the grey werewolf. A long icicle, with a needle tip, shot from his hand. It travelled at rocket speed and in less than a second found its mark—the wolf's temple. It tore through everything in its path—the rubber in the gas mask, skin, tissues, nerves, bones—before emerging from the other side of his head. The grey werewolf fell down, howling in pain. Soon, the vortex disappeared.

Maun dropped to the floor; half-burnt with a swollen mass with blood frothing out of his mouth. But he wasn't dead yet. His heart was still beating.

Besar could hear groans of insufferable pain from inside the igloo. His eyes filled with tears as he thought of Maun's plight. No, he couldn't cry. He couldn't be weak, he told himself.

'*Stalikrati*,' said Besar. But there was less force in his voice now—as if he was tired. The walls of the ice house grew thinner but they still held up against the fire. Besar threw a weary glance at Labya. What was she doing? How much longer did she want him to continue this fight? He was already so tired, so drained of energy.

Meanwhile, Ricchay's clay cast hardened because the air within the igloo was cold. He wondered how he could get his hands out and run from this place. How could he complete his mission? Dr Chary was nearly gone. The vampire's kick to his gut had been punishingly painful.

'*Anupanad*,' chanted Labya and opened up her fist. Twin beams of light shot through her braceband. One of them struck Ricchay while the other penetrated the corpse that she had dug out of the ground.

Ricchay found himself yawning. But it seemed to him that his tiredness was more severe than before. It was as if he was being drained of life itself. A smile spread across Labya's face. Her plan was working.

The brown werewolf howled watching the grey werewolf collapse in front of him. He was enraged. These vampires couldn't crush him. He was stronger than them.

He brought his sinuous arms down and now he was on all fours; a massive and menacing creature over seven feet long weighing about 200 kilograms.

'*Pavakgol*,' chanted the brown werewolf as he launched himself into a run.

Both Labya and Besar heard the magic spell. It was the death knell for Maun. The realisation jolted Besar. He got distracted and the walls of the igloo began to crack. Labya panicked! She was going to be exposed to the fiery downpour any minute now.

'*Anupanad*,' she chanted again and this time her eyes and voice were more ferocious.

Ricchay's head felt light. Everything seemed hazy and slow; the movement of those around him and his own heartbeat, which was dull and spaced. Was he on the verge of dying? Possible! But what was this heavy, sickening odour in the air?

'Yes, yes, yes,' exclaimed Labya triumphantly.

Besar was confounded. Why was Labya thrilled? And then he saw it; much to his astonishment, the lone corpse that labya had dug out began to multiply magically into a gigantic pile of corpses.

Maun, who was on the ground now slumped against the tombstone of a grave, held his breath, as the whole place reeked of decay. He turned around slightly to find corpses inside the igloo.

'Driver, tear his mask,' Labya screamed from within. Maun nodded, having now understood Labya's plan to thwart the werewolves.

He saw the brown werewolf charging towards him with an orange ball of fire atop his head. Maun couldn't move because of the pain surging through his half-burnt body. Still, he knew he had to stop the werewolf before it could attack Besar. He couldn't let any harm come to him. Besar was his brother. Just when the brown werewolf bent his head, to lodge the ball of fire into Maun's body, Maun flashed his claws and ripped the werewolf's gas mask. There was a brilliant flash of light. Maun felt the fireball slamming into his stomach; melting tissues and bones, steaming the blood and exploding inside before his body dissolved into a pile of ashes.The brown werewolf howled in delight. He had killed the vampire in the most amusing way. Now it was time to crush the other two vampires. But just as the burning smell of flesh, grass and wood cleared away, something more repugnant filled his nose. It was the smell of decay—sweet, pungent, insufferably redolent of bodies that had been rotting for over two weeks. The werewolf became nauseous and threw up without a pause. At first, there was blood and half-digested food on the floor but as the werewolf's nausea escalated, his very innards seemed to come tearing out of his throat. At last, the cloud of fire that had loomed over the vampires disappeared because the werewolf who had conjured it lay dead.

Besar magically removed the igloo—for it wasn't of any use anymore—while Labya smiled with delight.

'Let's make a few more corpses and kill the Council scum. This is so much fun,' she said. Now she wanted to completely drain the life out of Ricchay.

'*Anupa*...' she began but couldn't finish. She simply couldn't remember the rest of the verse as something else caught her attention. She opened her mouth again and strangely didn't know what to say. In the distance she saw two moons, cookie sized, hovering above brambles. And now as they drew closer, Labya could discern they were stuck to the eyes of a werewolf with conical ears, thick frizzy hair, a defined jaw, fangs, a bushy tail and a sinewy body covered with black, mottled fur.

'Impossible. You don't have a gas mask on. How can you survive this stench?' asked Besar, stunned by what he saw.

He knew who the werewolf was. The glasses gave it away; they belonged to Dr Chandrika Chetak.

The werewolf grinned.

'Let's just say, I have completely lost my sense of smell,' and added, 'if you can't get over the past then let me help you.'

'Labya, don't look at her glasses. She can delve into your mind and wipe away your memories,' warned Besar.

'*Himcaun*,' Besar chanted. An icicle materialised in his hand. As he aimed it at Chandrika Chetak's eyes, he broke into tears. After all, he had cast the same magical spell as his brother Maun, moments before his death.

'Ah! Tears of sadness. Besar, you grieve his death, don't you? Why won't you let me help you ease your pain? Why do you fight me?'

Chandrika Chetak stood still. The icicle was inches away from her. But she knew it wasn't going to touch her. And she was right.

Besar's hand quivered. He could no longer feel the hate to kill Chandrika. The sadness of losing Maun overwhelmed him. And he fell on his knees after losing his focus. The icicle aimed at Chandrika melted to water and fell upon the grass blades like beads of liquid pearl.

'Our Master, the all powerful, the eviscerator of Prana, the death-giver, the White Death, may your white light shine upon me, remove the grief I feel for my brother, fill me with hate so I can slay this werewolf,' prayed Besar before pressing his neck so hard that he nearly choked to death.

Watching Besar, Chandrika's face hardened into an ugly, twitching scowl.

'*Vapatat*,' she yelled while pointing at a tombstone. At once the heavy mass of rock uprooted itself from the mud, lifted up and plonked on Besar, severing his neck from his torso.

'Labya, my sweetheart. You've been quite helpful today, letting me get inside your head so easily and helping me learn an important magical spell for free. I like you. Hope you don't change my opinion by praying to the White

Death as your abettor, Besar, for the White Death doesn't exist anymore,' expressed Chandrika in a voice that flowed smoothly like honey.

Labya couldn't take her eyes off the werewolf. She was in a trance; compelled by a strange force to hold her gaze.

'Now Labya, I don't like fights. It is for brutes, isn't it? So be calm, show me the past and tell me what's been going on here,' said Chandrika, as a series of images flashed on her glasses and she easily disarmed Labya by removing the braceband from her wrist.

'Oh a Council scum and…and…a human who you think has the Corestone. Dr Chary? What a coincidence!'

'*Matcarak*,' yelled Chandrika and pointed her own braceband to the ground. Earthen tentacles sprung out from the ground and enclosed Labya, trapping her in a cage.

'Now, stay here while I deal with the others,' said Chandrika, and turning away from Labya, chanted '*Jagar*.' A hard jolt woke up the inactive. They looked traumatised as though consciousness had suddenly struck their minds like lightning. The spell hadn't awakened only Dr Chary and Ricchay, but Labya too, who after snapping out of her trance, tried to get her bearings. Chandrika evinced surprise; she didn't mean for the spell to work on Labya. A few seconds later, she realised that the spell roused anyone near the spell-caster whose consciousness had been compromised on either sight, sound, smell, touch or taste.

'Labya thinks the Corestone is with Dr Chary because the ringing noise is coming from him. But what about Vanhad? The werewolves can hear the noise there too. Surely, the Corestone can't be in two different places at the same time,' said Chandrika while scrutinising Labya's movements and wondering if she had other bracebands in her possession. Despite her suspicion, she maintained a great sense of calm.

There was no need to get on the offensive. Fighting was for brutes. She would only fire, when fired upon.

Dr Chary thought he was in a crazy nightmare. But that is until he felt a pain in his stomach where Labya had kicked him. The pain was real. Still, why did everything around him seem so absurd, so far from reality? His kidnapper had fangs and claws. And wasn't that doctor Chandrika Chetak with her moon glasses? Why did she look like a wolf now, swinging her bushy tail around?

Despite Chandrika's spell, Ricchay was yet to rise to full consciousness. He had lost a substantial amount of the Life Energy or Prana. But not all of it was gone, it was still afloat within him. Somewhere. He could feel it. Faint staccato sirens echoed in the distance. Ricchay heard them and realised the Council was on its way to investigate the scene where clouds of fire had emerged. He then turned around to find Chandrika Chetak glaring at Dr Chary. Ricchay panicked thinking she was going to kill the old man. He couldn't let that happen. Dr Chary was the only hope for the survival of mankind when the apocalypse, propelled by the White Death, struck. He had given his word to Ruchira that he would help her find the special one. And Dr Chary was the special one. But how was he going to stop the werewolf? He didn't have any weapons. His eyes roved around desperately until they fixed upon his hands encased in clay and he realised his hands were his weapons. But how was he to use them when he didn't have the energy to move a muscle? His eyes were drooping, white blurs hijacking his vision.

Death was coming for him.

Labya who had by now pieced together all the events that had led up to the present moment, let out an ugly moan of annoyance and defeat and then banged her back against the cage.

'Is this how a caged bird sings? SHUT UP. SHUT UP,' yelled Chandrika only to find Labya agitated again.

'Looks like I can't have a moment of calm at all. Now die banshee. *Maranamuthi*,' chanted Chandrika and the tentacles that had trapped Labya closed into each other, crushing the vampire's flesh and bones into a bloody, splintered mess.

After enduring Labya's ear-splitting cries moments before her agonising death, Chandrika witnessed a strange event. The piled up rotting corpses on the open field began spurting out black matter that penetrated into her, Dr Chary and Ricchay. The three of them were connected together in a triangle of fluid black curves. And it wasn't just them. Chandrika's eyes followed the trail that led from them to the birds in the sky, plants and trees, their barks and branches, roots, leaves and stems, the granite and marble slabs that the tombstones were made of, every blade of grass, animal life burrowed underground, even the tiniest worms and insects connecting them all in a massive black web. The whole event couldn't have lasted more than a fraction of a millisecond; impossible for the human, werewolf or vampire eyes to see, but Chandrika's magical glasses had caught it all; enchanting the enchanter.

Chandrika licked a spot on her wrist. The oily, sticky substance that had touched her body was the Life Energy, also called Prana or the dark energy. It was what gave life to the living. The network that she had been staring at ealier was the very web of life; in which everything alive was connected. She then wondered why the dark energy had leaked out. Recalling Labya's memories that she had accessed earlier yielded the answer. Labya had created the corpses using Life Energy drained from a victim. Now that she was dead, her magic that had bound the energy within the corpses had been undone, releasing the pool of energy back to the living; giving back what had been taken, restoring the balance. Understanding the mechanics of magic was Chandrika's true motive, and in the moment, she felt heady with joy like a school girl who had learnt something new.

Almost as soon as he was renewed with new life, Ricchay rose to the occasion. Thus, when he swung his arms back and struck with gunshot quickness, he surprised both Chandrika Chetak and himself. The effort paid off, for the werewolf was knocked out cold with the hardened clay that bound his hands.

The sirens grew louder in the distance. Ricchay knew the Council was going to be here soon. He had to plan his escape quickly or the Council would surely find out about his mission and take Dr Chary away from him. But before they could get to him, Dr Chary was ready to escape for he was already on his feet, stepping back, turning to run. Ricchay panicked. He dashed towards the writer, punched him in his gut once again but lightly and kicked his knees. The writer fell down again, moaning in pain.

The red lights of the Council cars now poured into the cemetery through the spaces between the branches of the trees. Fear coursed through Ricchay's body. He knew he had to flee; he would not be able to fight them. And then, he sprang into action. After hammering the ground with a force that cracked his cast open, he dragged Dr Chary into the van and sped away from the scene.

3

The White Death's Equal

Ricchay had been running scared all his life—the day bullies in his class taunted him for being fat and wanted to punch his belly; the day he failed in his exams and didn't want to face his family; the day his friend caught him stealing money from his bag because he didn't have any to buy food; the day his friend became blind because of him; the day Kadambari asked him to marry her; the day his father became paralysed because of him and when Ruchira entrusted him with the task of finding the challenger to the White Death.

And now he was running away because he was afraid of being caught by the Council. But his body, soaked with sweat and blood, was tired of running and tired of being scared. He wanted to pause—catch his breath, accept his fate, face his fears.

With this determination, Ricchay brought the van to a sudden halt. They had reached the outskirts of the city. He got out of the car and walked towards a nearby field of wild grass and denuded trees. For several minutes, he simply savoured the sensation of breathing the hot, silken Darmas air and loosened up his muscles, taut with fear.

Later, he headed to a pond with shimmering speckles of moonlight in it, in the middle of the field to wash himself clean. Dr Chary joined him shortly. Ricchay was alarmed when he saw the old man, for he had completely forgotten about the White Death's Equal. He kept a keen eye on the writer to remind himself of the importance of his mission. On the other hand, the writer hardly paid him any attention; he was busy quenching his thirst by drinking from the pond.

Meanwhile, Ricchay mulled over the whole situation. He was tired of living in fear all his life and wanted to give himself a chance to face his failures, mistakes, shortcomings—all the worst things that had happened and were going to happen to him—and accept them with grace.

Then, he thought about Padma and the other victims. They were never given a chance to go against him or refuse to be dragged into the Arabian Sea. How could they when he had threatened them by putting a gun to their heads? No, it was just grossly unfair.

But what about Dr Chary now?

'Do you believe in magic, Dr Chary?' Ricchay asked, remembering his own father who had asked him the very same question when he was young.

Dr Chary looked up with a start as though he had just noticed Ricchay and was now trying to grasp the reality of where he was, what he was doing and what was going on around him.

'Of course you do! How silly of me to even ask. Every book you have ever written has been about magic,' said Ricchay, before flashing a metallic object.

There was a flicker in Dr Chary's eyes. He recalled seeing the object before.

Ricchay walked alongside the pond and caught his reflection as he peered into it once. A look of disgust came over him. He had always hated his face—dark, lifeless eyes, a long, crooked nose, heavy jowls and cheeks full of pockmarks. Again, he was reminded of his father, not because he was the spitting image of him but because of what his father had said, 'You need to hate something really bad to kill it, don't you Ricchay? Like the neighbour's cat. It smells. It sneaks in and leaves a trail of mess. It annoys me day in and day out. But is that enough? Can just being annoyed put an end to the cat's menace? No, it can't. It certainly can't. I need to be able to hate the critter. Hate it so strongly that I feel like killing it. And that emotion is very necessary to unleash Destructika or the magic of destruction. With Destructika I can bend nature's elements—earth, fire, wind and water and put an end to this little menace.'

'*Calamana*,' Ricchay yelled. A blue flame materialised in his palm with a click similar to a cigarette lighter. Ricchay moved his hand closer to the ground. Blades of grass were now ablaze, wilting under the heat, turning to ash. Wasn't that how the neighbour's cat had ended up too when his father had cast the same magic spell on it, in front of him? He had been eight-years-old then. The incident had scarred him for life.

Ricchay looked at Dr Chary. There he saw it in his eyes—bewilderment, shock and horror. He had felt those emotions too when the cat had been burnt alive. The memory distracted Ricchay, causing him to lose focus and control over the fire. And now his shoe caught fire.

'*Paniyapata*,' he yelled, hoping water would shoot out of his palm and douse the fire. But the spell didn't work because, as he chanted it, he knew it wouldn't work. And that was the problem with him; he always doubted himself. The consequences of his self-doubts were grave. At crucial times, he couldn't use magic to save himself; like this situation he was in at the moment. And on other occasions, he had caused horrific accidents with his inability to produce the right magic; such as his friend's blindness and his father's paralysis.

Ricchay scampered towards the pond and then dunked his foot in the water. Loud hissing sounds resounded. Smoke arose. Luckily, only the shoe had been burnt and his toes were unharmed. Ricchay pondered. It seemed to him that his life had come full circle. He had chanted the same spell years ago to extinguish the flames that had trapped the cat's body. But the spell hadn't worked back then too. The poor cat had lost its life for no fault of his. Just because his father wanted to show him the power of magic—the power of Destructika. The cat had become a spectacle. No, his father wasn't nice at all. He was a heartless man. He had done many cruel things. It was good that he had become paralysed because of him. And then died!

The man didn't deserve his sympathy, tears or grief. Thinking about all this made Ricchay light and free. He wasn't responsible for his father's death. It was all *karma*! The realisation to face his demons head on made him feel a bit stronger.

Dr Chary squirmed with fear for he thought if he tried to run now, the man would burn him too. But how could the man produce fire? This man in front of him hadn't yet revealed his fangs or claws. But whatever he had seen was all very strange, absurd.

Ricchay cleared his throat.

'Dr Chary, do you remember writing the book, *A Dwarphant's Long Tale*?'

Dr Chary was perplexed.

'Do you know what a dwarphant is?' The man's voice was so strident, so intimidating.

'No... I mean yes... It's an animal, very much like an elephant, except it's really short and black,' replied the writer as if he were reading the words right out of his book.

'Right. But have you ever seen one?'

'Erm...no.' Dr Chary wondered what the man was getting at. Why was he asking such a nonsensical question with such profound sincerity like it meant something to him? Was he crazy?

'Neither have I. Neither has anyone in the past 20,000 years. It seems like they have just vanished into thin air.'

After a pause, Ricchay continued, 'Yet, you wrote about Kanlin, one of the greatest dwarcerers, along with Carsani. How did you do it? How did you get the idea?'

'I don't know. It just came to me.'

Ricchay laughed.

'It doesn't happen just like that, Dr Chary. There's a reason behind everything. And the way I see it, the story was based on your recollections of the past. But here's the absurd part. Kanlin was born 25,000 years ago and yet, you wrote a story about him now, in the present. You weren't even around when Kanlin was around. But what if Kanlin was known to your ancestor who existed around the same time? What if your ancestor witnessed Kanlin's triumphs and tribulations? What if your ancestor's memory was preserved even after his death and passed on to his descendants like you, Dr Chary? Just like you write in the book. You're a descendant, Dr Chary, a descendant of Haten. And the proof is your book, *A Dwarphant's Long Tale*. Haten wrote the same book, about Kanlin, but 25,000 years ago. What's striking is that you both used the same words, the same expressions, although in different languages. Surely, you couldn't have copied his work. There remains just one copy of Haten's book and that lies at the bottom of the Arabian Sea. The way I see it, Haten's memory somehow awakened within you and you thought exactly what he thought.'

Dr Chary was now intrigued. The talk about memories suddenly brought to his mind the image of Dr Chandrika Chetak; the weird doctor who had turned herself into a wolf in the cemetery. But how?

'Have you ever felt that you were different from everybody else at any point in your life...that you were special?'

A deluge of thoughts resurfaced in Dr Chary's mind. It was beyond him to suppress them any longer. He had seen a plethora of shockingly absurd things by now and was desperate to understand what was going on.

'Yes, I know I don't fit in. I am always restless,' Dr Chary admitted. His mind screamed at him, 'Tell him about the day you were desperate to chop off Romas's fingers and make him suffer.'

'Who are you?' asked Dr Chary. He was suddenly thrilled. Was this man going to explain the bizarre experiences he had had?

'I am so sorry I haven't introduced myself yet. I am Ricchay Gupta and I work for the Council.' Now Ricchay flashed what seemed like a police badge. It had banners, the logo of a pair of hands holding a black ball and words that read:

RICCHAY GUPTA,
Udal Officer,
The Council,
City of Coch

Next, he furnished a Police ID card.

He then explained, 'The Council is a covert organisation that operates under the police. You don't ever read about us in papers or see us on television. We provide our services to governments across various states and nations to keep the world safe. Indeed, there's danger everywhere with drug lords, kidnappers, rapists, mad men on the loose, and that's why you have the police and the military to protect the country and its citizens from harm. But what about supernatural threats that exists in the magical world? Indeed, the magical world has been intentionally hidden from the common man by governments since time immemorial because it is powerful and dangerous. But it exists, along with the magical creatures such as the werewolves and vampires. Like the ones you saw at the cemetery. They are evil; hungry for human flesh and blood. But that's not all. Their purpose is the elimination of life on earth. And to achieve this, they have the magical power to bend nature's forces, cause sudden earthquakes, storms, fires.'

With a grave expression in his eyes, he continued, 'That's why governments across the world fund the magical arts training of special servicemen called Udals to wipe out magical creatures like werewolves and vampires. I am a Udal, Dr Chary.'

Ricchay now pointed to the metal band in his hand, 'This is what gives them and Udals like me magical power. It's called a braceband. You see the stone in its centre?

It can control the four elements—earth, fire, wind and water—when you chant the right magical spell. It's magic, Dr Chary and I am sure you believe in it because every book you have ever written has been about magic.'

After a pause, he continued, 'Our enemy is very strong and has a purpose given to them by their Master who is death himself, the White Death.'

Dr Chary's ears pricked up. Hadn't the bodiless voice, the strange woman with fangs who had assaulted him in Akshay's house and Dr Chandrika Chetak, mentioned the name of the White Death to him?

'Do you believe in birth and death?'

'Yes,' replied Dr Chary.

'Your grandson was born just months ago.'

'How do you know?'

'I know a lot of things about you.'

Dr Chary's intrigue grew. Did this man also know that he could hold his breath underwater for as long as he liked?

Thinking of Naveen, Akshay and Meera and the ugly fight the couple possibly had because of him brought tears to Dr Chary's eyes.

'I know you miss your family. I do as well. Quite terribly so! I wish I could be with them right now. But Dr Chary I know things about you…that you're special…and that's why I can't let you go even if you miss your family.'

Dr Chary was shocked. The realisation that the man talking to him could in fact be his kidnapper suddenly struck him and supplanted the excitement he had felt before. He dropped to his knees, held Ricchay's legs and cried for mercy, 'Please show me some kindness… Do you want money? How much do you need? I'll write you a cheque. I am a rich man…a very rich man… Guess I don't have to tell you that...that's why you have kidnapped me, haven't you? But please let me go... I can give you all my money... I have no use of it... But please let me go back to my family... I am old and weak. Please show some kindness.'

Ricchay looked away. What if Dr Chary wasn't special? What if he died at the end of this mission, just like others? He didn't want to be haunted by another crying face and be reminded of his cruelty for the rest of his life. So, why was he doing this—talking to Dr Chary, building this bond? It was all because he wanted to be fair to the writer, make him aware of how important he was to saving mankind; most importantly, make him believe that it was his purpose too; for without belief, this battle against the White Death was already lost.

He took the writer's hands in his. They quivered! And Ricchay realised how gnarled and delicate they were. Could they really crush the enemy and save mankind? Ricchay knew he was doubting his beliefs again and it wasn't right. Every time a person was in doubt, the evil was bound to grow within him.

'This is not about money at all, Dr Chary. It's about self-discovery. This journey that we are about to go on, is about you finding out who you truly are.'

Dr Chary stopped sobbing at once. He was drawn to what the stranger had said. It was true he was a rich man who had never cared about money. But the one thing he did care about was finding out who he was. Maybe that's why he had been so restless. This man had told him just what he had wanted to know all his life; it was as though he could read his mind. Could he also help him explain the murderous urges, the white flashes, the strange voices, the ringing noise? Suddenly, the fear of "exposure" no longer bothered him. He was ready to reveal everything to the man. He had missed the opportunity with Dr Chandrika Chetak, but he couldn't keep throwing away his chances. Hadn't he suffered enough in silence, suppressing his abnormalities? He owed himself the truth now.

'Please tell me more,' he asked.

'Do you believe in God; his infinite powers that created this planet? We call him the Maker, the architect, the fount of kindness, love and so on...'

'I believe in energy. I can feel it. It is within me. It is what keeps me alive,' interrupted Dr Chary. He wasn't here to listen to a religious discourse if that was what this man had in mind.

'Ah...that's precisely what I was getting at. The energy, the life force, the air that I breathe keeps me alive. It's called the Dark Energy or Prana and Sura—the Creator—contained an abundance of this energy. Sura liked to build and shape things. Think of him as a sculptor. He came with his tools, built and shaped our planet; everything else—mountains, rivers, plants, animals, humans and everything around it, the sun and the moon. Finally, he let Prana or the Dark Energy flow out of him and into his own creations. That's how life first began on earth, in a place called Gawaan.'

'But what has this got to do with me?' asked Dr Chary, scratching his head.

'Oh! Everything, Dr Chary... Everything! Please bear with me. It is a long story and I will try to tell you only what you need to know for now.'

'A story,' muttered Dr Chary. It was always nice to listen to one. Maybe, he could use it in one of his books. He sat down on a flat rock near the pond.

Ricchay continued, 'In Gawaan, life thrived in all its glory. There was laughter and mirth everywhere. That was the time when dwarphants roamed about free and bold.'

Ricchay paused to look at Dr Chary. The old man seemed less sceptical. He hadn't interrupted him.

'With his work done, Sura now wanted to create other planets where life could thrive too. It was around that time that his brother, Asura, paid him a visit. Asura was awestruck and curious to learn how Sura had created such beautiful things in Gawaan. After sharing his knowledge, Sura set on his mission, leaving his brother alone in Gawaan. Initially, Asura was thrilled to take on Sura's work, filling the sea with fish, the sky with birds and the land with deer. But, they say one day, along his journey to create more lifeforms, he accidently stumbled upon something new. A new form of energy; fluid like Prana. But there was something different about it. Unlike Prana that was dark, this new energy was bright and infinitely more luminous than the sun itself, which was Sura's grandest creation. Asura was enraptured by it. He called it the Light or the White Energy or the White Power.'

Dr Chary trembled. Somehow the words had an ominous ring to them.

'The White Energy was different not just because of its colour. When it entered Asura's body, a change came upon him. His mind became disturbed, he could no longer focus his attention on designing and creating new life. Every time he sat to work, a constant thought kept coming up. His work was unoriginal, just a reproduction of Sura's designs. That he had simply obeyed Sura, had no identity of his own. He was Sura's copycat. The realisation made him aware of the presence of an emotion rising within him. It was strange, unlike love that was obtained from Prana. It made him feel a sudden revulsion towards creation; life itself. The emotion was hate. Hate was stronger than love for when Asura tapped into the emotion he realised how he could end life; remove Prana from Sura's creations. Asura was excited. Finally, he had discovered something new and original. Thus, he forged a weapon, a scythe, and set forth on a trail of destruction, completely uprooting life from Sura's creations. The massacre made him realise his true purpose. It was to…' Ricchay took a pause to drink some water from the pond. All the talking had dried his throat. Dr Chary waited anxiously for Ricchay to finish the sentence.

'We talked about birth and life. But what about death? Forget the story for a minute, tell me, Dr Chary, how do you think people die?'

The old man's eyebrows furrowed.

'Various reasons. Either nature kills us or we kill ourselves,' he replied.

'True. But how does that happen?'

'Well… You know them too.'

'But I want to hear it from you.'

'Well, you could be in an accident, die because of storms or earthquakes…sometimes people are just crazy, killing each other or themselves and then there are diseases of course and ageing.' Dr Chary was now reminded of his wife and her battle with cancer while Ricchay thought of his own attempted suicide because he didn't like himself.

'Well, they're all manifestations of one thing—the Light or the White Energy. We age because of it. We die because of it. It is destructive. It flows within us, around us, in every creation, just as Prana. It is present in the air that we breathe in. That was Asura's design. If there was life, then there had to be death. And that became his true purpose—to end life itself. Back to the story... Asura now called himself the White Death who was imbued with the White Energy and reaped death with his scythe. Apart from uprooting life, studying the White Energy also taught him how to bend the forces of nature—earth, fire, wind and water. It was a magical power and the White Death named it Destructika or the magic of destruction. Soon, he shared this knowledge with some of Sura's creations so they too could destroy things around them. With time, these creations turned into depraved, rapacious beasts that fed on flesh and blood and came to be known as werewolves and vampires.

'About that time, the creator Sura returned from his travels only to be appalled by the massive death and destruction in Gawaan. What do you think happened next?'

Ricchay's fierce gaze told Dr Chary that the question was directed at him. The writer tried to remember all that he had heard in order to answer Ricchay's question.

'Well, I suppose there was a conflict between the brothers.'

Ricchay nodded his head vigorously.

'Yes! A battle broke out...called the Battle of Gawaan. Asura's army of course was made of werewolves and vampires, while Sura's army was made of dwarphants. Yes, the very dwarf elephants in your book and the Aravans, who were basically humans, with the magical ability to survive in any environment: land, air or water. They were humans who wanted to use magic to avenge the death of their loved ones.'

Dr Chary closed his eyes. Ricchay's narration was so vivid. He could see the things that were being described to him.

'But the White Death's army proved to be stronger. Millions of lives were lost. Sura couldn't bear to see his creations dying in front of him. So, he challenged the White Death to a duel. They fought for days until Sura realised that he was no match for the White Death. Still, he knew he couldn't let his brother win.' Ricchay paused to catch his breath.

The break annoyed Dr Chary.

'What happened then?' asked the old man, impatiently.

'He yanked the White Death, or Asura's scythe, plunged it into himself and locked his Life Energy into it through magic. Then he struck the White Death with it. At once there was a brilliant, nearly blinding flash of light that stayed for days. Eventually, when it became less intense, the Creator was found on the floor, still as a...' Ricchay swallowed the lump in his throat. Talking about the Creator's sacrifice was always so painful.

'The Creator was lifeless. After all, he had removed the Life Energy from him and locked it inside the scythe. But what about the White Death? He was nowhere to be found. Still his weapon, the scythe, was on the battleground. No one was sure if he was alive or dead. The destructive energy he had discovered remained as a white flash in the sky and everyone feared it.'

Ricchay now stopped walking and looked Dr Chary straight in the eye. He wanted Dr Chary to take him seriously. He wanted the old man to believe every word of what he was about to tell him next.

Thus, he began in a grave voice, 'This is the part that concerns you, Dr Chary.'

The old man was excited. Was this the moment he had been waiting for all his life? 'But how am I going to fit into this story? Didn't these incidents happen thousands of years ago?'

'Let's find out. As I was saying, the white light still glowed in the sky. The evil White Energy was still present. Fear and confusion abounded in everyone's mind, except for the ancient soothsayers, who could perceive the past, present and the future. And as they held the White Death's scythe, they shared their insights.'

Ricchay's voice dropped low almost as if he was scared to even utter the next few words. Dr Chary felt feverish. Goosebumps prickled his skin and his heart raced.

'Their message was both hopeful and worrying. They said the White Death was alive. He could never die because he had been struck by the scythe which had been locked with the creator's abundant Life Energy or Prana. The Life Energy that sprang from love had flowed out of the scythe into his body and suppressed the White Energy or hate within him. Just when fear sank into the hearts of Sura's followers, the soothsayers offered some reprieve. They believed the White Death had still fallen. After all, he personified hate and without hate there was no White Death. What they meant was with time, he would lose his memories, forget who he was, even his own destructive powers and ultimately, his purpose to destroy all life, and would be reduced to a common man. Still, the threat wasn't over yet, they warned. As long as the White Energy lingered on in the sky, it would keep flowing into the bodies of men, women and children, urging them to do evil. And as long as evil remained in the world, the White Death's memories could be triggered, giving him a chance to realise his purpose and rise again.'

Ricchay trembled as though he could see the White Death rising right in front of him and unleashing his destructive force upon the world. He closed his eyes. The darkness within calmed him down, made him feel less fearful and more hopeful of the future.

He then continued, 'And when that day came, the only one who could stop him and save the world from its doom would be the Equal. The soothsayers prophesied that the Equal would be born to the Aravan clan, a descendant of Haten, the most powerful Aravan ever, yet be ignorant of his own magical powers. On him would be bestowed the power of immortality through the scythe; for the scythe still had the Creator's Life Energy. So he could truly become the immortal White Death's nemesis and fight him anywhere: space, earth, underwater, even the realms below the earth's crust.

'You're the Equal, Dr Chary, the only one who can end the White Death's trail of destruction. You have the blood of an Aravan flowing through your veins. That's why you can stay underwater just like them. Remember, I told you the Aravans are humans with the magical ability to adapt themselves to any environment.'

Ricchay now eyed Dr Chary with wonder. This was the moment of truth and Dr Chary was overwhelmed.

'Yes, I can stay underwater indefinitely,' Dr Chary stated, once he had recovered from his shock.

'That's because you're an Aravan. You have to believe it.'

'How do you know about my ability?'

Ricchay closed his eyes and recalled how he had made a family tree of Haten's descendants along with Ruchira, not an easy feat for there were hardly any records. Dr Chary's name hadn't come up, but it did lead them to a man called Arjun Nolachit. Although, Arjun Nolachit couldn't survive the water test, in his panic-driven interactions with Ricchay before his death, he had revealed knowing a schoolmate Raman Chary, who, on several occasions, spent disturbing amounts of time immersed in the water without the need to come up for air. Although Ricchay hadn't taken him seriously, when *A Dwarphant's Long Tale* came along, his interest in Dr Chary piqued.

'Arjun Nolachit,' replied Ricchay and scrutinised the writer's expression. For a minute, the writer seemed disconnected from the reference but when Ricchay brought up the name of his school, the memories came flooding in.

'But I don't know any spells like the one you used to make me believe in magic.'

'That's because you are ignorant of your magical powers, just as the prophecy states. Still, magic flows in your blood, Dr Chary. You don't need any spells. Your body adapts to any new environment it is thrust into, on its own. Call it survival instinct. It is a great power but with it comes an even bigger responsibility. You're the only one who can stop the White Death. Although no one in our present time has claimed to have seen him, it is certain that the evil in the world is rising—mothers killing their own babies, men gunning down innocent people, bombing buildings, and interminable wars being fought over religion, political supremacy.'

After pausing to steady his trembling fingers, Ricchay continued, 'The White Death's followers are behind these diabolical crimes. They're doing so because that was the purpose given to them by their Master. But that's not all. They're also hoping that these crimes will help their Master regain his memories, realise his purpose to destroy this world.'

Now, Ricchay breathed out, as if to release the nervous energy and added, 'But we don't want that to happen. That's why we have been desperately trying to find the Equal. Our efforts have been rewarded Dr Chary, for you are the Equal who'll overpower the White Death. And now that I've found you, it is my responsibility to ensure that you reach Vanhad in Kerala. An Aravan is waiting for us there. She'll take you to the mantle, the realm below the earth's crust, where you can absorb the power of the Creator through the scythe and stand up to the White Death. You must come with me at once, Dr Chary.'

'The what…the mantle… Are you insane? No, stay away from me. This is all rubbish!' Dr Chary's breathing had grown heavy. His face was hot and sweaty and his heart was pounding. He was ready to run. Ricchay sensed Dr Chary's fear. It excited him. He pointed his braceband at Dr Chary; ready to strike.

'You don't understand it, do you? You don't have a choice. You're coming with me. *Cala…*' he started, but stopped abruptly. A voice within told him what he was about to do wasn't right and so he drew his hand back. Ricchay couldn't force Dr Chary to do what he wanted. This wasn't right. He had wanted to be fair. Wasn't that why he had taken the time to explain things? He had wanted Dr Chary to believe him. Ha…belief! Did anybody have faith in anything anymore? People doubted everything because of the evil White Energy that floated in the air. It made you feel these negative emotions. That was why his partner in crime—Ruchira, the Aravan—was afraid to even step out of the water.

Dr Chary could suddenly hear the ringing noise and the bodiless voice again. The voice compelled him to repeat after her.

'Stop...wasting time...take me...to Ruchira at once,' Dr Chary drawled.

He now glared at Ricchay. Blood spurted from his ears. Ricchay was stunned. How did Dr Chary know Ruchira's name when he was sure he had not mentioned her even once in the conversation?

4

Solving a Mystery

By the time the ringing stopped, Dr Chary had lost enough blood to make him dizzy with weakness. But just as he was about to lose his balance and crash into the rocks below him, Ricchay caught him. He then washed the blood off the old man's ears and tried to revive him by spraying cold water from the pond into his eyes. Dr Chary opened his eyes. Still, Ricchay wasn't too relieved for the old man looked very weak.

'Can…can…you…get me something to eat. I'm hungry,' said the writer, with much effort.

'Yes, of course, of course,' said Ricchay, pitying the old man.

He then hoisted the old man with his arms, brought him to the car and drove back to the city where he was sure he would find many restaurants.

The car came to a halt at a Chinese restaurant; the very first one that Ricchay spotted.

'What would you like?' he asked Dr Chary while scanning the menu inside the restaurant.

'Anything…no meat…no meat,' replied the writer, feebly.

'Ah…yes,' said Ricchay and placed an order of dishes that could be made quickly.

Within 10 minutes, the meal was served, and in a matter of few minutes Dr Chary had wolfed down his share of the fried soya nuggets, noodles and corn soup. He seemed to be in a hurry.

'Please be...quick...we can't waste much time here... We need to meet Ruchira,' warned the writer, giving Ricchay a hint of the cause for all his worry.

Again, Ricchay was very surprised that Dr Chary had taken Ruchira's name when he was certain he had never told him about her. And why was Dr Chary so eager to meet Ruchira when just an hour ago the story about the White Death or the prophecy had seemed ludicrous to him. But Ricchay couldn't ponder much on these for he noticed people in the restaurant pointing at Dr Chary and calling out his name excitedly. That was when Ricchay realised that the old man had drawn attention because he was a famous writer. Ricchay panicked. Sooner or later Dr Chary's son would find out that his father was missing and file a case with the police. And no one was supposed to know of the old man's whereabouts until the mission was over. Ricchay quickly got out of the restaurant even though he was only halfway through his meal.

Their next stop was a supermarket where Ricchay picked up an electric razor. He then drove to a secluded spot on the road and used it to shave off the old man's beard and moustache so he wouldn't be recognisable. Dr Chary did not make a fuss; he was quite cooperative, much to Ricchay's surprise. With his wild hair gone, the writer looked refined; even 10 years younger. Ricchay then drove away from the supermarket; a less worried man.

On the way, he asked for directions to reach Darmas's central bus terminus. His nervousness returned once he got the directions. He realised that he was not only drawing closer to the mission, but that he was also drawing closer to his death. He took a deep breath, closed his eyes to calm himself down once again. He then pulled out his wife's picture from his wallet, kissed it and wondered if he should call her one last time. But he rejected the idea once he realised talking to her would only make him more emotional.

The terminus, home to Darmas's infamous buses that polluted the city with their effusive carbon emissions, was right before him. But Ricchay couldn't get inside immediately. He first needed to get rid of the car, which he did in a muddy plot of land behind the terminus, where some construction materials had been laid out.

'Two tickets to Vanhad please,' said Ricchay, as he stood before the ticket counter inside the depot, eyeing the bus schedule for Vanhad. He was in luck, for there was a bus departing in 10 minutes.

'Oh brother...not again! How many times have I got to repeat myself? Doesn't anybody read the papers? Vanhad is closed for visitors because of the flu. The last stop on this route is Uditgiri,' said the grouchy man at the counter.

Ricchay eyed the map of Tamil Nadu and the neighbouring states and postcards of Vanhad behind the man. He had been to Vanhad before. It was a hilly town in north-west Kerala, by far, the greenest place in India; replete with rainforests. One could hardly see any blocks of concrete there. Most of the houses there were made of mud and had plants growing out of them. Uditgiri was 20 kilometres away from Vanhad.

Of course, Vanhad and the surrounding forest had been cordoned off by the Council. Ricchay knew a thing or two about it. All this anxiety about the mission had made him forget about the situation in Vanhad.

'All right. Two tickets to Uditgiri then,' said Ricchay, thinking of ways and means by which he could get to the Vanhad Forest from Uditgiri. Ruchira was waiting for him and Dr Chary, at the Vanhad River that flowed through the Vanhad Forest. The Vanhad River drained into the Arabian Sea, where Ruchira lived. It was easier for Ruchira to come to Vanhad River and that is why it was chosen as the meeting point.

The man at the counter handed Ricchay the tickets and said, 'The bus will leave in the next five minutes.'

Ricchay got inside the bus along with Dr Chary. It was half-empty; there were about 20 passengers. Ricchay wasn't surprised. After all, no one would want to travel to Vanhad or any place close to it, for there had been an outbreak of a deadly flu there. Getting the flu meant death.

Ricchay squirmed, considering the possibility that he could easily get the flu, as he settled into his seat. But he was able to drive his fear away by looking at Dr Chary and realising the importance of the mission.

Soon, the driver climbed inside the bus and the engine roared to life. Ricchay scanned the bus once again as it trundled out of the depot. Maybe, it was a good thing there were fewer people on board and the seats around him were empty, he told himself. He didn't have to worry about anyone suspecting him or Dr Chary.

Moments later, the writer fell asleep after Ricchay gave him sleeping pills that he carried in his wallet. He didn't want the old man to run away from him or scream for help. Ricchay was planning to take the pills himself but only after he was sure there was no threat up ahead.

In the absence of airports and railroads in Vanhad and Uditgiri the bus was the safest way to travel and Ricchay had thought of it well before buying the tickets. The highway from Darmas to Vanhad was notorious for stray werewolves. So Ricchay couldn't have risked driving all alone in a car with Dr Chary. What if a werewolf attacked them? How could Ricchay defend himself when he didn't know how to do magic? At least there were more people in a bus and a lone werewolf would think twice before attacking it for the fear of being outnumbered and overpowered.

Ricchay put on his braceband just to feel secure that he was armed.

His eyes fell upon his wrist and the bright red bands of scars on it. They hurt even now, 15 years after they had been dealt by his father. His father was a very ambitious man and had expected Ricchay to surpass his peers while training at the Council. The day he learnt that his son had failed in his exams he was livid; breathing fire over the news. When he finally confronted Ricchay, he punished his son by tightening the braceband to such an extent that Ricchay had only been able to remove it with the help of pliers. Oh, how Ricchay had cried when the white stone in the braceband had burnt and scraped his skin and poked into the very flesh and bones in his wrist.

Ricchay now wondered if his father would have felt proud of his accomplishments, had he been alive. After all, he had made good money; more than he needed for a lifetime. He was well-respected and loved by all. He was even considered one of the most proficient spell-casters in the Council. All thanks to Vahne Roy! Vahne was the one who had helped him cheat during exams when the training was on, and rise to an important position within the Council;

all the while keeping Ricchay's inability to do magic a secret. But why had Vahne helped him so unconditionally? It was because they had been best friends. But that was all in the past. Now, they barely knew about each other's existence. Ricchay wiped the tears from his eyes. Thinking of the past hadn't been good at all.

The only way to snap out of the past was to stay in the present. With that, Ricchay picked up the newspaper folded in the seat pocket in front of him. Again, learning about the present didn't help his cause because the headline read:

EPIDEMIC RATTLES VANHAD

An unknown flu has rattled the peaceful, sparsely-populated town of Vanhad. Although there has been no official word yet, the flu is believed to have claimed over 34 lives in over two weeks. Amongst those affected, the flu shows no signs of abatement. Treatment is being provided, under close watch, at the Vanhad Government Hospital that continues to be out of bounds for the press

It's shocking to note the government is still maintaining its hostility towards the press given the gravity of the situation. Whatever information is known today about the flu was initially made available through an unnamed source who came forward after the flu claimed its first five victims. The source disclosed that the flu was highly contagious and caused by rabid jackals before making some shocking allegations about Kerala's chief minister and the ruling party supremo, Pramil Payankan. Allegedly, he had given explicit orders to the Government Hospital to hasten the deaths of those in the terminal stages of the flu so that the flu could be contained.

At first, the reports were rubbished by the chief minister and his party, but later, in a volte face, the spokesperson of the ruling party, Riyaz Ahmed, conceded that the flu was indeed caused by rabid jackals lurking in the Vanhad Forest, communicable but easily curable with the anti-virus Coviron. He also warned the residents to stay indoors, exercise vigilance and not to venture into the forest. Just after his admission, a leading daily claimed that the unnamed source who had spread the rumours about the flu was none other than the advisor to the Kerala Department of Health (KDoH), Mrs Preethi Payankan, Mr Payankan's wife.

The claim wasn't denied by Mrs Payankan. In a dramatic twist, the spokesperson, Mr Ahmed, called forth a press conference and revealed that Mrs Payankan was emotionally unstable ever since rumours were rife that her husband had a secret lover. In a bid to sully his reputation, she made these damaging allegations about his involvement in the quick deaths of those afflicted.

Trusted sources have now spilled the beans that Mrs Payankan has been made a lucrative offer by the opposition, the United Party.

In view of these recent developments, people in Vanhad seem to be infuriated for the attention seems to have shifted from the flu and the plight of the victims to politicians washing their dirty linen in public. On Tuesday, anguished protesters gathered outside the town square and demanded that the government be forthright and answer their questions such as: Is the flu indeed fatal? What are the symptoms? Is the anti-virus actually helping the patients? If so, why is the death toll increasing?

Ricchay knew the truth about the situation, didn't he? The flu wasn't caused by jackals, but werewolves who had occupied Vanhad's forest two weeks ago and were on a spree biting residents in the vicinity. The Council had then sent its forces to the forest to thwart them, rescued some of the victims, and admitted them in the hospital. Although there was no cure for the victims—they would easily transform into werewolves—the Council's doctors had tried their best to delay the transformation. However, once the transformation was complete, the doctors had no choice but to kill these victims lest they join the werewolves in the forest and fight against the Council. It seemed as if the werewolves in the forest were on a mission to increase their numbers and build an army. But why? Was it a mere coincidence that they were holed up there just about the same time as Ruchira? Was there something more to the whole story? Ricchay's restlessness grew while thinking about the motive of the werewolves and the chances of being bitten by one of them. So he decided to calm himself down by popping a pill. Sleep overcame him.

He awoke the next day, along with the rest of the passengers, when the bus rumbled and screeched to a halt and the driver announced in a loud voice, 'The bus is going to be parked right outside the dhaba. Passengers are requested to buy their meals and refereshments from there and return to the bus within 45 minutes.

Ricchay and Dr Chary followed the passengers out of the bus and crossed the road to get to the dhaba. Ricchay was glad that they had stopped for he was starving.

The dhaba was a fragile construction; made of colourful asbestos sheets. Inside, there were plastic chairs and tables.

Ricchay ate heartily, relishing every bite of the eggplant rice, spicy fish curry, kebabs, pepper rasam rice, butter dosas, garlic naans and dal makhani. Still, what really caught his attention was the frothy coffee, made with 100 per cent pure, unadulterated cow's milk; Ricchay drank many cups. On the other hand, Dr Chary didn't seem very interested in the food although he had wolfed down his share in a few minutes. His hurry reminded Ricchay of the previous night's dinner at the Chinese restaurant. Again, Ricchay was mystified.

'Let's take a walk outside,' said Ricchay while eyeing the people around him. There were so many questions running through his mind. Although he was sure the old man couldn't have the answers he was looking for, he just wanted to step outside for some fresh air. Dr Chary nodded and the duo set out towards the palm trees and bushes surrounding the dhaba.

Ricchay stared at Dr Chary and wondered why the old man was so meek and agreeable to everything he had asked him to do. Why wasn't he screaming for help when he was aware that he had been abducted? Was he scared of him? That he would use his braceband, his magical powers to attack him if he disobeyed? But what about the time, when right after fleeing from Chandrika and Labya, Ricchay had left Dr Chary all alone in the car to stroll around the field on the outskirts of Darmas? Why hadn't Dr Chary run away even then?

Ricchay stopped walking and put away his braceband. He looked at Dr Chary for minutes expecting the writer to run. But the writer didn't budge. Then he held the braceband for a while before throwing it into the distance; he couldn't use it anyway! No point in holding onto the bauble. The writer was still as a rock.

'Well Dr Chary, you surprise me. I don't have any weapons to scare you with, anymore. Clearly, you know I have kidnapped you, so why are you still here? Why aren't you screaming for help or running away from me?'

'I...uh...don't know. I am supposed to be with you.'

'But why... Wait a minute. The Corestone... The vampires thought you had it. Do you really have the Corestone? Do you know what it is?'

Dr Chary stared back at Ricchay. But he couldn't use this opportunity to run even if he wanted to. The bodiless voice was ordering him to stay with Ricchay. The ringing noise reverberated in his ears now. Oh, it was intolerable! His ears were throbbing red and spouting warm blood.

'Please help me. It won't stop. The ringing won't stop,' Dr Chary pleaded as Ricchay tended to him.

'What's that Dr Chary? What's going on?'

There were tears in the old man's eyes.

'I keep hearing this loud ringing sound every now and then... And then...this woman talks to me. She says things I should and shouldn't do. And I feel like I have to do what I'm told like I have no other choice.'

'What...the noise... The vampires talked about it too. Wait. Who's this woman?'

'I don't know. She wants us to leave for Vanhad right now. She says we are wasting a lot of time,' said Dr Chary as both the ringing and the bleeding stopped.

'Who? Ruchira... How do you know her?' asked Ricchay while wiping away the last remaining specks of blood from the old man's face with his handkerchief. This new information was baffling. How was Ruchira talking to Dr Chary and telling him things he was supposed to do? Giving him orders?

Ricchay looked around in confusion, his eyes searching for Ruchira. She was not around. How could she be? There was no waterbody here. So how could she be talking to Dr Chary, telling him what he should be doing?

'I am not sure...but I can hear her voice as I hear the ringing sound...and she keeps telling me that I am the White Death's Equal.'

Ricchay was stunned. But he couldn't probe Dr Chary any further. The old man seemed very weak once again because of the blood he had lost. In the distance, the furious honking of the bus could be heard. It was time to leave. So Ricchay made his way back along with Dr Chary. Although there were still many questions that flooded his mind, he knew he had answered the most puzzling one—Dr Chary couldn't leave his side even if he wanted to because his mind was somehow being controlled by Ruchira.

5

Friends or Foes

The uphill journey towards Uditgiri made Ricchay very nauseous. After all, the climb was full of stomach churning moments, courtesy the innumerable hairpin bends. All the milk he had drunk added to his discomfort. To keep himself from throwing up, Ricchay tried to distract his mind by admiring the scene around him. Indeed it was just jaw-droppingly beautiful—mountains spread out high and wide like the sky itself, the greenery bathed in the golden light of the sun, waterfalls cascading down rock walls, alongside the road, with the sweetest symphony that could make even an insomniac fall asleep. With time, Ricchay forgot about his nausea and fell asleep.

When he woke up he found that the bus had pulled over in a town called Nilambur; 15 kilometres away from Uditgiri according to the signboard. Ricchay let out a yawn; shorter than the one Dr Chary let out. The writer too had fallen asleep.

The duo now peered out of the window to find people queued up before colourful tents and three other buses parked alongside the road.

Just then, a man stepped into their bus. He looked like a doctor; dressed in a labcoat, with a stethoscope hanging around his neck and a scratch pad in his hands. He had a word with the driver, checked his licence and scribbled something on his scratch pad. Then, he walked along the aisle, casually glancing at the passengers.

Their eyes met. Ricchay felt a rush of emotions. The man felt it too. Maybe a little more than Ricchay because he was the first one to express it, 'Ri...Ricchay... How're you? It's been so long.'

'I never thought I would see you here, Vahne.'

'You've surprised me too. I wonder...'

'How are you?'

'Listen...there's work...I will see you in a bit,' said Vahne, before leaving the bus.

Ricchay's heart pounded with excitement. The man he had just spoken to was no doctor. He knew him very well. He was Vahne Roy; his former best friend, partner in crime who had helped him hoodwink the Council into believing he was a talented spell-caster. Ricchay hadn't seen Vahne in over five years now. All his childhood memories now flashed before him. There was a time when they couldn't spend a day apart from each other. But that time had passed... Their much-envied long friendship had ended bitterly with Ricchay's pride being wounded by Vahne's constant snubs.

Ricchay was both happy and distressed by Vahne's sudden reappearance in his life. He didn't want Vahne to know about the prophecy, his mission and the fact that he had abducted Dr Chary.

There was a commotion starting in the bus; people were wondering aloud why their journey had been interrupted.

Vahne Roy re-entered the bus and Ricchay walked up to him in order to keep him from noticing Dr Chary.

'You look good. Ahem... What's going on here?'

For moments, Vahne just stared at Ricchay. They had had a history. As his walkie-talkie buzzed to life he was brought back to the present. He answered it and then said to Ricchay, 'Not now. We'll talk later.'

Ricchay felt rebuffed once again, took his seat away from Dr Chary and watched Vahne. First, Vahne fixed his tie that was slightly askew, cleared his throat and then announced with a drawl, as if to ensure that everyone could follow every single word he was uttering.

'Good afternoon, everyone. I am Doctor Vahne Roy from the Kerala Department of Health, also called the KDoH. Welcome to Nilambur. As you all are aware, there has been an outbreak of a contagious flu in Vanhad. The KDoH has issued a health inspection order for all tourists visiting towns in and around Vanhad, just to make sure everyone's safe and those infected are quarantined at once.

'I'd request all of you to queue up outside the yellow tent. I can assure you that if you cooperate with us, this won't take more than 30 minutes of your time. Thank you.'

As Vahne Roy finished, a young, animated man climbed into the bus and distributed copies of the KDoH's order to the passengers, even willingly answered questions from the worried passengers.

Ricchay took a long, hard look at the three tents in bright shades of yellow, green and red, that were marked with the emblems of the KDoH. There were Udals interspersed with civilians; some wearing lab coats and others police uniforms with their bracebands concealed but their handguns clearly visible. He wondered if the Council really did suspect that the passengers could be bitten by werewolves? Maybe, if he had a chance to talk to Vahne, he could find out what was going on.

He stood behind Dr Chary in a line outside the yellow tent. The passengers from his bus had simply joined an existing line made up of travellers from another bus. The atmosphere was tense. After all, everybody worried that the person next to them had the flu. So they kept to themselves, eschewed touching or talking to each other, even breathing the same air by blocking their nostrils with hands or handkerchiefs. Only Ricchay knew there was no way one could get the flu through the air or just by touching an infected person. Still, he was tense. After all, there was a crowd around him and he didn't want anybody to recognise Dr Chary.

'I don't want them to know who you are. You hear me. Tell them your name is Mohan Kumar,' Ricchay instructed Dr Chary.

'Got that,' replied the writer.

There were doctors outside every tent, seated on chairs, examining the passengers.

The line moved ahead. Ricchay spotted Vahne now. He had just stepped out of the green tent and was speaking into the walkie-talkie. Soon, another bus pulled over and Vahne got inside it. There were altogether five buses parked outside the tents; four of these, it seemed, were returning from Uditgiri, Vanhad, Palam, Chemula to Darmas. After Vahne finished with his customary lecture, the passengers from the Chemula-to-Darmas-route bus joined the line behind Ricchay, who now asked Dr Chary to bend his head and avoid the gaze of the newcomers.

'Next,' yelled a woman in a doctor's costume seated outside the yellow tent.

'Mohan Kumar,' Ricchay whispered into the writer's ears just before the latter took his seat beside the woman.

Ricchay recognised the woman with braided raven black hair who was examining Dr Chary. She had studied with him and Vahne at the Council's training academy. But her name eluded him.

'Can I have your name please?'

'Raman… Raman Kumar,' Dr Chary said, giving away his first name, much to Ricchay's consternation.

The woman stared at the writer and for a moment there was a faint flicker in her eyes. Ricchay's heart hammered against his ribcage. He was afraid the woman had recognised the writer.

'Malini…Mala,' he said aloud, struggling to remember the woman's name. The woman was distracted. She beamed at Ricchay.

'Ricchay… How are you?' She seemed to remember his name very well.

Ricchay's eyes fell on the badge the woman was wearing. *Manasa Shetty*, it said. Ah! Now it rang a bell!

'It feels like a reunion now… I just saw Vahne,' replied Ricchay.

Manasa looked thrilled and quickly finished checking Dr Chary's body temperature, heart rate, his neck and arms for bite marks so that she could talk to Ricchay.

'Thank you. You can get back to the bus now,' Manasa instructed Dr Chary who then wheeled around to stare at Ricchay. Again, Ricchay was alarmed. He didn't want anyone to know that Dr Chary was with him. But now that the writer had made it obvious, he had no choice but to go with it.

'Wait for me in the bus, uncle. I'll be there in a bit,' said Ricchay. Dr Chary nodded and walked to the bus.

'Ah…Ricchay… As you can see, it's a crazy day. Everybody's in a rush to get out of Vanhad,' she whispered.

'How is it there?' asked Ricchay curiously.

'Very grim. The hounds are very strong...and we're struggling to comb out the forest,' admitted Manasa after making sure no one was watching her.

Ricchay gulped in fear. He had been reminded, once again, that his chances of survival in Vanhad were very slim.

'Are you here for the operation in Vanhad?' asked Manasa as she now examined Ricchay.

'Yes... No... I mean Kadambari's uncle lives in Uditgiri. He came to visit us and now it's my duty to make sure he reaches home safely.'

'Oh yes... Kadambari and you ended up together right? I was...um...'

Just then, the same frisky man who had distributed the KDoH's notice in the bus emerged before Ricchay and whispered into Manasa's ear.

'Yes, his tests are done. He's all clear,' said Manasa, before adding, 'Ricchay, Vahne Roy would like to speak to you. He's in the green tent.'

Ricchay's heart fluttered in panic. Why did Vahne want to talk to him? He didn't want Vahne to find out about the mission or that he had kidnapped Dr Chary.

'What's this about?' he asked the frisky man who was now acting as an emissary.

'I don't know... He's waiting for you.'

'Okay,' said Ricchay, as he was escorted inside the green tent.

Ricchay found himself in a formidable, cold and utterly uninviting setting. The silence was so deep that Ricchay could hear his own heartbeat. It was dark all around save the spot where Vahne sat beside a desk in a corner of the tent. A lone candle was fixed in an ornate stand. Its light fell upon umpteen files and bracebands scattered on the desk and Vahne's very face—his sallow skin, high protruding cheekbones and shock of prematurely white hair.

Vahne's head hung low, with his hands scratching his forehead as though he was in deep thought. It was not until Ricchay tapped the floor nervously that he realised he had company.

'How's everything, Ricchay?' he asked without looking up. Somehow the concern seemed forced.

'Yeah…err… It's all good,' replied Ricchay. The anxiety in his voice was palpable.

'How is Kadambari? Hope she's in great spirits,' said Vahne, and unlike before, the concern seemed very sincere.

'She's doing okay.' Ricchay was restless; chewing his thumbnails. He wanted to get out of the tent now and check on Dr Chary. What if he ran away?

'Why don't you sit down?' asked Vahne and then finally lifted up his head and stared at Ricchay. He could immediately perceive the change in Vahne's eyes. They were usually cold grey and severe, but now, there was a sort of tenderness in them that reminded Ricchay of the Vahne who was once his closest friend.

'Please sit down,' urged Vahne.

Ricchay sat reluctantly.

'I heard about your promotion to an officer. I was so thrilled,' expressed Vahne.

Ricchay didn't know how to respond.

'Have you still not forgiven me? I tried to get in touch but there was no response. I wrote several letters to you over the past month.'

Ricchay bit his lip. He didn't want Vahne to bring up the past. It was just too embarrassing.

'I...uhh...heard that Kadambari was in a lot of pain after the delivery... How is she now? Ricchay...forgive me... This silence between us has grown into an enormous wall. And now, even though we are in the same room, we can't see each other... I wish I could take back what I had said.'

'No, you shouldn't have to. It was a reality check for me. You were right, Vahne. I got my hopes up too high. The truth is that the day I heard you say you wanted to study and work hard to become the youngest head of the Council, I wanted to do the same. You were so confident. That inspired me. But I completely forgot that I was poor at magic and that I owed any success within the Council to you. The thing is I wanted to do everything you did, so we could be toget...' Ricchay's voice broke off.

Vahne pulled his eyes away from Ricchay. He couldn't look at this man. He was so weak and pitiful. He had no ambition, no sight. He was aimless like a plastic bag floating in the wind. No, it wasn't right. Vahne was doing it again—looking down upon Ricchay Gupta. Wasn't Ricchay his closest friend; the only one who talked to him in the training academy, and who never made fun of his dysfunctional family? Vahne knew that he owed it to Ricchay for his unconditional kindness towards him.

'I never meant it. I was just very stressed then,' Vahne lied. The truth was he was tired, annoyed with helping Ricchay fool the Council. But wasn't there something more to why he had insulted Ricchay?

'I am sorry. Let's forget it. I heard you and Kadambari had a daughter. What's her name again...forgive me. You know I have never been good at remembering those.'

'Ajari. I thought I was the one who was forgetful.'

After a pause, Vahne exclaimed, 'Ajari! Yes...wasn't Kadambari's great grandmother called that?'

Ricchay was taken aback. How did Vahne know this? Had Kadambari told him? Then again, Ricchay couldn't remember the two ever talking much in the training academy.

Suddenly, the tenderness disappeared from Vahne's eyes. He now caught his reflection in the polished metal of a braceband lying on his desk. At once, a memory was triggered.

Vahne saw his younger self standing behind the door of a classroom at the Academy, overhearing a conversation between Kadambari and her friend.

'I have never seen a face more handsome,' said Kadambari to her friend.

'Oh yeah. Who'd think of saying no to Vahne. He's a gorgeous beast. Ah, his eyes are like pools of silver. I have never seen a sharper nose in my life. And the way he smiles, he makes my heart skip a beat.'

'What Vahne... Ewww... I was talking about Ricchay,' blurted out Kadambari.

'Ricchay... Ricchay Gupta?' Kadambari's friend cried with disgust.

'Vahne's hideous... I can't imagine why anyone would like him. Have you ever seen him proper...'

Vahne couldn't stand there anymore. He was gutted! His eyes mirrored his disgust and anger with Ricchay. He could bear anyone bad-mouthing him but certainly not Kadambari.

Why had Kadambari liked Ricchay then? Ricchay was the one who was hideous with his pockmarks and droopy eyes. Ricchay was the one who was weak, aimless, full of self-pity and self-loathing. Kadambari's decision to choose Ricchay over him had deeply hurt

Vahne. After that he had begun to hate Ricchay and insult him whenever he got the opportunity. That was how their friendship had ended. Vahne swore never to talk to Ricchay again.

The anger had subsided but the hurt had remained. Vahne was compelled to break his vow now that Ricchay was before him.

Dwelling on the past had made Vahne emotional. He got up from his chair, with the candle stand in his hand, and walked towards a fridge in the tent.

'Why are you here, Ricchay?' he asked after gulping down some water.

'Th... The operation...' Ricchay mumbled. He couldn't lie. He knew that Vahne was very shrewd. He had his ways of finding out the truth.

Vahne looked shocked as he turned to him, 'At Vanhad?'

'Yes...Vanhad.'

'The situation is pretty grim there, Ricchay. They have already bitten most of the villagers living close to the forest and now they're making werewolves out of the Udals fighting them. They're on a rampage to increase their numbers. They're doing so because they don't want to be overpowered by the Council and want to stay in the forest at any cost. The Udals who entered the fight are decamping out of fear. Civilians in and around Vanhad are escaping in droves. The bottomline is everyone's fleeing. My team's been stationed here to check if any of those have been bitten. Already, there are reports that five civilians in Darmas, who had left Vanhad last week, have transformed into werewolves. It's getting out of control. You should go back, Ricchay.'

'No... I can't.'

Vahne was puzzled. He took his seat once again.

'Why not? We have lost 78 of our most able Udals; 10 of these were veterans who had dedicated their whole lives to serving the Council. But once they were bitten, the Council just killed them all, even though their families begged the Council to try delaying their transformation. Want to know why the Council didn't agree? Because it thought delaying their transformation was a big waste of time, effort and money. Would you want that for yourself, Ricchay? Death is inevitable if you enter Vanhad.'

'Death is inevitable anyway...for us all,' said Ricchay. The words seemed to allay his fears of death and dying for the moment.

'Where's the permit?' asked Vahne.

Every Udal who wanted to join the operation in Vanhad needed a permit for the Council's records.

Ricchay furnished the document and Vahne skimmed through it quickly only to realise that there was another permit stapled to it.

Ricchay bit his lip nervously. He had forged two copies; one for himself and the other for Dr Chary. Of course, in all his anxiety about the mission, he had forgotten that that he had kept the two copies together. And now he was prepared to take questions from Vahne about Dr Chary.

'So, you have a partner?'

'Ah...yes.'

'And he's on the bus with you?'

Ricchay nodded.

Vahne stared at him and questions ran riot in his head... But this is suicide. Why would he go there? He knows he can't cast a single spell right. It doesn't make any sense at all.

He looked at Ricchay closely and noticed that he looked nervous—he was scratching his forehead, biting his lips and there was alarm in his eyes. Why was Ricchay tense? Was he hiding something? Not knowing the truth made Vahne terribly restless.

But he had means to find out the truth even if Ricchay wasn't going to tell him willingly.

Vahne opened his labcoat, revealing a sceptre fastened to his waist. The sceptre was wrought of a white metal and crowned by a stone, the size of an orange.

Ricchay was shocked. The sceptre belonged to the head of the Council. Although they had been working in different branches of the Council and he was aware that Vahne was close to becoming the head of the Council, the truth was Vahne hadn't been promoted yet. So how had he come in possession of such a powerful weapon?

'What are you hiding from me, Ricchay?' asked Vahne. His voice shot an octave. 'Where's your braceband? How can you fight against the werewolves without one?' asked Vahne before drawing closer to Ricchay.

The sceptre in his hand was pointed at Ricchay now. The stone crowning it was called a Lumestone, just like the stone which was the centrepiece of his braceband. The Lumestone had the power to bend the forces of nature and unleash the magic of Destructika. If the Lumestone was the bullet then the braceband was the gun to trigger its power. That's how the White Death had purposed them to be, thousands of years ago after he discovered the destructive properties of the White Energy, infused it all within the Lumestone and went on to forge millions of bracebands fitted with millions of Lumestones so men and monsters could fight with it and kill each other. Every Udal who worked for the Council armed himself with a braceband. You had to fight fire with fire. How else could he protect his brothers, his neighbourhood and his nation from the magical force of the enemy? Vahne looked menacing now; his nostrils flaring, his grey eyes glaring down upon Ricchay. Suddenly, a loud crackle was heard and the flame of the candle (now resting on the fridge) grew bigger and brighter, lighting up the whole tent.

'Don't keep secrets from me, Ricchay. It drives me crazy. Remember Sine Nomine, that island we went to. I know something happened there. I asked you about it a million times at least, but you never told me anything. When we got back I was so mad at you. We never kept secrets between us. We told each other everything. I told you how I felt but you continued to be quiet. Your silence annoyed me quite severely. And then there was this whole issue with Ka… Well, I kept my distance. And then one day, I felt it. Pride! You were a poor, ugly weakling, a failure at everything that you did, a miserable loser, and an aimless wanderer. I hated you—hated you with every fibre of my being.'

What he did not tell Ricchay now was that once he began to hate him with a vengeance, he had been able to cast some of the most difficult magical spells. The accomplishment had thrilled him and given him the confidence that he could certainly fulfil his ambition of becoming the youngest head of the Council. What he also did not tell Ricchay was that this ambition had made him lonely and afraid. And there were times when he regretted the fact that he had destroyed their friendship.

Ricchay now felt a strange force penetrating his mind.

'Tell me, Ricchay. It has been years. What exactly happened in Sine Nomine? I have spent sleepless nights wondering about it. I wish I had never gone there, that I had never felt these emotions.'

Ricchay trembled. Words spilled out of his mouth involuntarily, 'I...uhh...found a stone. It was in a cave.'

'But why would you hide that from me?'

'Because I wanted to be more powerful than you...so that my father would like me more than you. The stone could help me be that person.'

'Huh? I'm lost here... What power?... What are you talking about? What did you find?'

'It was a grey stone with several inscriptions on it. I thought Ruchira could decipher them so I gave it to her.'

'Who's Ruchira?'

Vahne advanced towards Ricchay and the Lumestone in his sceptre poked Ricchay's forehead. Ricchay felt a searing pain, just like the day his father had tightened the braceband around his wrist.

'She's my friend.'

'What? I thought I was the only one you talked to apart from Ka... How is this Ruchira your friend?'

'She saved my life once.'

'Tell me more.'

'I wanted to kill myself by drowning in the water. She saved me, took care of me like I was her brother. I owe everything to her.'

'How come you never told me about her?'

'She didn't want me to because she doesn't trust those who are good at Destructika.'

'And why is that?'

'Within them, the White Energy is stronger than Prana.'

'But who is she? How have I never seen her at the Academy?'

'She is an Aravan. She lives in the Arabian Sea. She never leaves the water because she fears the White Energy will corrupt her.'

'An Aravan? I thought they had all perished during the Battle of Gawaan.'

Vahne was soaked with sweat now; his face showing his excitement. He was getting to learn new things; all because he had tapped into his hatred for Ricchay. Hate was such a powerful emotion. It had let him master Destructika, feel enlightened.

'What happened after the battle?'

'The White Death lost his memories and destructive powers, and disappeared, never to be found again. That is why his worshippers today are trying to find him by staging the most violent and abominable acts of destruction so his memories could be revived.'

'No, no, I know all that. Tell me, specifically, what happened to the Aravans after the battle.'

'Most of them hid in the water fearing the White Energy, while a few stayed back on land.'

'What? Impossible! Is this true?'

'Yes.'

Vahne pressed the Lumestone harder onto Ricchay's forehead. A voice within him said, 'Show him no kindness. He's weak, despicable. Only if you crush the weak can you gain power. Let the Lumestone tear through his skull and push the brain out from its dark vault. Let it spill on the floor. Let it be illumined by the Lumestone. The true purpose of the Lumestone is to bring light into the darkness.'

The Lumestone burned Ricchay's skin. And then, drops of his blood fell, staining the pure whiteness of the Lumestone. It glowed with a white fire now. As Ricchay let out a cry of pain, Vahne shuddered in shock. It wasn't because he had injured Ricchay, but because he had felt the urge to kill the weak, the aimless Ricchay Gupta in cold blood. Such an appalling thought had never crossed his mind before.

'Get out of here... Go. Go. Go. Just get out,' he yelled, disgusted with himself and afraid that if Ricchay stayed longer, he could harm him.

But Ricchay didn't react to what Vahne said. He was in a lot of pain. Soon, Vahne realised it too and was filled with remorse. He apologised profusely and tended to the man he had wounded, the man who had once been his best friend.

Ricchay's bleeding stopped because of the ice cubes Vahne was pressing upon his forehead. Vahne now looked at Ricchay with the same tenderness in his eyes as before, thinking of all the good memories he shared with Ricchay. Still, the voice within Vahne told him things could never be the same anymore, that Ricchay and he could never be friends again because he, Vahne, was powerful and Ricchay, weak.

He thrust the permits in Ricchay's hands and asked him to leave the tent, immediately.

6

Sine Nomine

'He's coming inside,' said a pot-bellied passenger in a white dhoti and a collared shirt as he looked at Ricchay walking towards the bus.

'Why was he called inside the tent?' asked another passenger worriedly.

'I'm telling you; he has the flu,' replied the dhoti-clad man.

A commotion broke out in the bus now. About five of the passengers led by the dhoti-clad man bounded out of the bus with their luggage, afraid that they would catch the germs from Ricchay.

'Get out of here. You have the flu,' yelled a woman with a scarf wrapped around her face as Ricchay stepped inside the bus. She was in two minds about whether she should waste her bus ticket because of one supposedly sick man who looked fine to her by the way, walking briskly on his own two feet.

'I can assure you, there's nothing wrong with me,' said Ricchay.

'Then why were you called inside the tent? There's blood on your shirt. I have heard victims vomit blood. You have the flu,' pointed a sweaty man hitching up his sweater to his nose.

'No, he doesn't. Why would they let him out of their sights then?' reasoned an old man before breaking into a series of coughs.

'You're coughing already... You are sick... Oh my god! He's infected us. He's on the run, I tell you. We should call for help,' said the sweaty man in absolute panic now.

There was now an uproar among passengers arguing with each other about whether or not Ricchay had the flu.

'Silence! Well, I work for the Coch Police Department. I was called in to discuss some confidential matters. As for the blood on my shirt, do you notice I have a gash on my forehead? Besides, do you really think the police would have let me go if I had the flu? They have guns in their hands,' said Ricchay and flashed his police ID.

He expected to hear sighs of relief from the passengers. Instead, the commotion resumed after the sweaty man said, 'I'm telling you he was in a scuffle with the police because he tried to escape. Now that he's here, the police will come looking for him.'

The man's words were prophetic, for soon, two Udals, totting guns, got inside with the five passengers who had fled the bus.

'What's going on here?' asked one of the Udals in police uniform. Ricchay flashed his ID card and explained the situation to the Udal.

'I am going to call a doctor now,' said the Udal.

'Yes, that's the best thing to do,' said Ricchay. They both looked at each other as though they had an understanding.

A doctor was called and Ricchay was re-examined in front of the passengers who now seemed relieved. The barricade was removed and the bus resumed its journey.

Ricchay sat down while sighing tiredly. It seemed like such a long day, given all the drama. He wondered what he should expect next. Dr Chary was seated next to him, unmoved by the commotion around him and not making use of the very golden opportunity to tell the police that he had in fact been kidnapped. Perhaps, it was because Ruchira was controlling his mind. Ah mind control! Hadn't he himself been a victim of it in the tent where Vahne had ordered him to tell him about Sine Nomine?

Now the memories of his adventure with Vahne in Sine Nomine washed over him.

Ricchay and Vahne—both in their teens and full of energy and rebellion—had ended up on the island that was surrounded by the Bay of Bengal, after running away from the Council's Academy for some adventure. The island was beautiful; pristine and green. There was untamed wilderness all around bearing the most delicious fruits and vegetables. The water was a clear blue and the air was fresh, with the flowers in full blossom. Still, it was all very strange for no one actually lived on the island. Not just people, there weren't even animals around; you couldn't find fish in the water or spot a bird on the trees. Though Ricchay and Vahne were spooked out by the eerie silence and stillness around, they couldn't leave. The possibility that they had discovered a new land filled their hearts with excitement and made them feel legendary as though they would feature in history books alongside some of the greatest adventurers such as Columbus and Magellan. They named the island Sine Nomine. Vahne was the one who came up with it. It was so fancy—a Latin expression for the nameless one. Vahne had picked it up from a book. He read all the time.

The island was a lot of fun. There was no one to bother them; tell them when to get up, what to do. No rules at all. Still, Ricchay wasn't all fascinated by living life with abandon on the island. Something made him very uncomfortable; it was his inner voice that kept telling him that the beauty he was gazing at was only an illusion.

One day, as Vahne slept, Ricchay went on foot to explore the island alone. He was thoroughly stunned. After walking aimlessly, he suddenly came upon a dry and desolate area. The air was intolerably foul there. The wilderness too was gone. The trees were but mere stumps without leaves and the river with its clear blue water had turned into a thick red pool, like tomato soup.

When Ricchay overcame his shock and his eyes moved away from the river, he saw a sight that sent chills down his spine. There were innumerable corpses up ahead rotting under the sun. Flies, worms, and other living things were feeding on them. Shortly, a body arose pulling away the worms and flies sticking on its neck.

Terrified, Ricchay galloped away from the scene. After some time, he stopped running. The desolation was still around, but he found a cave. It was no ordinary one; emitting an incredibly strong energy that excited Ricchay's senses and compelled him to probe further.

As soon as he stepped inside, he felt small and puny like an ant. The rock walls surrounding him seemed to stretch on, limitless and were lit up with torches. Indeed, the setting was new and unfamiliar, still Ricchay had no apprehensions about being there for his only goal was to find the source of the energy. Thus, he walked further, eventually making his way through what seemed like a maze of smaller caves. What guided him was the very same energy that had pulled him inside. With every step he took, his restlessness to find the source of the energy grew; such that when finally he sensed he was close to the source, his breathing became rapid and shallow and his head was soaked with sweat.

'What is this thing?' he exclaimed, his voice trembling with thrill after he was compelled to turn left. Upon entering a dark torch-less chamber, he saw it—the source of the energy. It was a stone; oblong and chunky, aglow with a shimmering grey fire, set atop a cairn. Ricchay reached out to touch it. The first touch set his heart racing, for a fraction of the energy seeped out of the stone and into his body through his fingertips. Ricchay felt so charged, so powerful. He wished to absorb all the energy from the stone. But a voice within kept telling him he wasn't worthy enough to acquire the full power of the grey stone. When it stopped glowing, strange writings appeared on the stone. The letters were fiery, free flowing, curved, capped by horizontal lines. Ricchay couldn't read the message but he was certain it was meant for him, as was the grey relic itself. And thus he grabbed it. Once the relic was removed from its place, all the other stones arranged in the cairn came crashing down.

Just then Ricchay heard a quick pattering of feet. The sound came from behind him. Was there somebody else inside the cave? The cold fingers of fear and panic squeezed his heart. He worried that the intruder too had felt the aura of the relic and was drawn towards it; just like him. Oh, but he couldn't possibly allow the intruder to take the relic away from him—it was his and only his.

'*Nivacira*,' he chanted and flung his arm backwards. A crackling bolt of electricity shot from his braceband and struck the intruder; a dark silhouetted figure.

A violent cry resounded in the cave. And it was followed by a heavy thud. The intruder had fallen. Ricchay pocketed the grey stone.

'*Nivacira*,' he chanted again and aimed at the wall in front of him. Now, the electric bolt struck the cave wall and burned a hole through it. He ran out through it with his breath rattling in his throat.

When he was outside and had left the cave far behind, he was gripped with panic once again. What if the intruder was in fact Vahne? After all, he hadn't seen anybody else over the course of a week on the island. And how had he actually been able to cast the spell he wanted to? And so easily that his best friend had been killed within seconds! Shocked, Ricchay fell on his knees and bawled for what seemed like hours.

'Ricchay, why are you crying?' he heard a familiar voice and realised it was Vahne.

'You're alive… It wasn't you,' screamed Ricchay and pulled himself together.

'Why should I not be alive?'

'I was in the cave and…'

'What cave?'

'If you want to be powerful, more powerful than Vahne and if you want father to like you more than Vahne…then don't tell him about the grey stone,' Ricchay's inner voice advised him.

'Nothing… Vahne we should just leave…right now. Go back to the Academy.'

'What? Why?'

Because I have to get help, find Ruchira, ask her to help me decipher the message on the grey stone. She knows a lot about ancient languages, thought Ricchay, but instead said, 'Because I am sick of this place.'

'Sick of it? I thought you said you wanted to stay here for a month.'

'I just want to go back.'

'Ricchay, what's going on? You're hiding something from me, I can tell.'

'I am not feeling well. I think I am going to get a fever soon. We should leave.'

And Ricchay and Vahne's Sine Nomine escapade came to an abrupt end.

A week after their return to the Academy, Ricchay was able to meet Ruchira.

He was very anxious that day. In fact, since the time the grey stone came into his possession, he had become restless.

'Please can you help me decode the inscriptions on the stone? I can't sleep because I want to know what they mean,' he begged Ruchira through laboured breaths.

'I can't recognise this language at all…I would need some time,' replied Ruchira and rubbed Ricchay's chest to calm him down. While doing so she unwittingly knocked out the grey stone from his hand. Suddenly, the pain in Ricchay's chest disappeared. His breathing also became normal. His head felt so light; like a great worry had been lifted off him. He told Ruchira how he felt but she left him quite abruptly with the stone in her hands.

Ricchay didn't see Ruchira for a very long time after that. But somehow, he wasn't bothered about the stone anymore. In fact, he forgot all about it, even his adventure in Sine Nomine once he got caught up with the intense training at the Academy.

7

The Grey Corestone

Recalling memories of Sine Nomine had excited Ricchay's grey cells into putting two and two together.

'So, Vahne got me to tell him about Sine Nomine by pressing the Lumestone to my head. Ruchira is possibly using something to control Dr Chary's mind,' he said to himself.

Dr Chary heard Ricchay. A minute later he heard the ringing noise and the voice of the woman. She demanded that he repeat after her.

'Ricchay... Please understand... I can't move out of the Vanhad River even if I want to help you... Therefore...I want you to come to me. You'll have to ward off the werewolves by yourself and bring Dr Chary to the river,' interrupted the writer.

Dr Chary seemed to be in a trance with his voice dull and slow, head hung low on his shoulders and his pupils bobbing between the lids.

Ricchay was baffled until he recalled the time when the writer had spoken to him in a similar manner, asking him to stop wasting time in Darmas and take him to Ruchira.

'Ruchira, is that you?' he asked incredulously.

After a gap of a minute, Dr Chary said, 'Yes...Ricchay.'

'How are you able to talk to me through Dr Chary?'

'Through…the…Corestone,' replied Dr Chary, again after a gap.

Ricchay was stunned. Wasn't the Corestone what the vampires and werewolves were desperate to find because it apparently belonged to their Master, the White Death, or so he had heard them say?

'Ruchira…how can you do that?' he asked curiously.

Ruchira's response through Dr Chary came after a short time, 'I can get inside Dr Chary's mind…and see what he sees…hear what he hears…and control his mind.'

'Just like Vahne got inside my head with the Lumestone. So, the Corestone and Lumestone are similar…both forged by the White Death… Ruchira, is this the very grey stone I found in Sine Nomine?' asked Ricchay. It was a guess based on the fact that when he had held the grey stone on the island he had been able to cast a very difficult Destructika spell with ease.

'Yes.'

Ricchay's face was scrunched up in worry.

'Ruchira, you have to stop using it. It's the reason the werewolves and vampires are attacking us…the werewolves are in Vanhad… The Corestone is evil; it belongs to the White Death. The vampires said it has the power to bring catastrophe upon our planet,' he warned in a whisper; making sure the other passengers didn't hear him.

'I can't… It has this power over me… I have been trying to…but I can't.'

'Unless you stop using it, the werewolves won't leave Vanhad… You realise you have invited trouble and made this a suicide mission for me.'

'I...can't stop Ricchay... I am so sorry, but I am trying to use it to control the minds of the werewolves and drive them away. It's not been working yet. But I promise you, I will find a way to...protect you from the enemy.'

'Ruchira, you have to stop. What if the werewolves kill you to get the Corestone or Dr Chary or me when we make it to the forest.'

'Dr Chary cannot die... It is his destiny to be the White Death's Equal.'

Just then, the driver slammed the brakes, bringing the bus to a violent, jerking halt. The passengers lurched forward, banging into the seats in front of them. Two of them—the man in the dhoti and the woman with a scarf—were knocked unconscious at once with blood streaming down from their gashed foreheads. Dr Chary and Ricchay only had slight bruises on their hands and knees. Sitting in the middle row possibly saved them from taking the brunt of the violent impact.

Two portly men climbed into the bus.

'*Find us the Corestone we will, as it ring...ring...rings*,' sang the man with long, shaggy hair falling in curls until the curve of his swollen belly, as he pointed his braceband at the passengers.

'*Unhissa*... Darn it... That was the spell we were supposed to use to make everyone fall asleep instead of standing in the middle of the road and scaring the driver into hitting the brakes... What if the Council heard the tyres screeching and got suspicious... Chandrika will kill us,' said another man with a braided beard, gulping in fear.

'You fool! If we had made the driver fall asleep, the bus would have crashed into the woods...gone up in flames... and that would have alerted the Council at once. We did the right thing… Now let me focus on the ringing noise and find out which of these passengers has the Corestone,' said the long-haired man whilst moving forward and leering at the passengers scattered in the bus.

'I can't hear it any more. What about you Bana?' asked the bearded man.

'It is very feeble. But I can…'

Just then, a passenger in the front row screamed, 'What's going on? What are you two doing? What's that in your hands?'

The long-haired man, called Bana, was annoyed. After all, he was trying to concentrate on the ringing noise of the Corestone.

'*Agnichad*,' he yelled. A wall of flame shot out of his braceband and smacked into the passenger. Screams rent the air now, as the passengers watched the man burning alive, flailing his arms, and the tongues of fire catching onto the seats and the glass of the windows shattering into fragments. Both the driver and the man crashed out of the bus through the windshield.

'Silence!' screamed Bana.

'What's wrong with you? Why did you use the fire spell? There's a commotion now. *Paniyapata*,' yelled the bearded man. Water gushed out of his braceband and doused the fire burning the empty seats behind the driver's seat.

'*Unhissa*,' chanted the bearded man next. At once, all the passengers in the bus felt drugged with sleep.

'Oh thank you for the silence, Kaban. I think it's this man… Oh wait, it could be the one next to him,' said Bana, whilst straining his ears to catch the ringing noise. It seemed to come from both Ricchay and Dr Chary.

'Let's get them both,' suggested Kaban, the man with the beard.

'Good idea!' said Bana. He and his partner now lifted Dr Chary and Ricchay—who were both asleep—and got off the bus.

Just as they stepped out under the murky night sky and laid Dr Chary and Ricchay on the road, they were confronted by their boss. The reproachful look on her face made them tremble in fear.

'I asked you to prove to me you weren't savages. And look what your raging White Energy just did,' said Chandrika Chetak with clenched teeth.

Her minions were quiet. They knew they were at fault, so it was best not to argue with their boss. Chandrika zipped up her jacket until her chin and slipped her icy, numb hands into her pockets. It was cold and windy here in Uditgiri which stood at 1793 metres above sea level. But to Chandrika and her minions, who were wrapped up in three layers of woollens, the weather seemed frosty; for the werewolves had little tolerance for cold.

'Why have you brought two men?' she asked after taming her unruly hair into a bun.

'The noise was coming from both of them and we were confused,' answered Kaban as his partner was silent.

'Well, did you search them? You could have found out who had the Corestone then.'

'No... Yes...I mean we were going to.'

'Use your heads, you morons. We can't win this battle with just our strength. We need to be smart, sharp and conniving like the vampires, so we can crush them and be the superior race once again. Why did you have to set the bus on...'

'They don't have the Corestone,' chimed in the werewolf who had started the fire.

He had been searching Dr Chary and Ricchay's pockets. After a pause, he added, 'Yet, I can still hear the ringing from both of them.'

'How dare you interrupt me?' Chandrika yelled. Her eyes were bloodshot.

'*Parabti*,' she chanted. The ground underneath Bana rumbled and cracked open, swallowing him into its dark belly.

'I guess you have to be a brute when you deal with brutes,' said Chandrika with a scoff.

She now turned her attention to the other werewolf.

'Kaban, bring them inside,' she ordered, while pointing at the woods abutting the road.

Kaban masked his fear, nodded his head vigorously, before chanting, '*Jagar*.' At once, Dr Chary and Ricchay perked up from their sluggish state.

'Come on… Step on your feet… Get going into the woods,' yelled Kaban while pointing his braceband at Dr Chary and Ricchay. A few minutes after waking up, Ricchay found himself sneezing without a break as though his nostrils were clogged with dust. That was odd. Wasn't the mountain air supposed to be fresh?

'Pipe down,' ordered Kaban.

Ricchay gulped in fear. Shortly, his sneezing stopped. Still, he didn't feel normal. He could hear a ringing noise, even when there seemed to be no source of the sound anywhere around him. Wait, wasn't this what Dr Chary was talking about too? Although, the sound was faint, it was annoyingly painful. He was puzzled. Was Ruchira now trying to control his mind too?

'Ricchay... I am doing this because I don't want the werewolves to target Dr Chary and separate you from him,' said Ruchira faintly.

Again, Ricchay looked about him. Ruchira wasn't anywhere around but he could hear her loud and clear as though she were right next to him.

'Ruchira,' he said, only to realise the words he uttered could be heard by the werewolves. Would Ruchira be able to hear his thoughts, if she had indeed got inside his head with the Corestone?

'Why can't you stop using the Corestone?' he thought.

'I can't... I told you... I just need to use it or I go crazy,' said Ruchira.

'It's not helping any of us. Do you want Dr Chary...the Equal, to die because you can't stop using the Corestone?'

'He can't die... It's what the prophecy says,' reasoned Ruchira.

'Ruchira...please, I beg you. Don't do this... I don't want to die.'

Ruchira didn't respond.

As Ricchay stepped into a thicket, where Chandrika Chetak was standing, brandishing her braceband under a waxing, gibbous moon, trying to recall the day he had seen her first, a change came upon him. He could hear his heartbeat in his left ear. The sound frightened him somehow. Was he going crazy? Suddenly, his left ear began to feel very hot as if all the blood in his body was rushing there; pooling into a single vein. And now that very vein was growing bigger and bigger. Ricchay knew at one point it was going to burst open from the pressure. Much to his horror, he also realised he wasn't the only one aware of the sensation. Having worked for the Council, he knew a thing or two about the werewolves; especially their hypersensitive noses. He was right. For as soon as the distended vein ruptured, Kaban had transformed into a werewolf and pounced on Ricchay licking the fresh warm blood that had spurted out. The sight terrified Dr Chary so much so that he fainted.

'Draw back…draw back…I need him to be alive,' yelled Chandrika, but she knew Kaban was beyond comprehension now.

'*Sicatimanca*,' she chanted while pointing at the ground and then turned into a vicious, howling, four-legged beast herself and pushed Kaban away from Ricchay with her brute strength.

A body of mud arose from the ground like a giant snake and coiled around Kaban, squeezing the life out of him.

'Ah…sometimes I need to release all that pent-up rage too. It's so hard to control it when you are a werewolf,' thought Chandrika as she changed back to her human self and glared at Kaban's corpse.

'How…did you evade the…Council?' asked Ricchay while bearing the throbbing pain in his head and ears. He wanted to distract Chandrika and keep her from targeting Dr Chary. He didn't have to try too hard for his sneezing fit returned soon and held Chandrika's attention.

'What's that? Oh! I forgot all about you. You're the Udal who knocked me out the last time.'

Ricchay pointed his hand at the sky just as his nose cleared up. He wanted Chandrika to think that he had signalled the Council. He wanted the werewolf to be afraid. Just then, his eyes fell on his empty wrist and he realised he had thrown the braceband long ago outside the dhaba.

Chandrika Chetak now laughed derisively.

'Even if you did alert the Council I wouldn't be afraid. After all, it was the head of the Council who released me when I was caught the last time around. You know why... It's because he's a werewolf.'

'That's impossible.'

'Looks like you're not aware of the goings-on!' she taunted, before adding, 'Stop fighting for the Council. It is absolutely futile as is fighting for...'

'And why do you fight for the White Death when you know he doesn't exist, at least not in the way you'd want him to be; as the all-powerful, the eviscerator of Prana and the death-giver. For all that you know, he could be a priest worshipping the Creator, Sura himself. That's what happened to him after the Battle of Gawaan. The Creator suppressed the hate in him and made him forget who he was,' interrupted Ricchay.

He didn't want to hear what Chandrika had to say. She was trying to shake his belief in everything.

Listening to Ricchay's words gave Chandrika a delirious pleasure more than feeding on human flesh and blood ever could. Finally, she hadn't heard a paean of fanatical devotion or an alarm of overblown panic but a scathing lampoon of the White Death. The words were raw and sharp like a razor that slashed the aura about the monster and exposed a mouse. This Udal has sense and is worth talking to, Chandrika thought.

'You're absolutely right. The White Death doesn't exist. I should know it better. After all, I have spent the last 200 years of my life trying to find him. I thought he could just be a common man, possibly a self-destructive loony because self-destruction was what fascinated the White Death the most. So, I went about sharing visions of the past that I had gathered, with over millions of loonies, hoping one of them could be the White Death and the visions could help reawaken his memories,' she said.

Ricchay seemed puzzled by what he had heard. But he was glad he had managed to engage the werewolf in this conversation and stall any acts of aggression.

After a pause, Chandrika continued, 'But nothing happened. And I realised I had just squandered my time trying to find the White Death when I could become the White Death myself by gathering more memories of the past, learning all the powerful spells only the White Death knew. And that is what separates me from his purblind followers,' she finished triumphantly.

'Now what is your business here with this man, Dr Chary and the Corestone? What else do you know? We have wasted enough time on chatter haven't we?'

With that Chandrika Chetak put on her glasses. As she tapped them they began to glow. Ricchay was drawn to them at once.

'Oh... It's been such a rough day I am tired of fighting. So be easy and considerate,' said the werewolf.

A force penetrated Ricchay's mind.

'Show me what's inside your mind,' whispered Chandrika Chetak in Ricchay's ears. Her voice was now warm, sweet and so very familiar. Ricchay thought he was talking to his wife Kadambari. He missed her terribly. He felt so burdened with all his secrets that he wanted to share them all with her. Myriad memories flashed on Chandrika's glasses. The werewolf saw them one after the other—Kadambari whispering sweet nothings in Ricchay's ears; the birth of his daughter Ajari; Vahne and Ricchay playing and practising magic together; Ruchira, the Aravan, telling him about the prophecy of the White Death's Equal, explaining her belief that Dr Chary was indeed the one who could thwart the White Death, but only after he was made immortal like Death himself by absorbing Sura's Life Energy or Prana from the White Death's weapon of choice, the scythe which lay in the realm below the earth's crust; also how Ricchay had discovered that Ruchira was using the Corestone to control Dr Chary's mind to ensure that he came to her in the Vanhad Forest.

The memories were compelling, so very powerful. Chandrika had to have them all. So, she lifted up her hands ready to remove them permanently from Ricchay's mind. Just then, a sharp hissing was heard.

'*Sicatayit*,' Chandrika said instinctively. In an instant, a hard mud wall materialised in front of her. The icicle which had cut through the air with a hissing noise, and was aimed at her, was now stuck in the mud wall.

'Just when I was ready to call it a day!' she said.

From the corner of his eyes, Ricchay spotted his former best friend, Vahne Roy, behind him. His face was marked with contempt.

'What are you doing here? Don't you want to savour your freedom after being released by the Council?' he asked, while looking at Chandrika.

'Aha! It's you. Weren't you the one who blew the head of the Council's cover and revealed that he was a werewolf? Very well! Why did you do it? Because you care about the Udals? Because you care that if they're led by a debauched leader their lives would come to ruin. That humanity would suffer the same fate. Naah! It doesn't make a difference to you. I have heard of your ambition. All you care about is power, don't you? You always wanted to be the head. And now you have the chance. I feel that hunger too. But being the head cannot empower you. Let me help you. Come closer. You don't have to fight me to become powerful. Let me bite you. I promise you, nothing can ever be as empowering as the transformation into a werewolf. You'll forget about mortality and morality. Every crippling worry will be gone as you let out that inner beast within you and experience raw, berserk, unrestrained power.'

'Doesn't that berserk power make you mindless! Well, if it didn't, you'd be careful about covering up your trails, not setting a bus full of civilians to fire just a mile away from the Council's camps. Aren't you plain foolish?'

'Enough. I haven't had a fight in days. Maybe it's time for one. And maybe it's time for you to fathom the power of the werewolves.' Chandrika growled. She was loud and nasty. Now her body began to transform again—it grew bigger, claws emerged from her hands and feet and dug into the ground, dense hair sprouted from everywhere, a wide jaw full of serrated teeth came into vision. She had indeed let out her inner beast.

'*Himayudh*,' chanted Vahne. A volley of icicles with sharp needle-like tips shot from his hand.

'*Sicatayit*,' chanted Chandrika in defence. A mud wall emerged to protect her from the onslaught of the icicles, once again.

'*Himakheti*,' Vahne screamed. A menacing spear of blue ice aimed at Chandrika's head bolted out from his braceband. But it was of no use. The mud wall remained inviolable.

This doesn't look good. She's using mud as a shield. How can I attack her? Vahne thought.

Just then his eyes caught Ricchay and he realised he had forgotten about his friend altogether. Chandrika, now on all fours, charged at him, baring her serrated fangs ready to rip his flesh with them.

'Ricchay, I want you to leave now. My car is right outside on the main road. I have signalled the Council. The Udals should be here any minute now. Head back to the camps. I will meet you there,' Vahne yelled.

Ricchay was confused. He didn't know what to do. Should he stay? But how was he to help his friend from being gored to death by the raging werewolf? He turned to find Dr Chary, awake and equally stunned by what was going on.

Just then, Vahne brandished that shining weapon—the head of the Council's sceptre.

'*Parabti*,' he yelled, pointing the sceptre downward. The ground underneath Chandrika rumbled and opened up. There was a wide fissure now waiting to gobble her. But Chandrika wasn't taken by surprise for she had seen Vahne aiming his sceptre at the ground. She knew he was going to cast an earthquake spell. She vaulted over the fissure. It was an unbelievable feat. She had to cross about 10 metres in length! She was now up in the air. Her muscles ached acutely for she had strained them to perform the impossibly long jump. But she wasn't ready to give up. Now, in mid-air, she flung her clawed forearm to maul Vahne, to tear down the very skin from his flesh and let him feel the brute strength of a werewolf.

'Why would you cast such a weak spell with a mighty weapon as the sceptre? Now look who's foolish,' Chandrika said dryly, while still in mid-air.

There was a smile on Vahne's face. Chandrika was perplexed. Why was he so happy when he was just moments away from suffering the most painful death? Vahne was looking up. But why? A loud hissing noise echoed in her ears. It seemed to come from above. Finally, Chandrika realised what had happened.

The earthquake was just a distraction. It was to keep me from noticing the second spell that he cast simultaneously using his braceband. He had planned a vertical attack all along; an icicle to impale me. I shouldn't have given in to the feral desire to fight, Chandrika now told herself.

'*Sicatayit*,' she said with vain hope. She knew it was too late. She had already felt the needle tip of the icicle puncture her back and now her heart. Blood shot out as though from a leaking hose. Bathing in it, Vahne rejoiced his victory and looked at Chandrika's face that was contorted in pain and shock. His happiness however, was short-lived for he soon realised that Chandrika was going to collapse on him. But before he could move away, the werewolf fell with a thud, crushing him under her colossal mass.

Ricchay saw his best friend struggling to free himself. He wondered if he should help him. Just then he heard sirens in the distance. The Udals were heading towards the woods. He had to leave now. Get on with the mission before the Udals cornered him and Dr Chary, and became suspicious. Then, he pulled Dr Chary to his feet and headed out of the woods. Shortly, Vahne Roy's car sped away on the highway without Vahne Roy in it.

8

An Unfair End

'I made it,' screamed Ricchay joyfully from Vahne's car. He had spotted the Council's base camps; skirting an impenetrable wilderness to his left. It was the final checkpoint and Ricchay reached it just before midnight. The Vanhad Forest beyond it was—his final destination. He now folded the pocket road map he had been referring to all this while and kept it inside the dashboard. It belonged to Vahne. Without it he would have lost his way for sure. And without Vahne's car he would not have reached the base.

Vahne had helped him all his life, Ricchay reminded himself. Yet, Ricchay had repaid his kindness by watching him suffer like a passive bystander, even abandoned Vahne as though he was a stranger who meant nothing to him. Slowly, the guilt that he felt grew so strong that it knotted his stomach, wrung his heart and seemed to clutch his throat making it difficult for him to breathe. Tears of pain and sorrow poured from his eyes until he heard a voice.

'Vahne is alive...now don't waste time... Come to me soon with the Equal,' said a voice. Ruchira was talking to him again!

Ricchay was reassured. He wondered if Ruchira had used her power of mind control to get inside Vahne's head and find out if he was alive and breathing.

'Now close your eyes for a minute,' she said next.

Ricchay obeyed and found his calm. Then, he turned towards Dr Chary and said, 'Just remember your name is Mohan Kumar and you work for the Council in Darmas.'

'All right,' said Dr Chary. There was no need to argue. No need to question anything. He was ready to follow Ricchay; not solely because he was under Ruchira's control but because he had seen fantastical things—like magic, werewolves and vampires. He had come to believe that Dr Chandrika Chetak was no ordinary doctor and that she was indeed a werewolf. He was gradually finding it exciting to believe that he too was no ordinary man, but someone very powerful. *The Equal*, that's what Ricchay had called him. Finding the truth about himself had made him happy. The restlessness that he had suffered all his life somewhat abated.

'These are the things you'll need,' said Ricchay, before handing out an ID card and permit paper to the writer. He had forged these documents knowing fully well that he would have to furnish them at the checkpoint.

Dr Chary took what was given to him.

'Remember not to open your mouth unless you are spoken to. Just stay calm and quiet,' Ricchay instructed and Dr Chary nodded.

Ricchay stopped his car just before a barricade, being guarded by a Udal. The Udal looked imposing in his military garb; camouflage-printed fabric, iron-plated boots and a beret. Ricchay saluted him first, flashed his ID and gestured Dr Chary to do the same. The Udal asked him to park the car in the shed up ahead and the barricade was lifted. With the car parked, Ricchay and Dr Chary ambled towards a cluster of tents.

Udals were all around them wearing long, black turtleneck coats and trousers, boots and helmets and flashing their bracebands. Their outfits ensured they blended well with the darkness around. A few were stationed in wooden towers, monitoring the forest through their binoculars. Dr Chary and Ricchay were led into the largest tent, amongst those present, by a Udal with a yellow-dyed moustache.

The sprawling interior was lit dimly by monochrome bulbs and sectioned with glass dividers. In every section, there was a flurry of activities—Udals practising magic spells in glass chambers, debating over the situation on the battlefield and planning war strategies with maps and blackboards.

Ricchay knew he too had to be outfitted and prepped up before joining the fight. But wasn't it a big waste given the fact that he couldn't do magic? And wouldn't it delay the whole mission? He couldn't wait to hand over Dr Chary to Ruchira, get back home to Kadambari, just hug her tight and stay frozen in that moment. The moment would come. He had to believe in it. But the threat was real too. He had to accept it. Prepping up was necessary, for the forest was swarming with werewolves. Perhaps, he could find out ways to evade them, even without magic.

Ricchay was now whisked away to a smaller, adjoining tent where an old lady was sitting by a desk with her head sunk into heaps of files.

'Evening, Mayram,' greeted the man who had escorted Ricchay and Dr Chary, before patting the old lady.

Mayram looked up with a start, then gawked at those around her as though it was the first time she had had any human contact in the entire day. The man with the yellow moustache whispered in her ears. Ricchay assumed he was telling her why Dr Chary and he were here.

'Hello Udals. Won't you sit down? Where are you from?' she asked, while reading the time on the clock.

'Coch and Darmas,' Ricchay replied.

'Okay. Can I see your IDs and permits?'

'Certainly,' replied Ricchay as he handed her the requisites. Mayram scanned them before making notes. For minutes, there was silence. Dr Chary seemed nervous; chewing his fingernails, as Ricchay looked on.

'Should I get them outfitted?' asked the man with the yellow moustache.

'Yes, yes. Do that Niran. They're both officers.'

'All right, officers. Follow me.'

Niran led them into the armoury room adjoining the old lady's tent. The room was full of metal lockers in different colours. He opened one of these with a key from a bunch and handed the duo their uniforms.

Dr Chary fidgeted with the coat he had been given.

'Are your bracebands intact?' asked Niran.

'No. We need new ones,' replied Ricchay as he covered himself with the coat.

'Very well.' Niran opened another locker and gave them their bracebands. Ricchay slipped his hand into one. It fit him perfectly for he was a big man with a big wrist. But he was sure that Dr Chary's braceband would have to be tightened for he was very frail.

Just as he was about to help the writer, the old man, to his alarm, started screaming, 'Make it stop. Make it stop... Make the ringing stop.' Ricchay noticed that his ears were also bleeding.

'What's going on? What's that noise?' asked Niran, as he too heard the ringing sound echoing in the room along with Ricchay. Just then the red bulbs on the ceiling began to flash and sirens started blaring.

'The base has been breached. Repeat. The base has been breached,' alerted a speaker.

'Let's go freeze those hounds,' said Niran spiritedly before scurrying out of the room.

Everything happened in a flash. Ricchay heard a babble of magical chants, then explosions, screams and cries. He understood that the werewolves had attacked the Council's camps. Then balls of fire came flying into the room, like cannons. Ricchay dragged Dr Chary to the floor as the whole tent was set ablaze.

'Close your eyes. Be calm. Hold your breath...or the werewolves will notice you,' he advised Dr Chary.

A pack stormed into the room now. Ricchay broke out into a cold sweat. He ignored his own advice to Dr Chary earlier and breathed heavily. He wanted the werewolves to smell his fear as he knew that fear excited them. And Ricchay wanted to be the one to excite them, so that their attention was diverted from Dr Chary.

Dr Chary was the Equal. No harm was supposed to come to him. Ricchay knew he had to put up a fight against the werewolves. He couldn't cast magical spells but he could certainly use the braceband as a weapon, couldn't he? He could lacerate their bulbous eyes with the sharp edges of the Lumestone. Death was imminent for him, but he vowed that he would die only after handing over Dr Chary to Ruchira. That was his goal. With that resolve, he clenched his fists; ready to strike.

But a surprise awaited him as he looked up; he found himself staring at sturdy black boots with skulls painted on their soles. The skulls represented the White Death. And he remembered that these boots were worn only by the Udals as a sign of disrespect to the White Death (for it was to signify that the Udals could crush the White Death under their feet). Surely, the pack that had stormed into the room couldn't be their enemy.

The ringing echoed louder than before. Ricchay clapped his ears as did several members of the pack. How intolerable the sound was!

'Ricchay, we…have been…sent…to take Dr Chary…and you to…Ruchira as soon as possible… She's near the… the…Vanhad River. Follow…us,' said a voice in the same staccato tone Ricchay had heard earlier from Dr Chary.

Ricchay recognised the voice but could not remember the name of the man it belonged to. Ricchay recalled that he had worked with him for a while. But why was he here along with a pack of five other Udals? What was going on? Was Ruchira controlling the minds of these Udals too? But why? Was this Ruchira's grand plan to get him to the river unharmed? The ringing had stopped now.

'*Calamana ruh*,' screamed a voice from behind. It was the old woman, Mayram. A blue flame spouted and spread from her palm, ready to incinerate the Udals.

'*Vatahata*,' chanted Ricchay's ally. Winds that magically shot out from his hand pushed the fire towards Mayram. Now, she was on fire and hollering in pain. Ricchay's friend laughed with pleasure.

'Stay behind us, you two. We'll take you to the Vanhad River.'

Dr Chary and Ricchay nodded. They followed the Udals out of the armoury through a burning hole in the tent. Outside, there was more pandemonium with certain Udals burning down one tent after the other and killing their own brethren who were trying to stop them.

Doubtless, Ruchira had controlled their minds too, Ricchay told himself, because she was getting impatient and wanted Dr Chary to reach her as soon as possible. But what had she done? All this violence and bloodshed wasn't acceptable even if it was for the greater good of finding humanity's last hope—the White Death's Equal. Indeed, she had forgotten her morals; callously killed people as if their lives meant nothing and turned into a monster consumed by the power of the Corestone. He had to warn her to stop this madness.

The pandemonium had spread to the forest too. Udals and werewolves came out of their hiding; curious to know why a pall of smoke hung over the Council's base. Soon, they were engaged in violent duels against each other.

Moving within the forest was now a highly risky affair. Though the Udals leading Dr Chary and Ricchay kept their movement slow and furtive, it was impossible to avoid getting caught in the midst of sudden fights. The werewolves were scattered everywhere.

Only one Udal—from the pack of six—remained alive and Ricchay and Dr Chary were unharmed.

'Are you okay?' asked Ricchay as he found Dr Chary gasping for breath near a pond. He was an old man and surely the journey had exhausted him.

The trio had landed in the heart of the rainforest, with a canopy so thick that only tiny patches of the sky could be seen here and there. The moonlight that was seeping through the gaps between branches was very faint and grey.

'We should rest here,' said Ricchay discerning Dr Chary's plight.

'What…erm…no. We cannot,' said the Udal. The left side of his face had been bruised; it was purple and swollen. He didn't look a day older than 18 to Ricchay. He was a child and full of restless energy. The restlessness seemed familiar to Ricchay, after all he too had been a teenager once. But now that Ricchay was older, it was his duty to impart some wisdom.

'We can't risk moving now. There's hardly any light. We can't spot our enemy. Besides, your Lumestone's nearly run out of power,' warned Ricchay as he drank the refreshingly cold water from the pond.

The young Udal checked his braceband. Ricchay was right. The Lumestone glowed very faintly. It had been used too many times to deal with the obstacles along the way.

'No…no…absolutely not,' he, however, said in protest against Ricchay's idea. And added, 'Your Lumestone is still intact, Ricchay. I can use it.' Then, he concentrated on finding his bearings using a compass and map.

'We are just five kilometres away from the Vanhad River!' he exclaimed.

He was right. Ricchay could hear the gentle gurgling of the water. But five kilometres was still quite a distance. The night was full of peril. Anything could happen.

'It would be best to lie low now and resume the journey at dawn,' Ricchay advised.

'Absolutely not,' said the Udal, as he attempted to take off his boots for a while. He let out a low cry of pain and realised he had torn his calf muscle while staving off the werewolves. Carefully, he freed his red and swollen right leg from the boot. Maybe, a little rest can help me heal, he thought. And so he sat down; ready to rest and massage his aching leg.

The repose however didn't last very long. A loud, grating, ringing noise all of a sudden signalled the end of it. It made the trio cringe and bleed from their ears. Ricchay was shocked. Why was Ruchira using the Corestone now? Why was she so impatient? Her impatience was going to cost them their lives for the werewolves could hear the noise too. Now, their whereabouts was exposed.

Suddenly, the ringing stopped. A heavy, brooding silence descended on the trio. Had Ruchira realised her folly and put away the Corestone? But it was too late.

A werewolf sprang from the darkness with a menacing growl. His body was distended. He must have been about eight feet tall. His long tale swished about thumping the tree trunks. He walked towards the trio, kicking up mud on their faces.

The Udal panicked like a child; no longer able to keep up the façade of a confident adult.

'*Khepaniyapata*,' he chanted expecting a jet of ice blue water to shoot out of the lumestone, instead only tiny blue drops squeezed out weakly from its surface. Much to his horror, the Udal realised it was the last dying breath of the lumestone and that he had forgotten to exchange his braceband with Ricchay's.

The taupe-coloured werewolf shook with laughter with its tongue sticking out at the Udal. It was an ugly and derisive laugh. In the next instant, the werewolf's mood changed to maddening rage as it pounced upon the Udal, jumping repeatedly, pounding his body with its massive bulk.

Horrific screams rent the air before the Udal was completely squashed and his blood-soaked innards popped out of the sides of his body. The repugnant sight made Ricchay throw up into the pond. He had wanted to intervene, but he was too afraid of losing his life or Dr Chary's. All he did instead was beg Ruchira to control the creature and stop it from torturing the young boy. Ruchira never responded. But he wasn't sure if Ruchira had heard him for the ringing noise had stopped. Just then, another werewolf entered the scene. His lime green eyes were livid with rage.

'Tivra. Stop. Condrol yorzelf,' his voice quivered as did the rest of his grey body. He spoke in a different rustic dialect and bit into the hard bark of a tree and growled.

'Why? A warewolf iz meant to let out his rage not bite treez.' Now the taupe werewolf, Tivra, picked up a leg of the Udal that had got detached from the rest of his body, and added, 'A real warewolf likes to rip flesh and break bonez.' He demonstrated the same with the limb as more blood splattered all over his body and he seemed more menacing than before.

'How dare you talk back to me? If you continue to be inzolent, I will keel you. So hold the rage, focus and lizen to the ringin' noiz. Juz minites 'go, it waz echoin' and now iz gone. And I had asked you to frisk thiz Udal, not trampol him to death. Stop disobeyin' me,' warned the werewolf with the lime green eyes, after drawing closer to the werewolf called Tivra and flashing its fangs.

'Well Nanke, I zmashed thiz Udal but hav wee been able to recover Master's Coresdone? Did it pop out from 'nywhere? NO. I don' care 'bout your threats 'nymore, just like I didn' care 'bout the ringin' noiz. The Coresdone isn' here. We are wastin' our time heer jus becoz you inzizted that the Master's object was here in Vanhad. And now, you are tellin' me the object iz with this Udal. You know you are wrong, but you won' admit it. You know the vampyres are right, that the object is in Darmas, not Vanhad, but you won' admit it.'

The werewolf called Nanke, with the lime green eyes, flared up in fury even more than before.

'*Sicatimanca*,' chanted Nanke pointing his braceband at the ground first and then at Tivra. A body of mud, long and thick like a snake, shot out and attacked Tivra by winding around his body and crushing his vital organs. Tivra fell on the ground—a dead werewolf.

'*Pavakgol*,' chanted Nanke with wild mirth in his eyes as a blazing, crackling ball of fire flew out of his hand and burned the dead—Tivra and the Udal—into ashes. He did so because he didn't want them to rot and reek, something that werewolves could not bear. Now, Nanke turned his attention towards Ricchay and Dr Chary.

Ricchay gulped in fear, realising he was possibly seconds away from suffering the same fate. Just then, to his surprise, the ringing sound echoed in his ears. Nanke's ears too pricked up.

Ruchira…can you hear me, Ricchay thought.

'Yes…Ricchay,' replied Ruchira.

'Please make the werewolf go away.'

'I can't Ricchay. If I could, don't you think I would have done it earlier? Somehow I can't seem to control the minds of the werewolves. Now what you need to do is…' began Ruchira.

The ringing sound was now much louder than before. Ricchay felt a great pressure inside his head. He half expected his skull to crack open.

'Tell him you can show him where the Corestone is buried,' Ruchira instructed as Ricchay grabbed his head. Even though he was in excruciating pain, he felt compelled to repeat what Ruchira was asking him to say.

Nanke eyed him curiously. He drew closer and frisked Ricchay.

'You don' have Master's object. But how can I sdill hearz it?' asked Nanke, perplexed.

'It's nearby. If you take me to the river I can show you where I hid it.' Ricchay could feel his nose tingling, a sneeze rushing up through him, but he stopped it by pinching his nose. He didn't know how the werewolf would react to the smell, if there was any smell at all.

'Hold on. How can the noiz come from thiz human as well?'

Nanke walked up to Dr Chary now and checked him. Again, the Corestone was nowhere to be found.

'I can show you where it is buried. Take me to the caves behind us,' said the writer, confounding both Ricchay and the werewolf.

Ruchira, what are you doing? Why did you make Dr Chary contradict me? Ricchay thought to himself.

'You just wait and watch,' replied Ruchira.

For minutes, Nanke stood still, staring at Ricchay and Dr Chary. He was confused. Was the Corestone in the river or the caves? Who was right? He looked askance at both of them. And then, he suddenly seemed to be struck by an idea. 'The two of you confuz me. I don' know who is right, or who is wrong. But that's why I alzo believe you. I like confuzion. It is bad, an evil forz that troublez the mind. So thiz is my plan. I will go to the river first.

If I don' find the object, I will kill you. Then I will go to the caves,' said Nanke as he inched closer to Ricchay.

Ricchay jumped out of his skin in fright as the werewolf got on all fours and lifted Dr Chary and him and placed them on its back.

'Now, hold on to my earz. If you don', you will fall and die and I will eat you two... You follow?'

'Yes... Yes we do,' replied Ricchay meekly as he watched Nanke's conical ears growing longer, turning back and reaching out to Dr Chary and him.

'Off we go,' said Nanke as he bounded through the darkness in the forest.

The ride was terrifying; full of back-breaking jerks, stomach-squirming leaps into the air and heart-stopping near-collisions with the tree trunks or the ground. Both Dr Chary and Ricchay's ear-splitting screams rent the air as they hung on for dear life. With time, however, the writer was tired of being afraid, and slumped on the werewolf while still holding onto its ears, ready to face death if it came for him.

Ricchay couldn't find his calm even though his body had got used to the precarious motions. Something bothered him. His sneezing had got worse. It was beyond his control now along with bouts of coughing. Both his ears and his throat felt sore and burned. Then there was the werewolf's fur. It was thick and prickly and made him scratch himself without pause. Red rashes popped up here and there and soon swelled painfully to cherry-sized bumps. In fact, the bumps on his eyelids were so big that he could barely open his eyes. All the while, his vision turned hazy and his body heat shot up.

Ricchay was desperate for water. That's when he began to smell the wet earth, seaweeds and fish. Were they near the river? He could feel his heart racing now. He guessed it was because he was anxious for the mission to end quickly so that he could rush back home to Kadambari. That's all he ever wanted. Thinking of his wife made him break into tears. Again, his heart hammered wildly against his chest. Ricchay doubted if it was due to anxiety. Soon, the bumps hideously and painfully multiplied, such that his whole body was swollen and felt like it was on fire. Indeed, the symptoms were typical of an allergic reaction. Could it be that he was allergic to werewolf fur? Hadn't he been sneezing whenever he had come in contact with them; while confronting Chandrika and her minions, and the werewolves in the forest? But he had never had such an outbreak before. Perhaps, because he had never had such prolonged contact with a werewolf. Ricchay panicked; his breathing grew heavy and his chest felt tight as if it was being squeezed, his heart was slowing down. Had it skipped several beats? Was this the end? No, no... he couldn't die now. At least not this way!

Just as Ricchay was wondering whether his end was drawing near, they plunged into the river. Ricchay felt the icy water sting him and swallowed large gulps of it to put out the fire within his body and bring himself back to good health. Unfortunately, the water couldn't help him as he had hoped. He felt terribly weak all of a sudden.

'Now where iz the Master's object, Udal?' asked Nanke gruffly.

Ricchay no longer had the energy to hold onto the werewolf so he let go. A white light flashed as he fell into the water. It was blinding. Soon, a figure emerged from the water. Ricchay struggled to lift up his eyelids. He hoped the figure was Ruchira.

Agonising yowls could be heard now. Ricchay was sure they came from the werewolf after it had been bludgeoned by Ruchira's hammer. The water reeked of blood. The cries stopped. Had the werewolf died?

Ricchay's eyelids stuck together and he saw moments of his life flashing before him. Indeed he was a failure—he couldn't do magic to make his father proud, couldn't repay Vahne's kindness to him, couldn't be the most confident, cheerful husband his wife deserved to have.

Still, hadn't he done one thing right? He had kept his word—he had delivered the White Death's Equal to Ruchira. And now that the mission was over, it was time to go home and hug Kadambari. Imagining Kadambari in front of him, Ricchay opened up his arms to hug her. Suddenly, his heart stopped beating.

Part III

Ruchira

1

Poort's Plans

'Wake up...wake up,' cried Ruchira desperately. She emptied the entire content of a heart-shaped bottle into Ricchay's mouth. But Ricchay didn't wake up. His body was as cold and stiff as the bed he lay on.

'Poort, can you make me some more Samras?' she asked aloud while kneeling beside Ricchay's bed.

Standing behind her was a creature which nodded its head vigorously. It looked like a reptile; about two and a half feet tall, with scales and scutes on its light taupe-grey skin, slits for nostrils, fins for ears, gills on its neck, a tail full of spines and a snout. But it wasn't just its appearance; there were other things very peculiar about it. For instance, its hands were gloved. It was reading three books at the same time; two in each hand and the third propped against its right foot. As soon as Ruchira had spoken, it dropped the books and exclaimed, 'Poort didn't know that!' revealing fiery eyes and mossy, curved teeth.

It now busied itself with a series of activities—weighing what looked like herbs on scales, tossing out what was in excess, grinding them to a paste using a mortar and pestle. Near the grey monstrosity was a pot lit by a burner and a tiny shelf full of jars, bottles and vials. With its gloved hands it now picked a bottle from the shelf, in which a purple liquid floated, and emptied it into the pot. Next, the herbal paste that the creature had prepared earlier was dumped. The pot simmered and sizzled, and spewed black smoke. The air smelled of pepper now. Even a single whiff of it could instantly clear a blocked nose.

'Your Highness,' said the creature, then sneezed repeatedly, removed its gloves, and continued, 'such an endeavour is futile. Samras is a potion that can cure life-threatening illnesses and heal the deepest wounds. It is powerful indeed but it certainly cannot revive the dead.' The creature now dropped the ladle with which it had been stirring the concoction bubbling in the pot. It let out a deep sigh, the exasperation evident.

'He's not... No...don't say that word... We can save him. Poort, please, you have to save him,' begged Ruchira after a bout of sneezing.

'Poort will prepare the potion for the Queen as she depends on Poort. Still, Poort says Ricchay Gupta is dead. His body is in *rigor mortis*. If your Highness could just look at his hands; they're stiff. They can't be moved,' pointed the creature, while pinching his nostrils to keep from sneezing.

Poort was right. Ricchay's hands were outstretched, locked together; fist to fist. Ruchira had tried to release them several times before but failed. She decided to try once more, just to prove that Poort was wrong. She grasped Ricchay's arms and applied all her strength to pull them apart. However, a voice within, told her that perhaps Ricchay was dead and perhaps, what she was doing wasn't right. So, she let go abruptly.

'He's gone, isn't he? And his hands are like that… because he was trying to hug his wife Kadambari before… He loved her so much… I'd be disrespecting his sentiment if I disturbed his hands,' Ruchira rambled. Tears pooled in her eyes and she was soon shedding copious tears before getting up from Ricchay's side to walk towards Poort.

'He gave up his life to keep his promise to me…and I didn't help him…and he did so much for me… He died because of me. I know it… But I couldn't stop…I just couldn't. I should have given him Samras before he went out on the mission,' said Ruchira, her guilt making her cry and Poort's concoction causing her to sneeze uncontrollably.

Poort didn't want to be distracted and lose focus from preparing the potion. So he tried not to look at Ruchira and tried to ignore her cries by plugging his ears with his little fingers. Still, some of Ruchira's words reached Poort.

Poort said, 'It's true your Highness, Samras is a medicine that can save lives. But when it's consumed on land it becomes poisonous, for the White Energy is concentrated there as opposed to here, underwater, where the energy is diluted. Anyway, what happens on land is that the White Energy leeches onto Samras and turns it into something that can bring about the end of life. When Poort warned your Highness of this risk she decided not to give Ricchay any Samras. Perhaps now with Ricchay Gupta's death and all that's been going on, the Queen has forgotten about it,' said Poort in a nasal tone with his nostrils pinched together. He then dumped two other vials containing clear liquids, with pea-sized bubbles, into the pot. By that time, Ruchira had stopped crying and there was pin-drop silence. The spicy, piercing odour of the potion brewing in the pot had also toned down.

'Poort says it is ready. Samras is ready,' exclaimed Poort as he filled the viscous black potion he had prepared into another heart-shaped bottle.

Ruchira was still quiet. Her silence seemed to disturb Poort.

'Your Highness, Poort says he is sorry. He has been... coarse. As you're aware, Poort states the truth as it is. Often he may appear unsympathetic, rude and aloof—entrenched in his studies, foraging for ingredients and brewing potions. But he chooses to be that for he is a medic, for he can't give into emotions. If he did, he could lose his focus—use the right quantities of the wrong ingredients or the wrong quantities of the right ingredients for his potions and harm his patients. Oh no! There goes Poort ranting again. He is trying his best to change. Please bear with him. Ricchay Gupta has always been loyal, kind and devoted to the Queen. The Queen treated him as if he was her own flesh and blood. Poort should have known better. Such a good man should live a long life. Poort will try to revive him.' With that, Poort walked towards Ricchay. The heart-shaped bottle, in which he had filled the fresh potion, was in his hand.

Ruchira was still sitting on the floor, shocked by what she had heard. Poort had mentioned the White Energy. Forget the land, it was here in this very room they were in; of an abandoned submarine sunk in the sea, concentrated in the Corestone that she carried in a pouch dangling from her belt. Ricchay had given it to her many years ago to study it after finding it on an island. And now, hadn't Poort prepared the healing potion in its very presence?

'Did I poison Ricchay? Did I kill him? No, no. Ricchay was gone when I found him. I couldn't hear his heart beating. Still, what I gave him was definitely poison, not Samras,' mumbled Ruchira. She then unclenched her fist to reveal an empty heart-shaped bottle in which a few drops of the healing potion Samras still remained. She stuck her thumb inside, rubbed it against the potion. Minutes later, white spots appeared on the tip of her thumb.

Suddenly a blood-curdling scream was heard. Ruchira turned around.

'Ricchay Gupta is dead. But…the…White Energy is here,' Poort stuttered in fear. He was standing on top of the bed, looking over Ricchay's face that was marked with white patches.

'Poort dropped the Samras on Ricchay Gupta by mistake. But this is what happens when Samras touches the skin in the presence of the White Energy. It turns into white poison,' Poort added, while pointing at Ricchay's face.

'I have it with me…the Corestone,' admitted Ruchira and flashed a heavy, radiant, grey stone.

Poort cringed and fell back on the bed, next to Ricchay.

'Your Highness… It's the source of the White Death's power—a vessel of the White Energy. Poort has heard his ancestors speak of it, about how it was used to bring about the White Age of Ruin in which the face of earth was lacerated; continents torn apart from each other. Rains of fire and acid poured from the skies killing flora and fauna. Indeed, death was everywhere. The great seas of the world turned red soaking in the blood of millions and millions of innocent children of men, Aravans, dwarphants and every life form on earth slayed by the White Death. So was degradation. Sura's creations, fallen to evil, began to plunder and pillage the homes of their own families.'

Poort took a pause to recover from the deep sense of foreboding his narration evoked.

'The Queen must explain how she found the Corestone? Why...why keep such an evil object?' Poort demanded, after getting up from the bed and moving towards Ruchira.

'I didn't find it... It was Ricchay Gupta. He found it, during one of his adventures and gave it to me to help him decipher the strange inscriptions etched on it. I didn't know what it was when I first saw it, but I do admit I was drawn to the stone. It was shiny...magnificent...and when I laid my eyes on the inscriptions, I became obsessed with decoding them. Something told me the words were solely meant for me. So, I went about researching tomes of ancient books for years until I figured out the message. The message was an instruction of how I could use the stone to get inside someone's mind, make them do what I wanted them to do. It has this great power of mind control and I felt compelled to use it on Dr Chary because he was the Equal and I wanted him to come to me at any cost.'

'But...surely...your Highness knew the Corestone belonged to the White Death,' pointed out Poort with alarm in his voice.

'I did...of course I did...because once I started using it...such evil, abominable thoughts came to my mind. I was horrified...I couldn't sleep...I was weak and nauseous. Dr Chary went through the same thing for I could hear his thoughts too... We had both been driven to insanity because of the Corestone. And then, the werewolves came to the Vanhad River where I was waiting for Dr Chary. I found out that they were there because they were searching for their Master's possession—the Corestone—that produced a ringing noise when it was being used. I knew without a shadow of a doubt then that I had the source of the White Death's powers in my hands, because from the very moment I began to use it, I could hear the ringing in my own ears.'

'But Poort doesn't understand... If the Queen knew it belonged to the White Death, why didn't she stop using it?'

'I couldn't... It had this power over me... Perhaps, had you known, you could have taken it out of my hands, for I simply couldn't let go of it. Even now it is with me; I can't let it get out of my sight,' said Ruchira, as she clutched the stone tighter.

Poort scratched his head as if he was thinking too hard.

'Indeed Poort has heard it is hard to resist giving into the White Energy...but...but if the Queen was overpowered by it why didn't she use it to drive the werewolves away from the forest to make...things...easier for Ricchay?' asked Poort while swallowing the last few words of his question.

'Firstly, it took me a while to understand how to control the mind of more than one person. It was difficult, like juggling balls. But even when I had figured that out, I could not control the minds of the werewolves or make them listen to me. Maybe I missed out something in the runes...maybe you could have helped me.' After a pause, she added, 'But it's not about you. I can't blame you for it. It's my fault. There was no need to control Dr Chary. Ricchay would have brought him to me anyway. If it weren't for the Corestone, the werewolves wouldn't have been in the forest and Ricchay would still have been alive...I am...I am a murderer, aren't I?' The blood drained from her face.

'Not to mention the blood on my conscience! I have killed Ricchay Gupta...and many before him. The ones I thought were the Equal mentioned in the prophecy... and...my own...daughter,' she confessed.

Ruchira's breathing grew heavy, her lips quivered. She then pulled out her weapon that was strapped to her back; a hammer wrought of a black metal with a solid head tapering to claws on one end. She was ready to drive the claws into her neck, puncture it and bleed to death, just like the werewolf she had killed. It was one of the most painful ways to die and she deserved it, given the horrific sins she had committed, she told herself.

'No...no...your Highness,' begged Poort. He then tried to yank the hammer away from her but Ruchira was stronger than him. The menacingly sharp claws were just inches away from her neck now.

'The prophecy... The Queen swore to her mother... She would find the Equal, make him absorb the Creator's power,' Poort yelled.

The hammer fell from Ruchira's hands with a loud thud. It had made a dent on the titanium floor where it had landed. Ruchira hadn't killed herself... She couldn't because of Poort, because of what he had just reminded her about.

Now, she sat still and stared blankly; frozen in the moment by an old memory.

'Amba...don't leave me...why...do you have to go?' little Ruchira asked her mother, who she called Amba, with tears pouring down her cheeks.

At once, her mother stopped packing the satchel she needed for her long journey from the sea to the land and ran to her daughter.

'You're but a small child Ruchira, but you should know this. The humans; their lives are full of suffering. Thousands of them; even newborns endure the most agonising pain and die every day while we live in comfort and security and outlive them easily only because the White Energy is concentrated on land. They are our brethren. They are our blood. My heart aches when they suffer and struggle. I must help them…help them by finding the Equal…for the Equal will be their healer… He or she will ease their pain,' explained her mother as she kneeled to wipe away Ruchira's tears and hugged her tight.

'But if you go on land…the White Energy will get you too…no, you mustn't go Amba.'

'If I don't, I will die in misery knowing that I couldn't help them. No, my mind is made… But you must promise me that if I fail, you will find the Equal… you will help humanity.'

'I…I promise Amba, but don't go now.'

Her mother only kissed Ruchira and continued packing even as Ruchira pleaded. Then, she was gone. Sadly, that was the last time she had seen her mother alive. Her death had come at the hands of bloodthirsty vampires who she had fought while protecting a human family. It was Ricchay who had searched for her body, even when Ruchira's father and she herself weren't able to overcome their own fears of stepping on land because of the White Energy.

'I am a sinner…and I deserve to die… But now is not the time. I won't renege on my promise to Amba. The prophecy must be fulfilled,' said Ruchira, after snapping out of the memory.

'The Queen mustn't give in to…' began Poort.

Ruchira was irked.

'Why do you call me your Queen? I am an exile…a "wanted" murderer… Vile and condemned by all. My own family's baying for my blood. I committed a grave, unspeakable crime of killing my own daughter. I was on death row... Poort, why did you save me? Why did you help me? Why do you not loathe me for what I have done? I am a sinner... Call me that and not your Queen.'

'Poort is a Pale One. For centuries, his kind were tortured by the Aravans, treated as inferior beings; the untouchables—slaves made to work until they dropped dead out of exhaustion. Your Highness, however, opposed this cruelty by the Aravans. She gave the Pale Ones respect, called them by their names, was moved by their suffering, decided to end it, saved them, freed them, let them study, make potions. The Pale Ones are forever indebted to the Queen.' With a bow, Poort showed Ruchira his gratitude and respect.

Poort continued, 'The death of the Queen's daughter was the result of a horrific accident. And the Queen took the blame for it. As for Ricchay, didn't he give the Queen the Corestone himself? What happened with him was merely a consequence of his own action. If your Highness could only listen to Poort's counsel. It's best to ignore these emotions for we have a lot of work at hand.'

Ruchira swallowed her tears. The consequences were always disastrous if emotions got in the way. Ruchira knew that very well. It was time to focus on the mission.

'Poort, tell me what's next?'

'The Queen must already know the way the White Energy works. Its nature is to find a host. A host can either be an object or a person. Once the host is found, it begins to leech onto it. Even the pure and most divine life-giving elixir, Samras is vulnerable to its influence. Leeching works faster, when matter is directly in contact with it. Now that the Queen has used the Corestone repeatedly, it can be said definitively that the White Energy within the stone has leaked into her body, and is growing stronger.'

'Yes…I,' began Ruchira, remembering all the bad thoughts she had had; how anger, greed, and every ill emotion within her had risen.

'And that she's corrupted. That her ruin and eventual decay have been initiated already.'

Ruchira knew Poort stated the truth. But somehow, the way Poort said it—like it was an unalterable fact—stunned her.

Poort suddenly flashed a mirror to prove he was right. Ruchira gazed at her reflection. What had happened to her eyes? They were pale blue now; no longer the bright sapphire she knew them to be.

'Perhaps Poort startled the Queen. He apologises. But it is the truth and the Queen should know it.'

'So…so the White Energy has leeched onto me from the Corestone. This is the end then…I have given into the White Evil. I am doomed.'

'No, no my Queen. It is not all bleak. Poort remembers something else his ancestors had told him. Would the Queen like to hear it?'

'Yes, Poort tell me…anything…give me hope,' begged Ruchira, desperately.

'The only way the White Energy can be thwarted is if there is enough dark energy or goodness. And there is still goodness within the Queen because she feels love for her daughter, love for Ricchay and guilt for bringing harm to them. Because she feels love and respect for her mother and wants to honour her sacrifice by believing in what she believed in—finding the Equal, and fulfilling the prophecy, humanity can be saved.'

Ruchira's lips quivered.

'But if she continues to use the Corestone, the evil in it could consume her completely and make her forget the goodness she once had, the love she had for her daughter, for Ricchay, for her mother.'

Just then a series of images from the past began to build up, rising up like a wave, showing her all the horrific things she had been compelled to do with the Corestone. It had been tough to pull away from that monster wave of memories. But when she survived it, there was something even more frightening to deal with. Thoughts of fear dragged her inside like a sinkhole. Ruchira had sunk for several minutes. What if she wasn't the only host for the White Energy? What if her actions had alerted the White Energy of Dr Chary's presence? What if the White Energy had leaked out and probed him too even though he hadn't touched it directly yet? Surely, that had happened, because she sensed the evil rising within him from the day she had used the Corestone. Hadn't he also been pushed to take his own life? Even if his eyes were dark, didn't he look a bit too pale as though he had absorbed the White Energy?

'Dr Chary could have…the Corestone,' she began, but the rest of the words died in her throat. Poort did not need Ruchira to tell it. By now, Poort's own powers of deduction had led him to consider the possibility. Poort wanted to explore it more, probe all the facts, to make sure there was logic. But after one look at Ruchira's trembling body, he realised that the ramifications of such a course would be devastating.

'He is an Aravan. He can stay underwater. He is the Equal. The Equal cannot absorb...He is the Equal. He is inviolable. Our saviour, Dr Chary,' remarked Ruchira, finding solace and strength by recalling the words of the prophecy. Poort wasn't convinced completely, but he knew better than to linger in doubt and suspicion at such a pivotal juncture.

'How do we stop this...my corruption?' She stressed on the "my," making it clear and final once again that she was the only victim.

'By destroying the Corestone.'

'And how do we do that?'

'The Queen's hammer.'

At once, Ruchira picked her weapon. But just as she placed the Corestone on the floor to strike it, she realised she couldn't let go of it. It was almost as if her fingers were glued to its surface.

Perceiving her hesitation, Poort reached for the Corestone.

When Poort first touched the relic he could feel his heart flutter, for, he could hear a mystical voice calling his name over and over again in a drawl as if to get attention. The voice was menacing at first, but as he kept hearing it, Poort felt entranced by it. Poort's eyelids drooped, and then the voice whispered, 'Power... Feel the White Energy... Seize the Corestone and crush the Aravan Ruchira. Rule Varmeer.'

Somehow, the message didn't tempt Poort; perhaps, because Poort never wanted to harm Ruchira nor did he ever want to rule over Varmeer, the sea kingdom where Poort and Ruchira grew up. It took an effort, but Poort was able to snap out of an induced stupor.

The stupor made Poort realise what Ruchira was going through as she grasped the Corestone, wrenched it away from his reach, and looked angrily at him.

An idea came to Poort's mind.

Poort removed from the shelf a vial with a dense oily concoction in which tiny purple flowers were immersed. Poort dipped his fingers into the vial, then jumped up to reach Ruchira and stuck his fingers close to her nostrils. Instantly, Ruchira felt drowsy and Poort took advantage by grabbing the Corestone—her weapon—away from her. Poort took Ruchira's hammer; it felt heavy and unfamiliar in his hands but he knew how the hammer had to be used. Poort drew it back and struck the Corestone with all his might. The force of Poort's effort was palpable through his deep grunts. A sound as loud as thunder was heard when the hammer and the Corestone collided. Poort was shaking. He stared at the Corestone in disbelief.

'Incredible! The Queen's hammer can make holes in mountains. There's not a scratch on the Corestone.'

Poort ruminated for minutes as he stowed the Corestone within a stiff fold of skin protruding from his stomach that closed up like a drawer. Then Poort woke up Ruchira by splashing water into her eyes. Ruchira felt lighter, peaceful now that the stone had been taken away from her. Poort narrated all that had happened when she was asleep.

'Why was my hammer not able to break it?' asked Ruchira with shock.

'This is no ordinary stone. It was forged by the White Death himself and imbued with his inconceivable powers. Still, Poort thinks there is something that can breach the adamantine surface of the stone—magma, hot, molten, sizzling magma. Its heat is known to melt the hardest of rocks,' Poort said. He could still hear the same whispers from the Corestone, but they no longer bothered him. Eventually, the whispers died as if the Corestone had sensed his disinterest.

'I hope you are right. We'll find an ocean of it in the Mantle. I am going there anyway for Dr Chary to become the White Death's Equal. I'll take the Corestone with me.'

Poort shook his head in disapproval.

'No, your Highness. You are too tempted by the Corestone and cannot possibly destroy it. Besides, do not forget you have already been corrupted. No, we cannot risk the Queen being completely ensnared by it or leave it here and let it fall into the wrong hands. And the Mantle is a long way off from here. We can't risk waiting that long.'

'You're right. It slipped out of my mind. What do you think we should do?'

'The Corestone should be destroyed in the pit that lies in Dehapat. It's along the way to Varmeer where the Queen and the Equal must go in order to reach the Mantle. But first, the Queen must come with Poort to Dehapat to destroy the stone. She has not swum in these waters for a very long time and Poort doubts how much of the route she remembers.'

Dehapat was an underwater crematory for the Pale Ones. There, the dead were disposed by dumping their bodies into a pit oozing with magma that spewed out of the earth's bowels.

'Yes, that sounds like a good idea, Poort.'

'The next thing we need to consider is of course dealing with Varmeer's guards along the way...at least a dozen of them. And well, the Queen is...' Poort cleared his throat and mumbled, 'an exile; a criminal in their eyes. Poort would like to warn the Queen that fighting the guards will draw attention. Poort has a plan of how the Queen can evade them without any risks.'

Ruchira felt slighted. First, because it brought back raw memories of the past that she had been trying hard to suppress, in order to carry out her mission. Secondly, Poort's tone was patronising.

'Aren't you a know-it-all? You must think I am stupid; ignorant of the danger that lies ahead of me. Ill-prepared, or even weak to face it. Let me tell you that I am not going to run away from the guards. I'll take them head on, crush their bodies to dust with this...' She wielded her hammer and continued, 'Evade the guards...ha! Why would I do that? Don't you dare talk to me like I am a coward! Cowardice is a trait of the Pale Ones. That is why they were so easily crushed by the Aravans and taken as slaves.'

Poort was quiet for minutes. He looked stunned and hurt. Such an outburst was unexpected. But then, after one hard look at Ruchira's pale eyes Poort broke his silence.

'Your Highness, beware! The White Energy is getting stronger within you, making you feel that you're superior and Poort is weak, creating this discord. That is the true purpose of this evil...evil device. Poort begs the Queen to think of good thoughts whenever a bad thought pops up so that the White Energy within her diminishes.'

Ruchira realised the grave implication of Poort's words and warning and asked for forgiveness. After a long pause, she asked, 'How should I handle the guards, Poort?'

'With this,' said Poort, and presented Ruchira with a vial. It was tinier than Poort's thumb and contained a viscous potion with a rich, golden gleam like honey and swirls of vapours rising from it that fogged up the walls.

'What is it?'

'The Living Corpse potion. It's the most powerful sleeping potion. It can knock out the guards within seconds. Make them have the most inert and soundless sleep for days, as if they were dead.'

'All right. Fighting them will draw attention. The sleeping potion could be helpful.'

'Indeed your Highness.'

'How do I use it?' asked Ruchira while poking the vial's cork.

'All the Queen has to do is uncork the vial when the guards are near. The vapours rising out of it will ensure they turn into inert corpses for at least two weeks.'

'That's a good plan. But what about Dr Chary and me? Surely the potion will knock us out too.'

'Your Highness, that's why Poort has the Isayu leaves with him. Here, take them. Just remember to rub them on your eyelids, so your eyes don't close and you don't fall asleep because of the potion.'

With the potion and a clump of the Isayu leaves stuffed in her pouch, Ruchira thought she was ready for the mission. Well, almost ready! She had to now wake up Dr Chary. Give him something to eat before the journey began. It was going to be a long one after all. She also had to tell him about the prophecy, what was going to happen next. But what about what had already happened? Ruchira's eyes then caught sight of Ricchay. His body lay there in a corner of the room; cold and neglected. That's what happened to the dead. They were so quickly forgotten. Life always moved on. It had moved on for her, after her daughter's death. How long had Ruchira remembered her daughter after her death and even grieved her absence? Precisely two months, not a day more, for after that she had come in possession of the Corestone. And the minute it was in her hand, she had become absolutely restless to uncover the power it held. The tragedy that had befallen her had been quickly forgotten. And now, just as her daughter, Ricchay was going to be forgotten too.

'We can't just leave Ricchay here. What about his sacrifice, his family? We can't forget all of that just because we have to carry on with the mission. His family needs to know what happened.'

Poort walked towards the quaint bed where Ricchay lay and covered his body with a blanket. Then Poort said, 'Your Highness, Poort hasn't forgotten him. Ricchay Gupta was an honourable man who kept his word. Although Poort fears the White Energy on land, he promises the Queen that he will find a way to deliver Ricchay's body to his family just after he returns from Dehapat and the Queen leaves for the Mantle with the Equal.'

'I believe you will keep your word just as Ricchay did,' said Ruchira. With that, she walked towards the other end of the room to wake up Dr Chary.

2

The Exiled Queen

There was no need to wake up Dr Chary. He was lying on the couch where Ruchira had left him but his eyes were wide open now taking in every inch of the strange environment he was in—walls made of metal plates bolted together, a yellowing world map as large as a blackboard with its frayed edges dangling from the wall, carpets depicting scenes of a bygone era spread on the floor, books and curios spilling out of shelves, portraits of the Russian Emperor, Peter the Great (he had seen one at the Chenpalle Museum), displayed on the walls, and an oval metal door that looked solid and heavy with bolts and a handle that seemed air-locked.

Just then a woman, wearing a grey scaly bodysuit made of animal skin, came strutting into his view.

'Dr Chary,' said Ruchira with surprise. She had expected him to be asleep. After all, she had given him a pint of the oily, sleeping potion with purple flowers in it, so he could get enough rest and get back his vigour.

'How do you feel?' she asked.

Before Dr Chary could answer, his stomach growled noisily and Ruchira realised how hungry the old man truly was.

'Let me bring you some food,' she said and left the room in a hurry. Dr Chary was highly puzzled, even disoriented. Where was he? Where was his family—Akshay, Meera, his grandson, Naveen? Everything was so unfamiliar, except the portrait of Peter the Great and the deep and raspy voice of the woman; he had definitely heard it before.

'Akshay,' he called repeatedly. No one responded. Was he dreaming?

Just then a creature resembling a reptile, with scales all over its body, came galloping towards him—its tail swished about. It bowed, with its head touching the ground.

Dr Chary jumped out of the couch in fear.

'It's an honour to make your acquaintance. The creature standing before you is named Poort and the Arabian Sea is his home.'

Dr Chary looked at what the creature was pointing at. To the creature's left, across the room, were silk curtains. But that wasn't what the creature was pointing at. Beyond the curtains was a glass window, wide and circular. On the other side of this glass window was a blue, smooth, undulating mass in which a shoal of eagle rays—with their mottled hides, pointed tails and wings—floated about. Was he indeed gazing at the sea just as the creature had said?

His eyes once again scanned the room he was in. He had but seen only one half of the room earlier. The other half showcased a bed, a tiny shelf full of glassware, cooking apparatus, and curious scientific instruments; vintage dials with numbers, directions and pointers hanging from the walls. He put two and two together to conclude that he was inside a submarine.

'Poort is sorry. He didn't mean to frighten you. How remiss of Poort,' said the creature, scratching its head, and continued, 'Indeed, you carry the blood of an Aravan. You're the White Death's Equal. Did you know you survived the entire journey from the Vanhad River to get here? That's nearly 12 and a half hours of being submerged in the water and bearing bone-crushing pressure to get here—15,000 feet below the sea. You know how you did it? It's because you are an Aravan and your body can adapt to any environment it's been thrust into. But you are not just any Aravan—you're the one destined for greatness, the one to save humanity and stop the White Death in his trail of destruction.'

What the hideous creature said, sounded familiar to Dr Chary and triggered flashes of the past—the ringing noise, the book-reading event, being abducted by Ricchay, running away from the werewolves and vampires. No, this wasn't a dream. It was all real. He had been a part of this mad world ever since he had first heard the ringing noise and the voice of the woman. His eyes now searched the room for Ricchay. Being around him was certainly better than facing this monster.

Just then Ruchira came into the room with her head bent towards a tray of food that she was holding. She placed the tray on an ornate table, lit by a lamp, positioned in the middle of the room.

'Dr Chary,' she said and looked up to find the writer with his back to the wall, scratching it with his nails and breathing fast. He was obviously afraid of Poort.

The fear in Dr Chary's eyes reminded Ruchira of her husband Nitrich who she hadn't seen in 10 years. But wasn't a fearful Nitrich more amusing to watch than Dr Chary?

An Aravan over seven feet tall and bearing 150 kilos of flesh, Nitrich would tremble all over, break into tears, climb up to the top of his high wardrobe and refuse to come down if a Pale One was anywhere near him.

'Oh Poort... Why must you always make a fool of yourself?' asked Ruchira jokingly.

There was a flicker in Dr Chary's eyes. He recognised the raspy voice. It was the same one that had commanded him to leave Darmas and go to the Vanhad Forest. He had undertaken that journey but he hadn't been alone. Where was Ricchay Gupta?

Just then another loud, rumbling growl echoed from the pit of Dr Chary's empty stomach.

'It would do us all good if we ate,' suggested Ruchira. She felt weak and dizzy herself because she hadn't had any food in a while.

'Dr Chary, please come and join us,' said Ruchira, as Poort and she sat on chairs beside the table. Although Dr Chary was terribly hungry, he was afraid to dine with the strangers in the room. He stood where he was, cowering close to the walls. But his manner changed when Ruchira removed the lids from the hot pots of food. At once, he darted to the table. The old man was so famished that he literally dove into a large pot of fried rice with peas, carrots and onions and did not bother with forks, spoons or even using his hands. He was soon chewing away. Next, he stuffed himself with what seemed, tasted and smelled like meat, floating in spicy blood-red gravy, even though he was a vegetarian.

Ruchira looked at Dr Chary gorging on the food. She was ravenous too. But she couldn't bring herself to eat. Every time she looked at the food, she wondered what

Ricchay had eaten last, even what her own daughter had had, and if they knew it was going to be their last meal.

Poort hadn't touched the food too. He was anxious about the mission; mulling over the past, present and future.

'Do you think Aravans could be around, your Highness? Do you think the smells from all this potion-making could have gone out and made them suspicious?' asked Poort. There was no response.

Poort repeated louder than before, finally shaking Ruchira out of her reverie. She now took notice of Poort who again posed the question to her.

'Well, they'd be too scared to come anywhere near even if they're suspicious. This is a man-made contraption. Aravans generally tend to avoid humans because they fear them, because humans come from lands where the White Energy is dense. That's why we chose this machine to be our hideout, remember?'

'That's true,' said Poort as he looked at Ruchira closely. She looked sad, faint and her eyes were brimming with tears.

'Poort knows the Queen is grieving Ricchay Gupta's death. But not eating doesn't do anyone any good. It augments the White Energy; makes you have ill and negative thoughts. You must eat,' advised Poort.

'If only all of us could snap out of our emotions as easily as you, Poort,' said Ruchira.

'Well you can, your Highness,' said the creature and handed her a baguette from the tray. It was cold and hard. They now held the opposite ends of it. A moment of silence followed after which Ruchira began, 'You brought the White Death's Equal to us. And for that you gave up your life. Your sacrifice won't ever be forgotten, Ricchay Gupta.

We will overcome our grief and be as tough and tenacious as this food we hold.'

They kissed the bread, said aloud in unison, 'Life goes on,' and then broke the bread.

Dr Chary was stunned. He dropped the bowl of porridge that he had been gulping down.

Ricchay Gupta dead!

'Dr Chary, I am Ruchira. Ricchay brought you to me because you're the...well. His death was sudden and shocking, caused by werewolf allergy. I am not sure what werewolf allergy means to you, what any of this strange world means to you. But you know Ricchay, you both talked and now he's...gone. There was only one thing he believed in. One cause he gave up his life for. That's you. But I want you to believe it. Believe that you're the White Death's Equal, that you'll save us from the White Death when he rises again and the White Energy that ensnares us all. Well Dr Chary, do you...do you believe it?' asked Ruchira.

Dr Chary clapped his ears, expecting to hear the strident, ringing noise that came in tandem with the woman's raspy voice. He was expecting his head to throb with pain and his ears to bleed. But nothing happened.

'He can't believe it your Highness. Not yet. He is not aware of the White Energy, knows nothing about its evil, how it takes countless lives,' Poort pointed out.

'Oh! He knows all about it. How it snatched his wife away from him. He has suffered too. He saw her die right in front of him like I saw my daughter,' said Ruchira. The words that had been uttered disturbed both Dr Chary and her.

The writer got up from his chair, staggered backwards to the wall because images of his wife choking on her pills, struggling to breathe just before her death, flooded his mind.

An equally devastated Ruchira found herself sobbing beside Dr Chary whilst recalling memories of her daughter.

Her convulsive cries reminded Dr Chary of his wife Aarthi, of the day when the doctor told his wife and him with absolute certainty that she had only two more weeks to live. Aarthi had been terrified.

'I don't want to die…I don't want to die, Raman,' she had screamed through her cries.

Dr Chary had hugged her and said, 'There's nothing to be afraid of. It's going to be okay, Aarthi.'

And then, imagining Ruchira to be his wife Aarthi, he pulled her closer to him with his eyes closed.

Ruchira felt it, the force of his pull, the tightness of his embrace, the saltiness of his skin and a sense of warm comfort and security in Dr Chary's arms. Soon, the pain in her chest eased and her tears fell no more.

She felt the writer rubbing his face against the curls of her long, auburn hair, his fingers stroking her cheeks and his warm lips pressing against her cold and clammy forehead.

'It's going to be okay, Aarthi,' said Dr Chary, and then opened his eyes and was shaken back to reality. The woman before him wasn't his wife Aarthi. She was the one whose voice had haunted him day in and day out and ordered him to obey her. Still, he could no longer be afraid of her, or push her away. After all, he hadn't ever seen a face more beautiful. It was so delicate, so dainty, like a doll brought to life. And the tears that sparkled in her blue eyes lent such a forlorn charm to her whole face that Dr Chary instantly felt an affinity towards Ruchira. He wanted to hold her tight, make her forget her sorrow.

Ruchira seemed to feel the same way too, for she said to him, 'I know what you're going through. You're not alone. You can talk to me. But I have something to tell you first. I tried to control your mind with an evil device—the Corestone—one made by the White Death himself, so that you could leave home and come here to me. It's the reason you heard the ringing noise. Every time I used the Corestone to draw your attention and make you obey my command, the ringing echoed in your ears. I know it caused you a lot of pain and I am so terribly sorry. I did it only because I knew you were special and I didn't want to lose you.'

For minutes they remained still with their eyes locked.

Meanwhile, Poort felt his cheeks burning hot and red, his hands curling into fists and his nails digging into his palms out of anger. After all that Ruchira had done for Poort, he thought she only cared about him and nobody else. But he was wrong. There was Ricchay of course. But that was different. Ruchira thought of Ricchay as her brother. Did Ruchira have a soft corner for Dr Chary? Couldn't she care for Poort the same way? Not out of pity that Poort was a Pale One and oppressed by society, but because she liked Poort as she liked Dr Chary. But how could Poort expect that? It was ridiculous!

'Your Highness! We shouldn't tarry any more. We should get on with the mission,' Poort said.

There was no response.

Dr Chary's eyes were now studying Ruchira's face as if it were a portrait, an artist's masterpiece.

Ruchira was well aware of the fact that the writer was enamoured by her. All her life she had been told that she was the most beautiful Aravan ever to be born! She believed it too and took pride in its knowledge. It was this pride that had caused the death of her daughter. The horrific memories came back again in waves and inundated Ruchira.

Ruchira saw her younger self in the dining hall of her grand underwater castle; simultaneously scrutinising the room and a checklist. Everything seemed to be there—tables, chairs, napkins, plates, cups, party caps, balloons, candles, confetti, candies, and a large birthday cake shaped like a turtle, a condensed milk fountain, clowns serving trays of food, a glass dance floor lit by chandeliers of phosphorescent seaweeds and gigantic towers of presents.

It was her older daughter Atali's 13th birthday and she checked everything to ensure that the arrangements were just perfect and grand. She looked at her watch. It was close to midnight—now was the time to call her family and surprise Atali, so she would remember this birthday forever. Ruchira was so feverishly excited that she scooted to her husband Nitrich's room. But as she climbed the last few steps leading to Nitrich's room, she heard loud wails.

The door was ajar. Ruchira was in two minds whether to go in or not for her younger daughter and her husband were talking. She decided to eavesdrop.

'There, there now…your Amba loves you,' consoled Nitrich. Amba was how children called their mothers in Varmeer.

'No, she…doesn't,' said Pamar, Ruchira's younger daughter while snivelling.

'Why would you say that?'

'Because I saw the dining hall. Amba is throwing Atali such a beautiful party. There's even a birthday cake that looks like a turtle. It's because Atali loves turtles. My birthdays are never so special.'

'That's because Atali is 13-years-old now. And in Varmeer, 13th birthdays are meant to be special. Believe me, when you turn 13, Amba will throw you the grandest party ever.'

'No she won't. Amba doesn't love me as much as she loves Atali. I am not pretty, that's why.'

Tears brimmed in Ruchira's eyes. She could neither accept nor deny what Pamar had said. Wasn't a mother supposed to love her children equally?

Another memory caught onto Ruchira's mind in a vice-like grip. She could feel her throat closing up.

Nitrich was frantically pacing around his brightly lit up room. He looked very worried; scratching his forehead, pulling his long black hair.

'What is it Nitrich?' Ruchira asked.

He turned around revealing his grim, grey eyes and a dog-eared page of a diary that he had been holding.

'Take a look at this,' he said.

Ruchira took the diary from him with a deep foreboding. She read aloud.

I hate school. I don't like to study for exams and be so nervous all the time. Still, I put myself through this torture for Amba. I want to be the best student in my class so Amba can be proud of me and like me more than Atali. Wonder why I bother? Everyone would still like Atali anyway. She's dumb—doesn't know what causes a high tide and low tide. And downright rude; she asked the janitor to clean her shoes for money. Still everyone's her fan...even Amba...I guess it's because she's so pretty.

Maybe that's all everyone cares about...Arnas proved me right yesterday. He's the cutest Aravan in my class. I really liked him, not because he's cute but just very funny, smart, kind and caring. I even thought he had a crush on me. Turns out that he showed me his good side because he wanted my help to score a date with...who else...but my pretty, blue-eyed, raven-haired sister, Atali.

I hate school. I don't have any friends. I am so lonely. Why won't Amba let me tell everyone that I am the daughter of the Queen of Varmeer? At least, then I could hope to make some friends. There are days when I feel people look right through me like I am invisible. Maybe that's what everyone wants...even Amba...maybe I should become invisible forever. That way no one has to look at my dark round eyes that have a bleak and cruel expression in them like that of a shark, my thick nose with its nostrils so far apart that half a finger could fit in the gap, and most of all my formless and ever expanding blubbery whale's body.

P.S. Guess where I read that description of me—Amba's diary.

Ruchira wadded up the page and asked her husband nervously, 'Where is Pamar?'

'Not in her room. Not anywhere in the castle. I have sent the guards to look for her.'

'I can't believe you're still here. Our daughter is missing, Nitrich.'

'Oh Ruchira! It's dark outside and you know how much I fear the darkness, how it fills me with dread and hopelessness,' said Nitrich. His eyes were wet with tears and his face was all scrunched up. He was just about to cry.

'But our daughter could be in danger. And all you're going to do about it is sit here and cry. I don't know why I ever married such a coward.'

Just then there came a rapping at the door, loud and urgent. Ruchira had an intuition that things were not okay.

'C...Come in,' she stammered.

A guard walked in with her head bowed down and announced, 'Your Highness, Princess Pamar has been admitted in the royal infirmary. She was found in the school's bathroom trying to cut herself. I regret to inform you that she has lost a lot of blood and hasn't woken up yet.'

Ruchira couldn't breathe. Her face turned blue.

Another memory assailed Ruchira's mind just as she was reeling under the impact of the second.

'Are you sure you only want me to do this, my Queen and not Poort?' asked Medav, a Pale One.

'Yes, Medav. Poort is incapable of it.'

'But the Queen is aware that Medav has been practising this skill only for a month. Won't she give this a second thought?'

'I have,' began Ruchira. She was however, a bit sceptical. Medav had already admitted he was a greenhorn. Not just that. She had just become acquainted with Medav and wasn't sure if she could trust the creature implicitly. But then when she thought of her daughter's suffering, she knew she didn't have a choice.

'Yes. She's tried to take her life twice and now she's starving herself to death...because...she thinks she's...ugly. I can't see her go through this pain any more. Do you promise me she'll look beautiful when this is over?'

'Princess Pamar will be the spitting image of you; your duplicate. For there isn't a face in all of the 10 sea kingdoms more beautiful than the Queen who stands before me. Medav promises the Queen, that no one will be able to tell her and her daughter apart.'

'You have my permission,' said Ruchira with a tacit acknowledgment of Medav's fine praise seen in a faint smile.

'All right, your Highness. Let Medav remind you that this process will take time and you'll have to bear with it. If there's any interference the consequences could be disastrous.'

Ruchira nodded with excitement. Life was going to change for Pamar. And it was all because of Alchemy. Alchemy was magic. It was the magic of bringing about change in matter. Put simply; changing the blind to the sighted, the ill to the healthy, stone to gold or the ugly to the beautiful. Its study and practice was forbidden in Varmeer by the Aravans because only the Pale Ones were capable of it and the Aravans didn't want them to be empowered. But that had changed when Ruchira freed the Pale Ones from slavery and issued a royal decree that encouraged the Pale Ones to become Alchemists and empower themselves.

Ruchira knew that Pamar was soon going to be the happiest Aravan for she would have a new face; not just any, but the most beautiful one in all of Varmeer. She would no longer compare herself to her sister, Atali for though the latter was pretty, she was no match to her mother's sublime beauty.

Medav shook an ornate vial. The fluid in it was a dazzling neon blue and full of sparkles. As he uncorked it, a sweet aroma arose. Pamar was asleep in her bed but when the smell spread through the room a smile came upon her face. Oh how serene she looks, thought Ruchira, confident that good things were going to come for Pamar.

Medav poured the fluid on Pamar's face. It spread at once, cool and smooth all over her—wrinkled forehead, her small eyes, bulbous nose, sunken cheeks, folded ears, thin, wan lips, pointed chin and the lines of her jaw.

Ruchira watched the process with bated breath. Nothing happened for some minutes. Then, her daughter's face disappeared behind what seemed like a blue mask that bore a likeliness to her own face.

'What's that?' asked Ruchira nervously.

'It's a process. Soon the princess's face will shape itself to the contours of the mask,' answered Medav.

A nightmare unfolded. Firstly, Ruchira heard a whimper. Her ears pricked up. Then she saw her daughter's fingers clawing the bed. She turned to Medav but he didn't seem to be disturbed. Soon, a muffled scream followed.

'What's happening?' yelled Ruchira.

'It's a process. You have to bear with it.'

Pamar's whole body convulsed violently now—her arms and legs thwacked the hard stone bed and bled.

'She's in pain,' Ruchira howled and ran to her daughter.

'Do something, Medav. Stop this.'

'You are not to stop the process in between. The consequences could be disastrous.'

'Can't you see, she's bleeding? You never told me this was going to be painful.'

She panicked. She tried to pry open the mask but she couldn't. There was only one thing that could help her now; the hammer. And it fell with a soft thud upon the blue mask. A thousand cracks appeared on its surface and the tiny fragments of the mask dropped on the bed. What Ruchira stared at now was a mess of blood—Pamar's skull had split open and her brain was spilling out of it, her eyes were black and bruised and the bones were poking out from her hollow cheeks. A deafening scream tore out of Ruchira. Pamar's body became still. Her suffering had ended.

Just then the door was thrust open. Nitrich walked in. He stared in horror at Ruchira and the blood-soaked hammer in her hands and said, 'What have you done?'

The memory disappeared and Ruchira dropped to her knees, her chest tightening up. She felt as though her heart was being squeezed out of her. The pain was agonising and was surely meant to kill her for the heinous crime she had committed—she had murdered her own daughter.

But the horror of the act hadn't taken her life. She was still alive; even 10 years after Pamar's death.

'Why, why, why?' Ruchira screamed. Just then her eyes fell on Dr Chary and she knew she was alive and breathing only because it was her duty to ensure Dr Chary became the White Death's Equal and saved the world from the Apocalypse.

'Is the Queen all right?' asked Poort.

She got up and nodded. It was time to let go of the past and stay in the present.

3

Dehapat

Ruchira took Dr Chary's hands in hers and squeezed them.

'Please have faith in me…I promise you, no harm will come to you, that you will return to your family soon… I know you have wanted to find out who you truly are. Hasn't this journey already given you the answer you have been seeking all your life? I know you'll save the world, bring an end to the White Death's scourge. I want you to do something for me. Just close your eyes for a moment and believe in it too that you are destined for greatness.'

Dr Chary was puzzled. He pinched himself and looked about frantically. He was still here in this bizarre world. Oh, how he longed to go back home, to be with his family and for this nightmare to end.

'Dr Chary, please do it. Just close your eyes and believe it; that you are destined for greatness,' urged Ruchira. There was conviction in her eyes, her voice. It compelled the old man to listen to her.

'I am destined for greatness,' Dr Chary said. At once, he felt a hot jolt. It was like he had been struck by lightning. He was excited. Now, he reflected on all that Ruchira and Ricchay had said to him. Suddenly, everything seemed to make sense to him. He had always been restless in the real world. Perhaps his place was here—in this fantastical, magical world. That could explain how he could stay underwater. And perhaps he was destined for greatness. Dr Chary smiled and squeezed Ruchira's hand in glee. Ruchira nearly let out a scream in pain. Ah! The force was just unexpected and belied Dr Chary's frail appearance. It made Ruchira's heart flutter.

'The Queen must hurry. Dehapat is only open for another hour,' warned Poort, while eyeing a vintage timepiece with Roman numerals hanging from the wall.

'Yes, let's leave,' said Ruchira.

'Here, you'll need to wear this,' said Ruchira as she handed Dr Chary a scaly bodysuit.

The new attire was highly uncomfortable—tight and thick enough to make Dr Chary break into a sweat. Also, it gave off a musky odour that repulsed him.

'This way please,' said Ruchira as she walked towards the glass window and stood there. Poort and Dr Chary joined her.

After tying her hair up into a tight bun, Ruchira dipped her finger into a vial containing a sticky bright green liquid and then pressed the glass window.

'*Animisa,*' she said. The liquid coursed through the surface of the pane that soon began to shake. Now, Ruchira poked it. Her finger passed through. Then she took a deep long breath and slowly pushed her head through the glass and into the water outside. Seconds later, when her whole body was outside, she gestured Dr Chary and Poort to follow her.

'Dr Chary, just pass through this nice and slow like Queen Ruchira did. Remember to get your finger out first, then your head and then the rest of your body. Don't hurry. Nice and slow!' advised Poort.

The writer nodded. He was no longer afraid of the strange creature for he was excited about what he would come across next in this strange, magical world. He prodded the pane that now had the consistency of jelly. Out went his finger through the jelly and into the water. Dr Chary looked bemused. Was this all magic?

'We are heading into the sea. So you'll need to fill up your lungs with oxygen. Breathe in all the air you can. Then, get your head out of the window and then the rest of yourself,' repeated Poort as he loaded his stomach pouch with vials containing colourful liquids and grabbed a torch.

The writer followed the creature's orders. Soon, he was in the cold water, enjoying the sensation of being wet and weightless, watching Poort roll out of the submarine—a cigar-shaped vessel that was longer than a hockey field.

Poort's torch lit up the dark surrounding they were in. Ruchira and Poort, now discussed the safest routes to take in order to avoid unnecessary confrontations with Aravan guards. As for Dr Chary, he was lost in his own thoughts. His eyes kept darting back and forth from the bottomless abyss where he floated all the way to the top through the staggering volume of water that separated them. He stared at the vastness of the undulating body for several minutes until, he suddenly thought it was staring back at him, perhaps in equal awe, at the vastness of his own potential. He wondered how he could survive breathless underwater, how the fate of humanity—the world—rested upon him as Ricchay, Ruchira and the creature had stated time and again. Indeed, there was something larger than life about him and if he wanted to discover it, this was the right place to be in.

With the thrill of discovery coursing through his body, the writer turned his attention to the other sights around him.

A carpet of sand, sea cucumbers and molluscs lay underneath him. Water was all around them, a gurgling, bubbling, infinite blue in which floated eagle rays, tortoise, fish and gigantic rocks that stood like pillars colonised by anemones, polyps and corals. At a distance were rays of the sun penetrating the very dense mass of water and silver fish dancing about them, trying to absorb their warmth.

'Let's go,' said Poort before leading the trio towards the rays.

Once they swam past the rock pillars and the rays, they found themselves staring at what seemed like a dense forest of coral reefs and an undergrowth of algae. Soon, they entered it. It was truly enchanting, bustling with colourful life like a kaleidoscope and bizarre animals that looked like feather dusters, plants with tentacles, roving eyeball-like pods and nets weaving out of them, sponges that resembled harps, eels as big as pythons, fish with fins, fins without fish whipping up the water into foam, ant-sized sea horses perfectly camouflaged with the corals, starfish with spines like cacti. Here, it was difficult to tell plants and animals apart, for everything around moved. Nothing was still, not even rocks; everything moved either to get food or get away from becoming food. There was chaos. And now the trio found themselves being dragged into this chaos; breaching endless shoals of fish, warding off predators scattered about and weaving through the coral labyrinth. At the end of the excursion, the trio was thoroughly exhausted. But there was no halt. Time was of the essence.

Poort studied the new territory they had waded into by rubbing his feet on the coarse soil, tasting the warm water and touching the plants that had sharp sword-like leaves growing out of the sea floor.

'We're in the right direction. Let's move,' Poort said and Ruchira and Dr Chary followed. Poort knew his way around, far better than Ruchira, because he was always travelling, foraging for ingredients for his potions.

The temperature of the water climbed steadily. It was a welcome change as the water had a therapeutic effect on the trio, lulling them into sleep.

'No...no... Your Highness! Keep pinching yourself. We can't afford to sleep now,' warned Poort as he noticed Dr Chary and Ruchira lagging behind.

'Yes of course, I forgot that. I haven't been around here in a while,' answered Ruchira before following Poort's instruction; waking herself up and then Dr Chary.

After a few miles, as the floor underneath began to slope downwards, the water began to boil and churn menacingly.

'Ah,' screamed Ruchira, as the scalding water singed her face and hands that were not covered by the bodysuit. Almost immediately, a change came upon her; a rocky layer, made of highly dense minerals, magically grew over her entire body to protect her from the heat. But around the head it turned into a thick, transparent shell so that Ruchira could see what was outside. She then stared at Poort, who seemed unaffected, for his scaly hide was tough enough to keep him safe. However, she noticed that Dr Chary's exposed skin was full of raw red marks, strands of his hair were burning, and his body too was writhing in pain.

'Isn't he an Aravan? Why isn't his body adapting to the heat?' asked Ruchira with alarm.

'Well...Poort is rather flummoxed. It is peculiar, but if Dr Chary wasn't an Aravan, how could he have stayed underwater for so long?'

The redness on Dr Chary's face and hands deepened; his skin was charring now, peeling away, to reveal his blood-soaked tissues and bones underneath.

'The Queen ought to use the spell now,' yelled Poort as he sprung towards Dr Chary, grabbed a burnt finger and stuck it into the bottle of the healing potion Samras. The writer fell back, passing out. His head and hands were burnt masses. Gradually, these parts were replaced by new ones. Ruchira shook her head in dismay.

'But Poort, he is an Aravan. His body should be able to adapt on its own without my help.'

'He's burning. Help him,' yelled Poort.

Ruchira then took notice of Dr Chary and the redness creeping up on his exposed skin once again because of the heat.

'*Agnilot*,' she chanted urgently and held the writer. The writer woke up by then to notice his body disappearing behind a shiny rocky bodysuit.

'Without Samras he could have been burnt completely,' said Poort with a sigh of relief.

Ruchira on the other hand didn't seem happy about Dr Chary's recovery.

'But why did his body not adapt? Why did I have to use the spell?'

After a long pause, Poort said, 'Poort doesn't have an answer to that.'

'No… I know what you're thinking. Don't say it. He is an Aravan; Haten's descendent. All this effort can't be for nothing. He is the Equal,' said Ruchira and shook her head vigorously.

'Your Highness, Poort never doubted that. Not even once. Perhaps, Dr Chary's body needs more time to learn how to adapt. After all, he's never been exposed to this environment before. Now, we must not halt our progress. We ought to keep moving ahead.'

'You are right, Poort. Those are wise words and we shall heed them,' Ruchira's voice was bold.

'Are you okay?' asked Ruchira turning her attention towards Dr Chary. The writer nodded his head. He felt quite all right; completely relaxed, breathing the pure, cool oxygen that floated within the suit. In fact, he had forgotten all about the ordeal. The suit that covered his body was quite fascinating. It made him feel light as a feather. Also, the specks of glitter on it shone with such brilliance that Dr Chary couldn't take his eyes off it.

'Let's go,' said Ruchira. The trio resumed the journey.

Soon, they came upon a cavern; a formidable one with double-headed tentacled creatures crawling about and a mouth so narrow that only one person could fit in at a time.

'P...Poort will go in first,' stammered Poort. Ruchira barely nodded. The sight of the tentacled creatures with eight pairs of gibbous, green eyes had made the trio squeamish.

They squeezed inside the cavern, one after the other. Poort went in first, Dr Chary next and finally Ruchira; all three were reluctant. The space within was equally formidable. Although the creatures with tentacles weren't around, just clambering through the narrow tunnel with its roof pressing upon them filled them with dread. What was worse...an eerie darkness descended upon them as Poort's torch died all of a sudden.

The darkness lasted only for two seconds before Poort's torch flickered back to life. But in that time, Dr Chary was consumed by an inexplicable fear—as though he had been sucked into a black hole; trapped in its inescapable darkness, dropping further and further into the void.

Once the light came back on, his trembling ceased and the trio resumed the journey. Moments later, they reached a dead end, or so it seemed, until Poort pressed his hand upon a circular wall and green sinuous lines spread over the surface.

'*Animisa*,' chanted Poort.

Now the wall began to wobble.

'Your Highness, please let Poort go in first. He just realised something. This isn't exactly a place visited by the Aravans and if the guards saw you they'd raise an alarm,' said Poort sagely.

'But why would the guards be here? In a place of grief and death.'

'Poort has heard that it is to keep a close eye on those who enter and leave Dehapat. To kill human intruders, anyone suspicious and send truant slaves, who try to end their lives here, back to their masters.'

'What slaves? I thought I freed the Pale Ones from bondage,' remarked Ruchira.

'Well, it all changed after Queen Atali gave up the throne and Tamasar was made King.'

'Who's that?' asked Ruchira with surprise.

'Your Highness's husband.'

'Who, Nitrich?'

'Yes, your Highness.'

'That's the most ridiculous thing I have heard. Why, Nitrich was so afraid to even step out of his room, how could he rule Varmeer? Why did he change his name?'

After a pause, Ruchira asked again, 'He hated seeing the Pale Ones anywhere near him. If he really was the

King, he would have got rid of them…killed them all, not enslaved them, right?'

'Your Highness, Poort doesn't know. He isn't aware of all the goings-on ever since he was exiled with the Queen.'

'And I have lost track of everything ever since I left you and was holed up in the Duram Mountains to carry out my research on the Corestone. Anyway, Poort, let's not waste any more time and get on with it.'

'Yes, certainly. But does the Queen know her way to Varmeer from here?'

'Yes, of course Poort. Getting to Dehapat was the problem. It's very straightforward from here on. No need to worry. Now let's get moving.'

Poort nodded now, poked his finger first through the wobbly, gelatinous wall, then his head and finally his body.

'The coast is clear, your Highness. Join me.' Poort's voice echoed after a couple of minutes.

Dr Chary and Ruchira soon found themselves on the other side of the gelatinous wall; in a chamber with a high vaulted ceiling, ornate pillars and panels of impressive sculptures embossed on the walls lit by phosphorescent seaweeds.

Poort appeared before them. His eyelids were green.

'You won't need the Isayu leaves. You're hermetically sealed in the suit, that's why you can't smell the Living Corpse potion that Poort mixed with the water. Everyone's been knocked out, the Pale Ones working here and the Aravan guards.'

'Wait a minute. How did you knock out the Aravan guards? They would have also been in their suits to protect them from the blistering heat here, right?' asked Ruchira.

She got her answer, in a minute, as she swam up ahead. The water had turned a turbid brown owing to the Living Corpse Potion and then she spotted two Pale Ones (with their eyes closed) sinking to the bottom and two Aravan guards (their bodysuits were marked by green lines) floating and bouncing off the walls and floor as if they were made of jelly. Clearly, Poort had used the *Animisa* spell on them just at the entrance to Dehapat. Ruchira was sure the Aravans had suffered. And somehow, their suffering reminded her of her daughter, Pamar. She looked at Poort—their punisher. Poort's eyes were full of eagerness.

'This way,' said Poort and led Dr Chary and Ruchira to the end of the chamber where two arched doorways stood on either side. The trio entered the one on the left only to be greeted by deafening bombardments and big menacing clouds of poisonous gases streaked with fire. The water here was bubbling and hissing violently. The sandy sea floor was rumbling and rolling like waves.

When the black poisonous clouds of gases lifted up to the ceiling, the trio witnessed a sight so spectacular that their skin prickled with goosebumps.

There was a depression on the sea floor a few metres away. Surrounding it were conical vents, not higher than a feet, from which an amalgam of liquid fire and rock flowed with violent hisses. The magma ooze drained into the depression or the pit, and it was there that the dead bodies of the Pale Ones were disposed of.

Dehapat was a violent place, like a war zone, and it destroyed anything that interfered with it. And that was precisely why Poort had come here with the Corestone.

Ruchira watched Poort swimming towards the pit with the Corestone. Was this the last time she would ever get to see the precious jewel? Yes, it seemed so, for Poort's intention was to destroy it by throwing it into the magma pit.

Poort's body trembled. It was terrifying getting closer to the pit, closer to the fire that could melt him if he wasn't careful. At the same time, another odd thought came to his mind. Hadn't a strange thing happened back in the sea when he treated Dr Chary's burnt hands and body with Samras? The writer had recovered well. No harm had come to him. Yet, when Poort had used it on Ricchay he had seen it turning into poison. Also, he wasn't really sure if he had seen gill slits on Dr Chary's hands. Didn't the gills grow once the body of an Aravan sensed it was in water? Shouldn't he point this out to Ruchira? Maybe later. After the mission was over. The thoughts distracted Poort and kept him from noticing a rock right in front, and within a fraction of a second, he banged into the rock and lost grip over the Corestone.

Ruchira bolted to check on Poort, but just as she neared Poort, the Corestone floated into her vision. She reached for it; her fingertips touching its surface and she felt a hot jolt running through her body. But before she could seize it, Poort had oriented himself and pulled the relic away from her.

Touching the Corestone had done something to Ruchira. Perhaps, it had once again sparked that yearning in her—for power, for control—and she knew that the Corestone could give her that. She felt so weak, so incomplete, so unlike herself without it. She had to have it. Something strange was happening; she could feel her eyes throbbing in their sockets.

Poort didn't notice the change within Ruchira for he focused on the task of destroying the Corestone. He was now almost near the edge of the pit.

Ruchira felt her anger, her fear, her greed—everything ill within her—rising up.

'The Corestone is evil. And Poort will destroy it,' said Poort resolutely, shaking away the nervousness that he felt.

'Enough...Draw back, you slave. How dare you decide what gets done; making the Aravan guards suffer while sparing your clan with the sleeping potion...and now destroying the Corestone.' Ruchira shrieked.

Poort turned around to notice luminous white spots popping up on Ruchira's irises.

'The White Energy is rising... My Queen, please, please think of good thoughts; think of your mother,' said Poort and muttered to himself, 'Poort shouldn't have brought the Queen here...It was a terrible mistake... Now it must be destroyed at once.' With those thoughts in mind, Poort ran to the pit.

'No,' cried Ruchira who reached where Poort had been, in a flash. But it was too late. Poort had already flung his arm. The Corestone had fallen to its doom. In less than a second, the magma liquefied the relic.

Wild with anger, Ruchira kicked Poort's head and then picked Poort up like a toy, putting his legs into the hot smoke rising from a vent before casting him aside.

Poort endured excruciating pain for his legs had been broiled. Even then, he tried to move towards Ruchira, screaming in agony and begging her to listen. But Ruchira paid no heed. All she cared about was the Corestone. Her eyes were now fixed on the remains of the relic; lustrous grey pools shining in the magma. She was ready to stick her hand into the magma, just to know if the remains held any power and didn't bother that doing so could melt her hand too. At that very moment, the grey pools in the magma amalgamated to magically reconstitute the Corestone again. After which the relic bounced off the pit and fell into Ruchira's hands. Doubtless, she was stunned not just by how the stone had salvaged itself but also by its very appearance. Its radiance seemed to have doubled and Ruchira was thoroughly enraptured. The jewel was hers and only hers. She would let no one take it away from her and despoil its beauty. She was its custodian and would guard it till her dying breath. And then, with a firm hold on the relic and the Equal, she swam out of Dehapat.

4

Into the Mantle

Dr Chary however couldn't forget Poort's horrific screams hours after the incident. They tore into his mind every now and then and made him dreadfully afraid of Ruchira. Wasn't she the one who had so gruesomely tortured the tiny, defenceless creature? What if she did that to him too? And what about Ricchay? How did he really die? She told him it was due to werewolf allergy. But should he believe her at all after seeing what she was capable of?

Ruchira moved unsteadily. The rocky-hide that had covered her in Dehapat had disappeared, now that the water was no longer hot. Her mind zoomed through the events at Dehapat. Horror and guilt exploded within Ruchira; paralysing her for several minutes and making her cry. They were tears of guilt, and as they fell, her eyes stopped throbbing, the white spots in the irises disappeared. When she recovered, she stared at the long chain of mountains right in front of her. She had to enter them for they would lead her to the Mantle.

'Dr Chary, let's go,' she said and turned around. But the writer wasn't there. Again, she panicked, until she caught sight of the old man drifting away towards a dark graveyard of wrecked ships and boats far in the distance.

'Dr Chary, come back here,' she yelled, but the old man moved further and further away from her. Ruchira chased him for some time and then stopped quite abruptly for she could hear whispers. She knew they echoed from the object she held.

'Power... Feel the White Power... Seize the Corestone. Control Dr Chary. Make him listen to you.'

'*Carnterti Cahler,*' she chanted, brandishing the lustrous relic and focusing her mind on Dr Chary and the task she wanted him to do.

Immediately, she felt a thrill run up through her legs.

The old nightmare returned for Dr Chary as he heard the ear-splitting ringing noise again. The voice of the woman followed. She ordered him to come back. Dr Chary turned around and swam towards Ruchira as he felt the blood leaking out of his ears.

With Dr Chary once again under her control, Ruchira resumed her journey towards the mountains.

Magic gave them access to the space within the hollowed out mountains. She then dropped to the floor and remained there fisting the sand and crying. This was the entrance to her homeland Varmeer and she hadn't been anywhere near it, for over a decade. She felt nostalgic. Everything excited her: the strong mineral odour of the water, the phosphorescent seaweed lanterns lighting up the whole space and the popping echoes of the water bubbles.

It was this nostalgia, this love for Varmeer that suppressed the White Energy within her and calmed her eyes that had begun throbbing again when she used the Corestone.

'Follow me,' said Ruchira when she realised she had to get on with the mission.

The writer kept up with her; swimming through long, winding passageways, never pausing to ask her where they were going, or even daring to tell her that he was tired. Clearly, it was because he was terrified of her.

The long journey made Ruchira think. Maybe the Corestone was evil. Maybe it made her hurt Poort. But it couldn't overwhelm her because there was still love and remorse within her. Wasn't that what Poort had said? If she had been overwhelmed then she would have killed Poort, but she didn't despite how angry she was with him. Maybe she could use the Corestone for good too. Transform Varmeer to Gawaan; the first land to be created by Sura, where people were never jealous of each other and lived in perfect harmony and peace. Hadn't that been her vision all along? Unfortunately, when she had explained it to her compatriots, some of them had objected strongly and skirmishes had broken out. But that situation could be avoided now because of the Corestone. They would now listen to her; realise she was right all along. And so, Ruchira was convinced there was no need to destroy the Corestone at all.

And then, Ruchira saw something that convinced her all the more that she needed the Corestone. At some distance up ahead, there were flagpoles displaying Varmeer's flags that had been shockingly changed to include Nitrich's face in the centre of a spoked wheel. Right below the flags were gruesome, dismembered, foul-smelling bodies of Aravans tied to the poles and hanging above the water.

These Aravans were criminals no doubt, for their crimes were etched on their chests. The blood around the letters had now dried. Some of these read: *Guilty of not bowing to the King's statue at the public square*; *Guilty of sneezing during the King's speech*; *Guilty of calling King Tamasar by his former name*, *Guilty of not keeping the house clean on the King's birthday*.

These were ridiculously petty crimes, Ruchira analysed. But the intent behind such harsh punishment was clear. Nitrich had realised that in order to gain the respect of his people, he would have to instil fear in their hearts and the only way to do that would be to become a tyrant and kill those who didn't obey him and his commands.

As Ruchira swam forward, towers came into view along with the royal army called the Guracs. They were dressed in menacing spiked bodysuits, berets and totting guns. Quickly, she rubbed the Isayu leaves on her eyelids and on Dr Chary's and turned her head down, so her face couldn't be noticed. Dr Chary too followed her instruction and pulled his gaze down.

A few minutes later, a green light flashed upon her from the towers and a voice echoed, 'Stay where you are. If you try to cause trouble you will be shot.'

Ruchira asked Dr Chary to stay still. The Gurac who had given the warning now swam towards them, heaping abuses on them through his megaphone, to show his authority.

As she stood there waiting for him, Ruchira was in two minds. Was she to use Poort's Living Corpse Potion or the Corestone to stop the approaching Gurac from interrogating her and Dr Chary? Of course, the potion had the power to knock out the entire army. But could the Corestone do that as well? The answer could help her determine if she could, if at all, control the minds of her fellow Aravans in Varmeer, in the future.

Now, instead of the potion, Ruchira had her hands upon the Corestone and chanted, '*Carnteti Cahler*.'

Instantly, a loud ringing noise was heard. And as it echoed, the Guracs fell unconscious, one after the other, and the water carried them away as though they were dead.

The coast was clear.

Ruchira placed the relic inside the pouch hanging from her belt. A smile played on her lips. Now, she knew she could go back home and transform it into Gawaan.

'Let's go,' she said to the writer quite cheerfully, before pulling him to her side.

The duo continued on their way; swimming past the floating bodies and the towers, and advancing towards a bifurcation in the passage. Although Ruchira was tempted to take the right turn, which would lead her to the heartland of Varmeer, she opted to go left because the mission was of paramount importance.

It was fairly straightforward from then on—no more obstacles, no more confusion. The duo seemed to be traversing a long straight passage. Although there weren't any phosphorescent seaweeds anywhere and the darkness was deep, Dr Chary wasn't seized with panic like before. For as soon as the darkness set in and the water began to heat up, Ruchira magically equipped him with a humongous pair of eyes that let him clearly see things around him.

The further they swam, the water turned more agitated—hissing, bubbling, churning, smoking and exploding. They came upon a depression on the floor. Just looking at it made Ruchira's stomach clench up in knots, for it reminded her of a death-defying stunt she was about to attempt—a 40-kilometre plummet from the depression, at breakneck speed, into the Mantle. But she had to do it; defy death for the sake of this mission. So, she repeatedly told herself that she could do this, closed her eyes and fell through the depression, hauling Dr Chary along into the very depths of the earth.

5

Fear is Power

While in mid-air, wings—large and wide—shot out from Ruchira's shoulder blades, and beat vigorously, slowing and steadying the breakneck descent. Even then, the experience was harrowing.

Ruchira could feel her blood, bile and her very intestine being pushed out of her body. And so, she clutched at her throat, as if to hold them all back in. Dr Chary was no different from Ruchira and looked down, with horrified eyes, at the abyss through which they were falling, and enduring the same horrific sensations like Ruchira.

Moments later, as the gap between her and the ground narrowed, and the speed of her drop also slowed down, Ruchira fixed her eyes on the point where she wanted to land and stretched out her wings and feet so that the landing would be smooth. But she hadn't flown in a while, so things didn't go as she had expected; and with a loud crashing thud she hit the ground.

The sudden jerk caused her to lose her grip over Dr Chary. The writer bounced off the ground, rolled down a slope to the very edge of a rock cliff where his movement finally stopped. Ruchira couldn't immediately go after him for her heels were stuck to the ground and she had to drag through for several minutes before she came to a complete halt.

Although Dr Chary had only minor bruises thanks to the bodysuit that had cushioned him from the fall, he was yet to recover from the trauma of the plummet.

Lying face down on the cliff, he looked down and saw something so magnificent that it made him forget about his nightmarish ordeals. A river was flowing beneath the cliff. But it was no ordinary river. From its glistening black viscous surface, liquid fire erupted with a loud hiss every now and then, rose gloriously above the cliff and collapsed into the river.

Suddenly, he felt an arm on his shoulder yanking him away from the site where there was a burst of fiery spray. He stared back at Ruchira in surprise. The sight before him was just staggering.

'This is the Mantle, Dr Chary, and what you are looking at is magma; liquid fire. This suit can withstand the searing temperatures here which could easily climb over 300°C but if it ever came in contact with the magma, it would light up like firework, and become liquefied in seconds.'

Dr Chary seemed astounded. He looked around, observing the mineral-encrusted colossal cave they were in, and the light show of the magma, and all the while feeling the mild tremors that shook the ground beneath every now and then. Was this really the Mantle?

'But it doesn't make sense. Even the pressure here is high enough to crush the hardest of rocks. How can I survive that?'

'It's because you're an Aravan and the magic that flows in your blood can help you adapt to any environment,' repeated Ruchira, then added, 'but beware the magma, Aravan bodies cannot survive in it.'

'Magic…it's fascinating!' said Dr Chary in awe as he witnessed another wave of fire soaring above him.

'It sure is… Now let us not waste any time. Let's get to the Temple of the Creator where we can find the scythe and fulfil the prophecy,' said Ruchira ecstatically.

'Let us not waste any time,' repeated Dr Chary.

For a moment Ruchira was puzzled about why Dr Chary seemed less terrified of her than before and more eager about the journey until she guessed he was under the influence of the Corestone and merely obeying her command.

'The Temple of the Creator… The prophecy… What are you talking about?' asked a voice.

Ruchira turned around to find an intruder at a distance harnessed in a sparkling armour made of diamonds.

The intruder caught Dr Chary's attention too. But unlike Ruchira who was rooted to one spot out of shock, Dr Chary found himself oddly moving towards the intruder. What had piqued his interest was an image carved on the intruder's helmet. Dr Chary had seen it several times before, in his nightmares, and seeing it had always made him break into a sweat and lose the rhythm in his breathing. The image was of a white-cloaked figure; the white phantom in a graveyard standing atop a pile of corpses brandishing a scythe.

'Dr Chary, come back,' screamed Ruchira.

'*Alorand,*' chanted the intruder and his arm stretched out of its socket and pummelled Dr Chary. It was a hard blow right to the head, knocking the old man unconscious almost immediately and throwing him off the edge of the cliff.

'*Vegadvij,*' cried Ruchira. In a flash, wings grew out of her body and flapped wildly. In the next instant, she had skimmed the distance that separated her from the old man, grabbed him and saved him from falling to certain death in the magma river.

'My, my, you risked your life to save his. He must be someone very special, more than our *own* daughter, Pamar,' remarked the intruder in his sardonic tone.

'Nitrich…is that you?' asked Ruchira as she stared, baffled, at the intruder.

'Not Nitrich… Arghhh…no…I have nothing to do with that name anymore! I am known as King Tamasar—the one who embraces his fears—and you will refer to me as King Tamasar from here on,' yelled the intruder.

Her husband seemed very hostile, very powerful. Was he here to avenge their daughter's death? But she was in no position to fight back, for her weapon was inside the rocky suit and she had to draw it out without Nitrich noticing. She decided to bide time till she could do that.

'But your voice sounds so different,' she remarked, remembering her husband's thin voice.

'Surprised to see me so confident and powerful? Well everything about me changed once I embraced my fears. Fear is power.' Now, Nitrich walked forward. Ruchira was clueless about how she could keep Nitrich from attacking her.

'Nitrich…Tamasar, I know I committed the most dreadful crime. I never meant to harm Pamar. I only wanted to help her…because she hated herself…hated her face so much so that she tried to take her own life. You know all about it. The Pale One, our servant Medav, promised me he could change Pamar's face to mine, so she would love herself. And then things went horribly wrong… Tamasar, there's not a day that I haven't repented my sin, thought of killing myself. But I figured that wouldn't be so punishing.

What I deserve is to be humiliated and tortured in front of the citizens of Varmeer and be known to posterity as the Queen who killed her own daughter. I am ready to turn myself in but pray, let me just finish one important task that could save humanity from the White Death's...' and then she stared at his helmet in shock. 'Why...you are a minion of Death himself.' She could now decipher the image on Nitrich's helmet.

'Yes, I am. So spare me this sentimental bosh about guilt and repentance. I was the one who killed Pamar. It was a ploy to oust you into exile and become the King. Power is all that matters. I learnt that from you. Now hand me my Master's Corestone... You wretched thief... I know you have it. I heard the ringing and you better tell me what you have been using it for. Why are you in the Mantle with this human?' he demanded while walking towards his former wife.

Ruchira was stunned by this sudden twist, still unable to believe Nitrich could be so monstrous. Nothing made sense, except Nitrich—or Tamasar as he now called himself—was drawing closer, ready to attack her and that she had to defend herself with her hammer and not the Corestone.

'*Animisa*,' whispered Ruchira, sliding her hand stealthily to her back, when her husband's attention shifted to Dr Chary, and touching it lightly with her fingers that were still stained with the alchemical green potion, because prolonged contact could turn her whole body into jelly and kill her. A second later, she knew she was lucky, for only a part of her back, that she touched, and not her whole body began to vibrate. But just as she was about to grab the hammer, Nitrich got a whiff of her intentions.

'*Alorand*,' he chanted. By the time his arm extended out to whack Ruchira, her weapon was in her hands and she struck vigorously. A painful howl was heard. Shockingly, Ruchira's powerful hammer hadn't been able to rend Nitrich's robust bodysuit. Still, the sheer impact had caused his knuckles to fracture. The howling continued for a while and disturbed Ruchira, as it reminded her of her daughter's agony on the day she died. She instinctively apologised for causing him pain.

'Shut up… You think you're the Almighty, and others around you are weak and vulnerable… Reminding me constantly of how strong you were and how weak I was, because of my fears, and how I could never be the King of Varmeer; pulling pranks to frighten me out of my wits so you could have a few laughs over my misery.'

'Nitrich… I was only trying to help. I thought if we made light of the situation you could see how silly and absurd your fears were and overcome them.'

'Well, you don't help anybody but yourself. You only want things to go your way. I am now here to ensure they don't. Want to know what power this so-called cowardly husband of yours has? It is "fear." And the one who made this caitiff, ridiculed by all, realise the power within him and achieve the unthinkable by becoming the King of Varmeer, was none other than the all-powerful, the eviscerator of life, the death-giver, the White Death…until death.'

He then pressed his neck as a customary sign of reverence to the White Death.

Slowly, the truth sunk in for Ruchira.

'I should have known when you feared the darkness, that evil was already there in your heart. So you colluded with Medav just to get back at me and prove that you could rule Varmeer? How could you kill your own daughter in cold blood and let me live with this agonising guilt? Is power all that matters to you?' asked Ruchira, unable to contain her howling cries, watching her husband pacing about casually.

'What makes you think you're good. Power is something that matters to you too. That's why you have the Corestone, don't you? To return to Varmeer, control the minds of all the citizens, make them live the way you have always wanted them to live and turn them into your puppets. Well, I won't let you have your way,' said Nitrich resolutely and added, 'The Corestone belongs to me. Through it, and the teachings of the White Death, I learnt how to create illusions for those around me using my nightmares. So, in case you didn't follow, let me make it clear to your dim-witted brain that there is no Medav. He was just an illusion. I was the one who killed Pamar. Now, that's not so tragic, is it, she wanted to die herself and I helped her. What is really tragic is that the Corestone was stolen from me years ago by someone who could see through my illusions. It wasn't you, for I caught a glimpse of that boy and he struck me with the most fatal lightning spell… how the stone came into your possession I do not know. And it is irrelevant.'

As he paused, Ruchira's pain, sadness and horror gave way to anger. And it was rising up with a hot fury like magma.

Nitrich cleared his throat and continued, 'What matters now is that you have something that doesn't belong to you and I need to take that away. But before I do that I want you to realise how powerful I truly am, having embraced the Light. And to prove that, I will make you suffer agonising pain, without even lifting a finger,' said Nitrich in a voice full of malice.

'No, you won't, you coward. This is for Pamar,' yelled Ruchira and bolted towards her husband with the hammer in her hand ready to unleash her rage.

Nitrich simply watched his wife charging at him. He wasn't disturbed. In fact, he didn't even duck when the hammer was inches away from his head. '*Mayabal*,' he merely chanted. Ruchira stopped, quite abruptly, on the balls of her feet, her weapon stuck in mid-air, staring into an eye that opened up on Nitrich's helmet just above his eyes. The third eye was entrancing; a pool of liquid gold swirling round and round, drawing her into a bottomless pit of yellow fire.

When the light disappeared, she found herself in her castle, peeking in through the door. Nitrich was right in front of her, in his royal robes, carrying their daughter Pamar, trudging along in his private chamber. The scene looked so familiar. Was this the night before Atali's birthday? But wasn't that many... A bawling cry interrupted her thoughts.

'No... She won't... Amba doesn't love me as much as she loves Atali... I am not pretty, that's why,' cried Pamar, repeating the words over and over again. Ruchira's heart broke listening to her sorrowful voice.

'No Amba loves you... Amba loves you,' cried Ruchira, running towards Pamar.

'She only loves Atali... I am not pretty, that's why...' said Pamar with resignation, clambered down from her father's chest and added, 'Goodbye Amba.'

> 'No, don't go... Pamar...stay with me... Give me a chance to show you how much I love you,' pleaded Ruchira with her hands around Pamar and wailed.

But Pamar and Nitrich mysteriously vanished from the scene. Still, Ruchira wasn't all alone. Nitrich's third eye was on the wall; waiting, watching, growing, inviting her into its yellow rapture.

After what seemed an eternity, Ruchira occupied another setting. Lying on a cold, hard bed of stone, Ruchira was once again, greeted by a familiar face, a familiar voice.

> 'All right, my Queen. Let Medav warn you that this process will take time and you'll have to bear with it. If there's any interference, the consequences could be disastrous.' It was her house-help Medav, standing beside the bed, looking upon her with faint amusement. But this time, it wasn't Pamar on the bed. Ruchira tried to get up but she couldn't. She felt so light-headed. Now the Pale One poured a neon blue, alchemical fluid over her face. It was so cool and smooth. A smile came upon her face. But it didn't last long for something thick and heavy seemed to cover her face leaving her in complete darkness. She could feel her own breath, hot and moist upon her face. Moments later, whatever covered her face lit up. She realised it was a mask. Suddenly, a knife materialised out of thin air, hovering in the gap between her face and the mask.

It seemed very irrational. Was she dreaming all of this? Ruchira thought. But that couldn't be because as the blade drew closer and nicked her face, she felt pain. Hot blood trickled down her cheeks, terrifying her. She screamed for help but her voice seemed to be stuck in her throat. Soon, the knife began to slash away maniacally, cutting through her skin, veins, and tissues, until the very bones underneath were exposed. Her skin now burned like it was on fire and her whole body writhed and throbbed in pain.

Her ordeal didn't end there! The knife soon split into two—the blade and the handle—and while the blade probed into her brain, cleaved it and scooped it out, the butt of the handle clobbered her until she stopped crying, her vision turned white and a deep exhaustion came over her. She was now too weak, too faint to feel pain, sadness or any kind of emotion. Soon, she couldn't feel her body too. Her thoughts were gone. Her consciousness was gone. Everything was gone. Only whiteness remained. This was nothingness. This was Death.

6

The Unfulfilled Prophecy

Nitrich watched his wife drop on the floor. She wasn't dead yet. But she could be if she continued to think that she was dead. It was all an illusion; the one he had yearned to trap his wife in for a very long time.

'*Animisa*,' he chanted and touched her body lightly. He didn't want to kill her with the spell. He wanted to amuse himself again by watching her suffer more. Maybe, he would wake her up to do that, but not now. The Corestone was what he desired the most.

Within minutes, he had found the relic and pulled it out. Holding it moved him to tears as though he had been reunited with a long lost companion.

'*Sucheti Ase*,' he chanted while pointing at the Corestone.

The relic now flashed countless visuals on its surface. They all seemed to be Ruchira's memories, right from her childhood to when Nitrich confronted her in the Mantle. But they played randomly, letting Nitrich learn about the prophecy; Dr Chary's role in saving the planet from its imminent doom at the hands of the White Death, and how Dr Chary could become the Equal by absorbing the power of immortality from the scythe.

'Oh, that's what you have been hiding all along from me, Ruchira! And no one in Varmeer knows. Wonder why? Now, I am enlightened. Knowledge too is power,' said Nitrich aloud.

Suddenly, a series of heavy thuds was heard. Nitrich turned around to find a rock spinning towards him. Before he could react the rock slammed into him with such force that he was thrown into the magma river along with the Corestone.

Nitrich's horrific shrieks rent the air.

The rock that had killed him stopped spinning and slowly transformed into a figure; it was none other than Poort, clothed in an olive green shimmering bodysuit. Now, the reptile hurtled towards Ruchira.

'Your Highness, wake up...wake up... Please tell Poort you can hear him,' yelled Poort into her ears before jostling her.

Ruchira lay in a comatose state until the whiteness disappeared from her vision. The nothingness was gone. Everything else returned—her thoughts, her feelings. She let out a squeal, feeling her body. She also felt a sting in her finger. She opened her eyes and saw the Mantle, Poort, and a long, glittering needle in his hands.

'Is the Queen... Are you all right?'

Ruchira got up with a start. Her face no longer burned. There wasn't any pain in her body except her finger right where the needle had poked her after managing to breach her rocky suit.

'Poort, you're alive?'

'Yes, your Highness. Fortunately, the *valkal* seaweeds in Dehapat are one of the main ingredients of Samras. It was because of their soothing powers that Poort was healed.'

'It was a heinous thing I did, Poort. I was livid, enraged. I couldn't hold my emotion in... Forgive me, Poort,' she said.

'It was because of the Corestone. The evil inside it urged the Queen to kill Poort and now it's gone.'

'How…where?'

Just then Poort explained to her all that had happened. When he finished, an extraordinary event occurred. An object spurted out from the magma river. It was a grey, radiant ball. The Corestone. For a second, shock paralysed Poort. The Corestone was intact, solid, unharmed by the magma. Was the evil inside truly inviolable? Then, a sudden fear impelled Poort to act. Ruchira's back was against the Corestone. She hadn't seen it yet, but she had heard the sound of it popping out of the magma river. She was turning around now out of curiosity. How could Poort stop her from noticing and using it once again? Just then, in a form of divine intervention to Poort's desperation for help, a super wave of magma erupted like a giant, swallowing the Corestone with its mouth of fire and crashed into the river. When Ruchira turned all that was visible to her was the agitated churning of magma along a particular edge of the river.

'But I don't understand. In Dehapat, the magma couldn't destroy the Corestone,' said Ruchira, her eyes searching the rest of the magma river, half-expecting the relic to pop out, bright and whole.

'Perhaps because the magma there was in contact with water and wasn't hot enough,' lied Poort at once. He couldn't see the Corestone anymore for the magma along the churning edges was far too bright and outshone the Corestone. Still, he could trace its outline, when it bubbled out every now and then and that was enough to instil a sense of foreboding.

'You're probably right,' remarked Ruchira, facing Poort once again. It was clear to Poort that Ruchira hadn't been able to perceive the Corestone at all because she wasn't attentive enough. That realisation gave Poort great relief; soothing his jangled nerves.

'But I thought I was dead. What happened here?' asked Ruchira, quickly changing the subject. She was disappointed that the relic was gone but she didn't want Poort to know it because it felt wrong.'

'Nitrich used a great magical power called *Mayabal* against you. He created illusions and made you believe they were real. He tried to…'

Ruchira interrupted him, 'But if it was all an illusion how did I feel pain?'

'That's how potent *Mayabal* is. It's evil magic. It plays with your mind, blurs the line between illusion and reality.'

'I thought I was dead… How did you save me?'

'With the needle… The only way you can snap out of the illusionary world is when something causes you physical pain in the real world.'

Recalling the illusionary world again, Ruchira realised the moments of pain and punishment weren't only hers… they were her daughter's too. Shock and sadness crushed her from within. But then, a thought came to her mind. Was it all an illusion or was it real? Had Pamar's death come because of Nitrich's magic…or her hammer? She chose to believe it was his magic, so that her guilt could diminish and she could find closure. She breathed. Drawing back to the present, she asked, 'Poort, how do you know so much about this evil magic?'

'Poort is a Pale One and your Highness knows very well that the Pale Ones once served the White Death. Poort has always been curious about his ancestors; their history and the powers they had. His great-great-great grandfather was believed to be an expert of *Mayabal*. It is evil, destructive White Magic.'

'But how did you know Nitrich was going to be here and try to harm me?'

'Because Poort was the one who told Nitrich where he could find the Queen.'

'I am not sure I follow you,'remarked Ruchira, stunned.

'When Poort got out of Dehapat to find the Queen, he was accosted by Nitrich. He told Poort he had heard the ringing sound and believed that Poort had the Corestone. Poort denied any knowledge of it. But the Queen's husband was still suspicious. So, he used *Mayabal* to torture Poort and find out that the relic was in fact with the Queen and that she had taken it to the Mantle. He immediately took off after the Queen. It took Poort a while to recover after which he came looking for the Queen and Dr Chary.'

'But I don't understand, how can you be here? Only the Aravans have the ability to survive in the Mantle.'

'The Pale Ones were once Aravans before they were corrupted by the White Energy and transformed into monstrosities by the White Death.'

'What? This makes absolutely no sense. How did…'

'It's a long story, your Highness. It can be discussed later. Right now, we must focus on the prophecy. Remember the time when it was written; when the only music was the sound of battle, when the only smile was on the face of the dead, the only goodness was knowing evil, and when the only creation was born from destruction. It was the great descent into the White Age, and it can happen again, when the White Death remembers his name and purpose and rises again. We must be prepared for the Awakening, by letting the Aravan challenger, the chosen one lead us.

But he can only lead, when he's made equal in power to the White Death. It is up to us to enable him by letting him absorb the power of immortality from the scythe that rests in the Temple of Sura. That is what the prophecy states and we must heed every word of it.'

Ruchira felt goosebumps prickle her skin, for what Poort said, stirred something deep within her. It was unlike Poort to quote such eloquent language, unlike Poort to say the words as if he felt them.

'Yes, we must do our part, Poort,' said Ruchira, with the force of conviction in her voice that she knew was expected after a rousing speech.

Dr Chary was sitting by the edge of the cliff; obviously astounded by all that he had seen since Nitrich's arrival to his dramatic fall into the magma.

'Dr Chary, it's time to go,' said Ruchira.

The writer nodded and got up. There was fear in him, but there was also curiosity. He wanted to hear more, see more.

'The path to the Temple is very precarious,' said Ruchira.

'Poort most certainly can fly,' said Poort, surprising Ruchira once again because flying was something only the Aravans knew.

'*Vegadvij*,' chanted Ruchira and Poort in unison. After being magically equipped with wings, they flew towards the other end of the cliff, with Ruchira holding on to Dr Chary with her arms.

The writer looked around him, observing the changes in the environment with great delight. For his flight was swift and smooth, unlike the last time. The magma river was no longer black now. Orange lines ran through it, dancing and shimmering around little pools of fire. The light from these shone in the cave and Dr Chary's eyes. Even the sight of the cliffs thrilled him as they were studded with rock-sized minerals such as olivines, garnets, zircons, topazes, rubies, even diamonds in their purest state and easily worth a fortune.

But soon, Dr Chary's wonder was replaced with pure horror for the environment changed into a hostile inferno. The river was completely orange now and more ebullient than ever before, hissing like a million serpents, the magma bubbling out so high every now and then that Ruchira had to carefully evade its waves to avoid being liquefied. Indeed, the magma river was ferocious. And its cruelty could be understood by looking at the cliff. The fire had consumed great big chunks of it and all that remained were a few boulders scattered here and there and a lone rock tower with a flattened top.

Shortly, much to Dr Chary's horror, Ruchira began descending upon this very tower that was surrounded by the high bubbling and hissing magma.

'We made it at last, Poort,' she said to the creature with tears spilling out of her eyes.

'Yes, your Highness. It is time.'

Ruchira and Poort bowed their heads in front of a curious statue that crowned the tower and stood far out towards the edge—a sinuous torso from which two pairs of hands stuck out. The ones in front were fastened around a black rock and the ones in the rear wielded a flute and a scythe with its blade pointing backwards.

After reaching the edge, Ruchira grabbed the scythe with its long, narrow, cylindrical handle wrought of a white metal and fixed to a curved blade.

Ruchira now turned around and walked towards the old man with the scythe.

A sudden chill grabbed Dr Chary's heart as he stared at the weapon's handle.

His hands and feet shook and dripped sweat. His bowels turned to water and his heart pounded louder and fiercer with every step that Ruchira took.

She chanted…

Hear one, hear all, of the heir of Haten, who'll save us all.

Pure of heart, strong of will, ignorant of magic, the heir would be still.

It is ignorance that'll be the heir's shield from the White Power, that the wicked wield.

The White Death and the heir will be two of a kind, made immortals by the power of the scythe.

Nonetheless, when the two duel; the one to triumph will be the heir—the White Death's Equal.

Just as Ruchira adjusted her grip on the weapon, she saw Dr Chary's body convulse.

'*Alopahar*,' a voice tore out from the pit of his stomach, but something stopped its rushed and restless ascent. A presence. A symphony; a piece of melody, then the image of his grandson lying in his cradle; his cradle rocking to the music, both elements bringing back the memory of the day Dr Chary had first seen his grandson, and calming his inner voice. In the end, what came out of his mouth was a whisper; barely audible, stripped of any emotion. He turned his head around to look for the source of music; although his instincts told him it was contained within him.

But there was also fear inside of him. Somewhere deep within. Moving. Slithering like snakes. Their lengthy bodies winding around each other, tighter, tighter…

Ruchira was drawing closer, turning the weapon around, to let the blade face the old man and stab him. The writer caught glimpses of the white fire that masked the surface of the blade, and the black ooze staining its tip. Unable to bear the fright anymore, Dr Chary squeezed his eyes shut. The snakes were going to bite into each other. Their knotted bodies were going to snap any second… Instead, the notes of the old familiar melody trickled into his ears again.

'*Alopahar*,' he cried in a heartbeat, before the rhythm could set, before he could see his grandson again.

A loud clang was heard as the scythe flew out of Ruchira's hand and fell on the floor. Dr Chary's hand that had extended unnaturally out of its joint had slapped it off. Even though he had struck first, it didn't seem like he had power or was in control. He was still shaking like a leaf. His reaction had been a nervous response as a rabid man who had just been offered a glass of water.

Now, with his eyes open, the writer pointed his hand at Ruchira. She looked at him in horror.

'*Ma…ri…ta Vi…ha…ra…ti.*' It was a slow, heavy voice bearing effort and struggle, pain and suffering; as if uttering every syllable was like injecting poison and venom into the artery.

Poort was stunned but he had seen and heard enough to know that the Queen was in danger.

'*Parnive*,' Poort chanted instinctively. At once he transformed into a boulder whirling on its own axis.

Before Dr Chary could react, Poort slammed hard into him and threw him off the tower. Poort looked on as Dr Chary disappeared into the seething, bubbling magma river crying out horrific screams.

'Poort, why did you kill him? He was the Equal…he was the Equal,' howled Ruchira, thrashing the floor with her fists and calling out Dr Chary's name hysterically.

'Your Highness… He was going to attack you, just as he attacked the scythe. Poort had to stop him. He's not the Equal… How can he be? You heard him. That was a magic spell spoken in the White Tongue. The tongue in which the magic of Destructika was written. The prophecy says the Equal is supposed to be ignorant of magic. How then did Dr Chary cast a magical spell to attack you?'

Ruchira was not listening to him for she was still reeling under the shock of what had happened; how her efforts in finding the Equal had been made futile because of Poort.

However, she tried to calm down to hear Poort muttering to himself.

'He isn't an Aravan… He isn't one.'

'What…do you mean?'

'While Poort was treating Dr Chary's horrific burns, he didn't find any gills on his hands.'

'What! That sounds ridiculous. How could he have survived underwater?'

'Well! Poort doesn't know… The Queen is right. Poort can't be too sure about the gills because he wasn't too attentive. But…but can the Queen tell Poort why Dr Chary's body couldn't adapt to the extreme heat on its own?'

'Because you said it yourself Poort, his body needs time to get used to the conditions here.'

'But isn't adaptation instinctive for the Aravans? They don't need to chant exclusive spells. When there's a threat, their bodies sense it and adapt accordingly. That is why we put so many humans to the underwater breathing test to find out who could, when pushed to their death, grow gills to breathe and survive; just like how it works for all the Aravans.'

'Well, it is, but there's no way Dr Chary could have survived this journey without being an Aravan.'

'The Queen could be right...but there is something else too. Poort is most certain of this fact. Samras is supposed to turn into poison in the presence of the Corestone. It happened in the submarine and both the Queen and Poort saw it. So how was it that Dr Chary remained unharmed when Poort treated him with the same Samras when his hands were burnt?'

The question was valid and Ruchira struggled for some time to come up with an answer.

'Maybe because you treated him in the water. And we both know how water dilutes the White Energy.'

'Well yes...brilliant. Logical... Why couldn't Poort think of that?' Poort looked relieved only until his eyes fell upon the weapon on the floor.

'But how did he do magic? That was a magic spell meant to attack the Queen... He isn't the Equal at all because he knows magic... But how...how did he do it?' Poort pointed aloud.

Ruchira's stomach squirmed uneasily. Poort had brought up something valid, but she didn't want to admit it. Indeed, what she heard was the white tongue. Hadn't she studied the ancient languge while deciphering the message marked on the Corestone?

'Well...Poort doesn't know how Dr Chary did it. But he certainly knows why he did it. Why would anyone have the urge to protect himself and fight? It is when they fear something. And Dr Chary feared the scythe because the Queen was going to stab him.'

Just then a loud hissing sound was heard followed by a series of crackles. Ruchira and Poort turned around to find a fiery mass shooting out of the magma river.

Ruchira shrieked in shock and a stupefied Poort looked on as a strange body hovered just above the tower; it was strange because it was alive and its heartbeat reverberated all around the Mantle. It was made entirely of fire and changed to a form in flesh within an instant.

And when that form came on before being claimed by the fire, Ruchira said, 'What... He's alive. Dr Chary is alive. The magma couldn't harm him because he is the Equal. He can't ever die; he is the immortal, he is our saviour and I found him.' Then, as tears pooled in her eyes, she called the writer. But he didn't respond. Desperate to get his attention and make him realise his purpose as the Equal, Ruchira flew up to Dr Chary.

With his head stooping to the floor, Poort found himself agreeing with his Queen's conclusion and nodding vigorously. But when his eyes caught sight of the scythe once again, a thought popped up, jolting him in its wake.

'Your Highness...we must,' Poort began only to realise Ruchira had left his side.

'*Vegadvij*,' Poort chanted immediately and a pair of wings shot out of his shoulder blades to let him zoom towards Ruchira.

'We're in grave danger... We must run,' Poort said with his hands grasping Ruchira.

'But why... What's wrong?'

Just then Poort noticed how Dr Chary's eyes were closed and his head hung about limply over his shoulder. If he was indeed asleep, Poort didn't want to wake him up. But he still had to tell the Queen what he was thinking or she wouldn't believe him.

'Your Highness... It is the scythe which has the Creator's power of immortality. And the Queen never struck Dr Chary. So how could he have that power?' Poort whispered in her ears.

Ruchira shifted her focus towards Poort. The sick feeling in her stomach rose. Maybe Poort was right.

'What should we do?' asked Ruchira.

'Please come with Poort...he begs you.'

Even as she hesitated, she found herself listening to Poort. As they flew, Poort pleaded with her to keep as quiet as possible. But Ruchira showed signs of restlessness and Poort knew if he didn't talk to her right away, the situation could get out of control.

'Dr Chary is still alive because he is indeed immortal. Immortal because of the scythe...for it is only the scythe that is known to have that power. But it's not through the Queen's efforts...the prophecy remains unfulfilled. He has the power in him because he was struck before by somebody else.'

'But nobody else knows about the prophecy except us. We're the only ones alive who do.'

'Poort begs you to be patient with him. He will get to the root of it...but only once we reach a safe distance from Dr Chary... Please do understand or we could die before ever finding the Equal.'

'All right Poort...tell me what's going on in your mind,' said Ruchira finally noticing the panic in Poort's voice.

'It is hard for Poort to explain himself...because there are too many thoughts, too many questions running amok in his mind... Perhaps, if the Queen would answer his questions Poort can become absolutely certain about what he thinks is right.'

'Poort... Get on with it,' said Ruchira, her restlessness returning.

'How did the Battle of Gawaan end?' he asked quickly just when he noticed Ruchira's attention wavering.

'The Creator locked his Life Energy into the scythe and struck the White Death with it, thereby filling his body with Life Energy and making him immortal.'

'And why did the Creator do that?'

'Because Life Energy sprang from love and now that the White Death was filled with Life Energy, it meant that there was also an abundance of love within him. That love suppressed the hate in the White Death. And without hate the White Death forgot his purpose in life and who he truly was.'

'Exactly! They say after the Battle of Gawaan, the White Death lost his memories and disappeared altogether. But everyone believed he was still alive because he had the power of immortality. And there's every bit of truth in that tale for the heartbeat we can hear now is of the White Death himself and perhaps his old memories were triggered...once he saw the scythe because there is nothing the White Death is more terrified of than the scythe which has Sura's Life Energy locked inside it. Fear made him remember everything.'

Absorbed in his own thoughts, which both thrilled and frightened him, Poort added, 'Dr Chary is not the White Death's Equal... He...is the White Death himself. That's why he can stay underwater for as long as he likes. Not because he has gills to breathe like all the Aravans. Nothing can kill Dr Chary, not the heat of the magma itself, not pressure, nor breathing the most toxic gases here.'

Although the fear within her was rising, choking her throat, the rational part of her brain was still trying to process all the information.

'It doesn't make sense. If Dr Chary is indeed immortal, how can he grow old? How can he have a heart attack?'

Poort seemed confused, until Ruchira narrated the book-reading episode.

Poort was stunned. What Ruchira had brought up was a conundrum, contradicting his ingenious conclusion. Poort welcomed the challenge. Delighting in straining his brain muscles for a logical answer, he said, 'It's a clever question. Very puzzling. Perhaps, because the White Energy wasn't completely removed by Sura at the battle. It was only suppressed. It's still within Dr Chary, causing changes. That is the true nature of the White Energy, to get inside one's body as they breathe in the air, interfere with Life Energy, impair its regenerative powers and cause the death of cells. And perhaps, once the Queen started using the Corestone to control Dr Chary, he also began absorbing some of its White Energy.'

'Does that mean he can die through ageing?'

'That remains to be seen. Perhaps, not. The Life Energy is still strong within him. We have enough proof of that. And as long as it is there, we can be sure it will obstruct the evil White Energy from augmenting. In essence, he's more Good than Evil.'

'But it was me...I helped Dr Chary discover who he is by bringing him here and showing him the scythe.'

As Ruchira said this, a sudden sound reverberated throughout the Mantle, sending cracks through the walls. It was a scream. An outburst. To Ruchira, it sounded like a cry of shock and horror from an Angel looking in the mirror and finding the Devil smiling back.

Her heart froze in her chest.

Acknowledgements

My heartfelt gratitude goes out to the following people:

Mom, for asking me to read non-fiction to write good fiction.

Dad, for being disciplined, following tradition, and becoming an engineer, while asking me to break the rules and dare to be different.

Archith, for reading the gazillion drafts of this novel, criticising and guiding me, without whom this novel would have been titled 'Doodle Do'.

My better half, Shriram, for his unconditional love and support, being the zookeeper and taming the gorilla in me.

My grandmother, Saroja Chary, for inspiring me through her resilience.

To all the math teachers in my school, for letting me get away scot-free, while I scribbled story ideas underneath my math text book.

My publisher, Ajay Mago, and Dipa Chaudhuri, Editor-in-Chief, Om Books International, for their warmth and cordiality extended to all first-time writers, constant encouragement, having deep faith in my story and giving me my first break.

Shoili Sarkar-Seth, my editor, for her sincerity, working through sleepless nights to edit and refine my last-minute rewrites, especially saving me from public embarrassment by punctuating sentences like, 'It's time to eat Dr Chary.'